Light of The Sun

David Costa

I dedicate this book to my family and to all the brave men and women who stand on the wall.

Acknowledgements

I would like to thank Conrad Jones, Author, and Red Dragon Books for all their advice and support in writing this book.

Take therefore no thought for the morrow: for the morrow shall take thought for the things of itself. Sufficient unto the day is the evil thereof.

Matthew 6:34 KJB

Chapter 1

Barcelona

'Allah will bless you and keep you in the palm of His hand.'

The text on the phone screen was her signal to proceed. The Arab had told her the same words when he had helped her strap on the vest. With screws, nails, and TNT in the pouches around her, she noticed there was no smell only that from her sweat. She left the hotel and walking in the warm sun made her way to the La Rambla area of Barcelona. This was the main tourist area of the city, over one mile long with its pedestrian tree lined walkway through the centre. She had walked here twice, once with the Teacher himself. The streets were already filling with tourists and shoppers. The famous living statue street artists were picking the best spots to surprise those same tourists encouraging them to donate their money into the buckets, tins, and caps on the ground. No one looked at her, no one cared, they were all lost in their own little worlds, heads looking down at the phones in their hands or browsing the shop windows for bargains and holiday mementos. The pavement cafés were also

1

filling up, with the loud chatter of conversation carrying across the street on the morning air. The suicide vest under her coat wasn't heavy or bulky, and her clothing was that of a Western woman with blue jeans and a coloured headscarf, leaving her face fully visible to all around. He had told her to go to the indoor market for maximum effect. Being early morning, the market was packed with local shoppers out before the severe midday heat. She could see figures of people in front of her, but not in any clarity, just the outline, her eyes did not want to settle on any one person, she didn't want to be weak, she was a soldier of Allah. He had told her to expect the fear, but that it would pass quickly as she passed through the gate into paradise. In her final moment she hoped someone would stop her, but then her voice took over, 'Allah Akbar, Allah Akbar,' she shouted. Her loud voice surprised her for a second and she could see some of the people closest to her turning their heads towards the sound, some faces already with the shock of the realisation of what was about to happen, death was here. She pressed the button on the handheld device.

The explosive blast with the force of the TNT in the crowded space caused complete and utter devastation. Her body was blown asunder into minute fragments of bone adding to the shrapnel already created by the flying packs of metal spread through the crowded market with the speed of bullets. Forty died immediately: men, women, and children, with fifteen more who reached hospital dying later, 150 victims were injured many of them losing limbs. All that was left of the bomber was her head, almost intact with her brightly coloured scarf still in place around her face.

When the blast sounded and vibrated through the city the Arab was strapping himself into his passenger seat on the 10.30 a.m. flight from Barcelona to Rome. He had sent the text message before boarding, breaking the SIM card, he had thrown it with the burner phone into a waste bin. *God is Great,* he thought. 'Allah Akbar,' he whispered quietly to himself.

'Keep your face to the sun and you will never see the shadows.'
Helen Keller.

Iran.

The sun was at its hottest as Colonel Ali Shafi of Iran's elite Republican Guard drove the Jeep through the third security gate allowing access to the Parchin military site. Parchin was supposed to be a secret site southeast of the capital city Tehran. According to reports from the UN nuclear watchdog the International Atomic Energy Agency (IAEA) it was suspected of being a possible location supporting the Iranian nuclear enrichment programme working towards the production of a nuclear bomb capability.

Intelligence reports from the CIA and Mossad confirmed the fears of the IAEA inspectors. Iran continued to tell the world that it needed the nuclear material for a medical research reactor, yet despite numerous requests by the UN team to inspect the site, they'd been delayed; until, as they now believed, to allow time to hide the true purpose of the site.

Satellite pictures had shown the site had been sanitised to protect its secrets in an effort to remove and cleanse any evidence of illicit nuclear activity.

The clean-up activity had taken several months and included a large covering being placed over a steel chamber; this the IAEA believed was being used for explosive experiments in an apparent effort to prevent satellite monitoring of the location.

The IAEA report had detailed that significant ground scraping and landscaping had been undertaken over an extensive area in and around Parchin. Buildings had been demolished and power lines, fences, and paved roads removed. The IAEA assessment was that this activity was a deliberate operation by the Iranian government to protect the real work that had been going on at Parchin, and to deliberately hamper its investigation if the IAEA was to be granted access to the site. Their most recent report which was now available to the UN and other interested parties stated, 'The activities observed... further strengthen the agency's assessment that it is necessary to have access to the location at Parchin without further delay.'

This delay of access was not only of concern to the Secretary of the UN and the President of the United States. The Prime Minister of Israel had explicitly stated that Israel couldn't allow a government who had called for the state of Israel to be wiped off the face of the earth, to have a nuclear capability on its doorstep. The threat was implicit, 'we will act before you do.'

Over the last two years as commander of the secretive base Shafi had overseen the security of Iran's biggest gamble; to become an independent nuclear power. Today as he parked inside one of the covered bunkers, he knew that the Western powers and supporters of the Zionist state of Israel would shudder with fear as the cause of Allah came down on them with the wrath of thunder.

Tel Aviv to Malta.

Rachel Cohen looked down on the landscape of the island of Malta as the Air Malta A319 with 141 passengers on-board made its landing approach to Luqa, Malta's international airport. The flight from Rome had only taken one hour and twenty minutes. Rachel knew touchdown was only a few minutes away when she saw the cabin crew strap themselves into their seats facing the passengers in the aircraft's cabin. Looking at the ground below she picked out the landmarks on the almost treeless surface that she remembered from the many times she'd visited the island in the past. Then she'd come as a tourist. Looking now out the window she could follow the roads as they wound their way through the island and the small villages and towns to the larger tourist developments on the coast. She could pick out the hilltop town of Mdina. The fortress town had been the original capital of the island before the residents moved down to the coast for work. When most of the inhabitants left, the city became so quiet it soon became known as the Silent City. Yet she remembered it as a beautiful place to walk through its narrow-cobbled streets, then dine in one of the restaurants on the battlements that looked down on Malta spread out below. Now ahead to her left she could pick out the current capital Valletta, with its Grand Harbour one of the best deep-water harbours in the world, and the lifeline for the survival of the British Forces in the Mediterranean in the Second World War battle against Rommel's Afrika Corps and the Italian Axis forces in the battles across the North Africa and the Libyan desert. For the bravery shown by the Maltese people in that campaign the island was awarded the George Cross by King George VI. To this day it is displayed on the national Maltese flag as a symbol of pride. The people of Malta were fiercely proud of their history, not only during the Second World War but also when the Knights of Malta fought off a Muslim Army from the Ottoman Empire in the Great Siege in 1565.

Now as the ground rushed up to meet her Rachel thought of how she'd fallen in love with the island and its people. This time her visit would not give her the chance to relax. This time she would be looking through the eyes not of a tourist, but of a field agent in the employment of the Israeli Secret Service, Mossad.

Now, she would be going through customs using her cover name of Anna Stressor; the Italian housewife; accompanied by her husband Palo now seated next to her. Palo appeared to be resting his eyes but Ari Rosenberg, also a member of the elite Mossad Kidon teams was, as always, alert.

Passport Control was as usual simple enough to go through, with just a cursory look from the female officer behind the desk. '*No problem so far,*' thought Rachel. Was it only yesterday she was sitting in her apartment on the outskirts of Tel Aviv, when her mobile phone had buzzed a text alert? The words in capital letters *RETURN TO OFFICE* meant, 'Urgent get there now!' Less than an hour later Rachel and Ari sat in the office of Mossad HQ in King Saul Boulevard in downtown Tel Aviv. Sitting behind the desk facing them was Kurt Shimon, head of the Mossad Counter Terrorist Kidon teams.

Rachel had met him a few times when training for the Kidon teams in the Negev desert. His reputation was legend in the Mossad. He had a desert tan with thick white hair; he looked fit and spoke with great confidence and authority. The Kidon or Bayonet in English, were the elite of the Mossad. Most members of Kidon came from a military background having served in the Israeli Defence Forces, IDF, and most of them had served in its Special Forces or elite regiments. On rare occasions a Mossad member could transfer into the Kidon when it was found they had that special gift or qualification. The training was tough, and few made it through to join the special clandestine killing arm of Mossad.

'We have a situation which needs your expertise immediately. Our intelligence sources in Iran have identified a clear threat to an unknown target somewhere in Western Europe. Scientists in Iran have perfected a small nuclear device using a small amount of plutonium which we believe is already being transported to Europe. This device could demolish most of London and leave a radioactive cloud to spread to the south of England and the coast of France, that's if London is the target. We do not know how it's being transported, but the triggering mechanism is travelling separately, and this is where you come in. An Iranian Colonel is travelling as we speak to Malta, with protection from the members of the Iranian Quads and possibly Hezbollah. In Malta he'll be handing the plutonium over to someone who will smuggle it into Europe where they'll meet up with members of a terrorist organisation, as yet unknown. We believe this Colonel is travelling from Iran on a container ship which is going to put him and his friends ashore at the Grand Harbour in Valletta in two days. This team will have the plutonium, and when it reaches their people in Europe, they will supply the explosives and trigger to set it off. The final target, and who their people are in Europe, are still unknown. That is where you come in. Get to Malta, pick up the trail, and try to identify the rest of these people. Combined with the explosive and the plutonium, this

8

will be a dirty nuclear device. Anything information we get here we'll let you know immediately.'

Every Mossad and IDF member knew the danger posed by the Iranian regime.

Iran had supported the terror group Hezbollah for many years, and its main operating base was in Lebanon, with Israel its main target. The Iranian Quads were really the Paramilitary wing of the Iranian Army, highly trained killers. Iran had told the world that the destruction of the state of Israel was their main priority. The Prime Minister of Israel had made it quite clear; Israel wouldn't allow a threat of nuclear attack against its people. Israel would carry out a pre-emptive strike before Iran had the capability to launch a missile attack on its country. The Western powers, especially the United States, feared such a scenario and that's why they'd put pressure on Iran to cease its nuclear strategy through inspections and sanctions. *This would be no picnic*, thought Rachel.

'Why Malta?' asked Rachel. 'It seems strange that if they want to get it into Europe, why tie themselves up on an island in the middle of the Mediterranean?'

Kurt Shimon smiled at Rachel when he answered.

'Believe it or not the Iranians still have contacts they trust in Malta even though we eliminated one of their friends there in 1995.'

Everyone knew the legend as part of the Mossad story. A Kidon team had travelled to Malta when intelligence was received that placed the leader of the Palestinian Islamic Jihad (PIJ) Fathi Shaqaqi, who had

9

links with Iran, and who had been meeting with the Libyan leader Muammar Gaddafi in Tripoli, to organise training, weapons, and money to be supplied to his terrorist teams had stopped off in Malta. The Kidon team, that was quickly dispatched to Malta, soon tracked him down and shot him dead outside his hotel. It was a well planned and executed Mossad operation, once more showing the terrorist leaders, nowhere was safe from their reach.

'Anyway, it does not matter why they're back in Malta it's our job to find out why, so I'm sending you two. All the information you need will be sent by encrypted message to your smartphones. Go over to operations they'll supply you with false identity, weapons, and any information on this Iranian Colonel and his friends. I'll be keeping an eye on this, and in the meantime I'll be contacting our friends in the European Security Services to bring them up to date.'

The file on Colonel Ali Shafi was thin. A ten-year-old photo showed a round faced man with a heavy dark moustache and dark brown eyes. His family and military background were standard for a Colonel in the Islamic Revolutionary Guard Corps. Not only was he a Colonel in the guard but also a member of its Quads Force, the Unit with a specific remit to carry out unconventional warfare and intelligence activities, and responsible for extraterritorial operations. As Rachel expected, the Mossad files showed that the Quads worked closely with Hezbollah, Hamas, and the PIJ; all enemies of Israel. The interesting thing was his family. He had married into the family of the Grand Ayatollah of Iran Sayyid Ali Hosseini Khamenei. *This was no ordinary soldier*, thought Rachel. The files had been downloaded to the two Mossad agents' smartphones which could only be accessed through their thumb print to the screen. Anyone else trying to access the phone, would lose a finger or two when it blew up in their hand. A bit of *Mission Impossible* stuff but the science boffins of Mossad don't mess around. Next stop was the Grand Hotel Excelsior in the capital Valletta. Rachel had stayed there once before in another world a long time ago. The weapons would be supplied to them by one of Israel's Sayanim living in Malta. These are Jews and local residents living and working as normal citizens in every country outside Israel. They are recruited by Mossad to help its operators with everything from transport to money, safe houses, weapons and access to communications networks and other facilities, including official documents exclusive to that location. Sayanim dedicated their lives to the state of Israel and its existence and had indicated their desire to help in whatever way they could. First stop after booking into the hotel would be to contact the local Sayanim and collect their weapons.

A final piece of the message sent on their phones surprised both operators telling them that they would be contacted at the hotel by an agent from the British Secret Intelligence Service, David Reece.

Chapter 2

'I heard the voice of the Lord, saying, who shall I send, and who will go for us? Then said I, Here I am; send me.'

It was raining in London, which made the River Thames that flowed through the nation's capital dark with churned-up mud, its colour more brown than usual. Sir Ian Fraser was looking out the window of his office on the top floor of Vauxhall Cross, the headquarters of MI6, the Secret Intelligence Service of the United Kingdom. Sir Ian head of SIS who was also known in the secret world of intelligence services and his employees simply as 'C', had his back to the room and the three other people sitting around the conference table. Still looking down at the river he could see the spires of the Houses of Parliament to his right and the outline of Thames House the home of MI5.

'So, what you're saying is she was British?'

The voice from the room behind Sir Ian was that of Sir Martin Bryant the Chairman of the British Joint Intelligence Committee. Fraser turned to face the three people in the vast office.

'Yes, that's what I'm saying. Interpol have identified her as being British. She was originally plain Margaret Brown from East London.'

'But how did Interpol identify her as Margaret Brown. Surely there was nothing left to identify the woman?' again it was Bryant asking the question.

It was now the turn of the only woman in the room to speak.

'DNA and fingerprints.' Caroline Aspinall was the head of the Security Service or MI5 as it was better known. MI5 have responsibility for intelligence operations within the boundaries of the United Kingdom, while MI6 has the responsibility for intelligence gathering and operations on all borders beyond the UK and throughout the world. Both organisations have as their main remit, the protection of the citizens of the UK and its assets. Aspinall was a career Intelligence Officer having joined MI5 straight from university in Cambridge. She had earned her stripes and the respect of the men in the room working her way up the ladder, first as a field agent then as a top-class analyst. Her clear thinking and dedication had saved many lives, and as she progressed through the Security Service ranks, her qualities were noticed. After serving for ten years as head of operations, she had recently been promoted to the top job when her boss had retired.

'What do you mean, that the Spanish have the DNA of a British citizen?' asked Bryant.

Aspinall looked at Fraser and the other man in the room Jim Broad for approval to continue.

'Go ahead please Caroline,' said Fraser.

She looked back to Bryant before continuing. Aspinall pressed a button on the table in front of her and the screen on the wall brought up the video of a young woman.

Margaret Brown looked every bit her young age. Her clothing was Western, her dark hair pulled back severely in a ponytail, her blue eyes looked straight ahead at the screen, and she seemed to be speaking without a script. There was a white sheet hanging on the wall behind her with words written in black in Arabic across it. She spoke clearly in English her London accent was still strong as she spoke.

'All praise to the father, Allah be his name. I am Margaret Brown, but my chosen name is Fatimah, and I am a soldier of the Islamic Jihad. My eyes were covered by the scales of the many false gods of the Western devils, but the work and love of the Prophet all praises to his name removed those scales and filled me with the desire to serve him however I can. Now I will bring his wrath as a soldier to those same infidels who blaspheme and ignore the will of the one true God that is Allah. I call on all our brothers and sisters to join our cause and attack these infidels wherever you find them.'

She then seemed to look at a space above the camera at someone hidden there for approval, then a male voice spoke in English with a slight Middle Eastern accent, 'Allah be praised, God is Great.' Just before the camera was switched off and the screen went blank.

'You see Sir Martin; this was no ordinary woman. Margaret Brown was originally as has been said from East London. The family still

14

live there, and Special Branch are raiding the family home as we speak but I don't think they'll find anything. Margaret Brown left the UK over five years ago and as far as we know has never returned. When she lived here she got involved with a crowd of Palestinian activists and was arrested during a demonstration outside the Israeli Embassy here in London. She was only sixteen at the time but because of that arrest she was fingerprinted, and her photo and DNA taken. When she was questioned the report showed that she was into the whole Middle East scenario as she felt the Palestinians were being persecuted by the Jews and the rest of the Western World. She was thought by her interviewers to be a low risk and not of any use from a recruitment point of view. A few years later we find her name popping up again logged as a passenger on a flight to Egypt, but it would now appear that the trip was one way and she never returned to these shores. We, as you know Sir Martin, share a database with other European intelligence agencies and Interpol. After the Barcelona suicide bombing last week, the Spanish fed the bomber's DNA, fingerprints, and a photo of the woman's head, which considering she'd blown herself up, was pretty much intact, into the system and up popped that long-lost file of Margaret Brown. The video was released to the various Arab and Islamic Networks and put on social media sites which proves that the DNA and fingerprint evidence is correct confirming the bomber was indeed Margaret Brown or as she has now identified herself Fatimah.'

'Can we find out where she went, who she got involved with and why she did this,' asked Bryant.

Aspinall looked to Sir Ian Fraser once more before replying.

'As with all these situations, it will have to be a combined effort. The Anti-Terrorist Squad have already started with the searches and follow-up enquiries where she lived and grew up. They will be looking into her school life and any other involvement in Middle East activities. Five will chase up any information here at home, we'll also be checking the family's phones and computers for any contact with her. Then I believe it will be over to Six to see what she did outside the country.'

Now it was the turn of Fraser to present the part MI6 would have to play in researching the life of Margaret Brown.

'You have to understand Martin, although we have Embassies in most of the countries in the Middle East and Africa, we have very few actual agents on the ground. We have sent out the usual request, asking them to find out what they can as a matter of urgency. However, between ourselves and the NSA we do have good technical and eavesdropping coverage. The people at GCHQ and the NSA at Fort Meade have become experts in giving us a heads up on what they call chatter.'

'So, no heads up this time then?' asked Bryant.

'Not as such. They got nothing in the build-up, they're getting too smart for that, a few seconds conversation on a mobile phone can bring a Hellfire Missile fired from a drone down on their head. But GCHQ and the NSA did get some chatter afterwards when the jihadist groups started to cheer and celebrate Barcelona. They all started to mention the Arab. We have an idea who he is, from years

16

of following any mention of him. The file shows he has been at this sort of stuff for some time. He may have even lived in this country for a time as a student.'

The MI6 chief sat behind his desk and pressed a couple of buttons on a remote control. The curtains on the large windows closed and the video monitor on the wall lit up to show a grainy headshot of what looked like a bearded man wearing sunglasses and the traditional Arab headdress a red and white checked shemagh. From the background it looked like the picture had been taken in what could only be described as any Middle Eastern town.

At the same time, a man of around thirty-five years came into the room and stood in front of the screen.

'Can I introduce for those of you who don't know him Matthew Simons our head of the Middle East desk.' said Fraser. 'He will talk us through all we know about the Arab. Matthew over to you.'

Simons was about six-foot-tall, slim, short dark hair with the tan and brown eyes of someone who might have been born in the Middle East, clean shaven wearing a short sleeved open neck shirt he had the body of someone who looked after himself.

'Thank you, Sir Ian.'

The voice was Oxford educated as Broad knew from his many past meetings with Simons. He also knew Simons was born in Gibraltar where his father met his wife while serving with the Royal Navy. He spoke Pashto and many of the other Arabic languages with the gift of sounding like a local when he did.

'This photo was taken at a Palestinian camp in Gaza by an agent working for Mossad. There was a party going on in the streets to celebrate 9/11, and the Mossad agent was there celebrating with the rest of them taking a few snaps with his camera phone. It turned out after questioning by the agents' handlers, the man in the photo seemed to be important. He had a few bodyguards and people referred to him as the Arab. Mossad then took up some interest in this man, and they've spent some time in finding out who he was. The reason Mossad told us all this and gave us some access to the file, was because it turns out our Arab friend here may have attended university in this country. Plus, we are inclined to think the job our SG9 people did in Manchester taking out the joint IRA and Islamic Jihad team might have endeared them to us for a little while. We like to think that when it comes to the Islamic threat, we are all in this together when sharing intelligence that affects everyone of us.'

These words stirred some recent memories in all present, especially those of Jim Broad who, as Director of Operations for the SG9 unit during Operation Long Shot, had seen his team take out three terrorists and arrest one with one escaping. The operation had prevented the assassination of the Prime Minister of the UK. SG9 was now, to put it crudely, the killing arm in the clandestine war against terrorist groups operating against the people of the UK wherever they might raise their heads, it was now the job of SG9 to find them and eliminate them. The decision to create the Department or SG9, was known to only a few, as a necessary evil to combat the rising war of terrorism that was attacking every civilised country in the world, especially in the West. It had been decided that prison only made Islamic Terrorists more dangerous for three reasons, being Martyrs to the cause, they indoctrinated their fellow inmates creating more terrorists, and they cost countries a fortune in security before eventually having been released after serving their term in prison, then they inevitably went straight back to their old ways, deadlier and wiser.

Broad remembered the words of Winston Churchill, when he said in the context of the Second World War 'The only way to defeat terror is with greater terror.' The Israelis, the Russians, the Americans had all come to realise this and formed their own Black Ops units to combat the disease that terrorism, especially Islamic Terrorism brought to the world. Broad thought you couldn't negotiate or talk to these people, they did not want to talk, they only wanted to kill you. It was now the job of intelligence agencies throughout the world to track them down and kill them first, 'Big Boys Rules' as it was known in the undercover war the Secret Agencies around the world now had to work in.

Matthew Simons turned once more to the screen on the wall and pressing a button on the remote once more brought up a file page marked *TOP SECRET.*

'Now let us have a look at what we have on the Arab, the man in the grainy photo. This file has been compiled by the analysts from many agencies working together, including our own intelligence agencies from Five, Six, and GCHQ. If Mossad are right, then this man did attend university in this country some time ago. If you can keep your questions until after I've finished we can discuss further at length. The file shows the basic background, and I have to say we should not get bogged down in all this, a lot of it is guesswork and speculation. Our friend is better known as Abdullah Mohammad Safrah. Born in Gaza in 1978 we first find him in this country attending the London School of Economics between 2002 and 2005 where he obtained a First in Economics. This part is fact, five have checked the records and he was here during that time and lived in a bedsit on Edgeware Road. The usual student life, but no sign of student politics or groups. After leaving the LSE; he then, according to Mossad, turned up for more educational training at the Bir Zeit University on the West Bank, where he studied Physics, before moving to the Mansoura University in Egypt to study medicine, graduating as a Doctor in General Practice. Mossad believe this is where he may have been fully radicalised, becoming involved at first with the Islamic Brotherhood, and then moving on to the PIJ, an offshoot of the Palestinian Liberation Organisation. Founding members of the PIJ believed that the PLO had become too soft, and their founding charter is the destruction of Israel by Holy War or Jihad as we know it. Our friend Abdullah, it would appear, put his education to good use at first; practising medicine in Kuwait, Bahrain, and then back in his homeland of Gaza. It is believed he then joined up with his comrades in the PIJ to help Hezbollah in Lebanon in their war with Israel. While in Beirut we have him in the hospital there, putting his medical knowledge to good use, and according to reports from the Red Cross and the UN, he was good at his job and well liked. He is the eldest of seven children and the thing that might have changed his whole outlook on life from helping people to killing them, may have been an airstrike by Israel on a suspected PIJ commander in Gaza in May 2008. The bombs not only hit their target, but one at least overshot hitting a civilian area killing two of his family - a brother Hassan and a sister Yasmin. He then disappears off the radar in Lebanon, but it's believed he ended up in Iran, specifically Tehran where his links to extreme Islamic Jihad movements, such as Hezbollah and al-Qaeda, became stronger. Again, his masters recognised him as a leader, a man of quality. He was trained in all the terrorist ways on how to kill, using bombs, guns, knives, and his hands. But where he excelled, was as a planner. He would impress his trainers with his ideas and how to carry them out. As I said at the start, a lot of this is second-hand hearsay, but from our experiences of the Middle East and how these groups operate, it can be assumed to be fairly accurate. Over to you if you have any questions.'

As he spoke Simons had changed the pictures on the screen from the Red Cross and UN symbols to what looked like a terrorist training camp somewhere in the Middle East for effect.

Sir Martin Bryant spoke first.

'I can see your concern with the fact he went to university here, and that Margaret Brown also spent time in this country, but how does this link the two. I need to confirm there is a threat before I see the Prime Minister?'

'I understand Martin,' said Ferguson, 'but as we said at the start it was through the chatter picked up by the technical spooks that has linked the Arab with Margaret Brown. We will put all our people on it and come back to you when we have more. In the meantime, I would suggest the PM say as little as he can about Margaret Brown. He should only state that for a time she lived in this country many years ago, and after she left there is nothing more known. That way we make the Arab and his friends think we are totally in the dark. In a slight fog maybe, but not totally in the dark. As you know, Martin, I'm taking the opportunity to meet with my fellow Directors of the CIA and Mossad in London before the end of December. At the same time, I've already asked them that we put the Arab top of the agenda when we meet.'

'So, while we wait for more information, we don't need to upgrade our state of alert for the moment?' asked Bryant.

When there is intelligence that indicates a threat to the UK mainland it is assessed by the Joint Terrorism Analysis Centre (JTAC) which makes its recommendations on the level of threat to the country, independent of government. Bryant knew that the threat level was currently at its second highest level out of a list of five, judged as severe meaning a terrorist attack to be highly likely.

'No,' answered Fraser, 'it should remain as severe for the moment, and I think we can leave it there for now.'

The highest state of alert in the United Kingdom was imminent and that would be only announced when clear information indicated an attack was going to take place. For now, severe indicating a threat of attack which realistically was always the case, would be enough. *No need to panic the population, the press, or most importantly the politicians just yet,* thought Fraser. The meeting broke up with Bryant leaving to brief the Prime Minister on how to spin the Brown girl's story. But Fraser asked Jim Broad to stay behind.

Chapter 3

The Arab had stayed in Rome for three days, taking in the sights and relaxing in the sun while drinking black coffee outside the many pavement cafes. He always drank his coffee black when he travelled outside the Middle East. The Western coffee was not strong enough, and he missed the coffee of his homelands of Egypt, Palestine, and Iran. The coffee there would always be sipped with a side glass of water, and when he could get it some fruit, an orange or apple. His days spent in London had been good training on how to keep below the radar and fit in to the picture around him. People and waiters would pass him by, taking no notice of the clean-shaven well-dressed man of Middle East appearance with the Pilot Sunglasses, smart suit, and Italian leather shoes. After three days the Arab had booked out of his hotel. He took connecting flights first to Istanbul in Turkey then on to Damascus in Syria. There he had a meeting with his contacts in the Syrian intelligence to discuss a weapons supply across the border into Iraq, to be used by Islamic Jihad fighters. From there he took a plane to Iran. When he arrived at Imam Khomeini International Airport in Tehran the taxi from the airport took him north on the Tehran South Freeway to his villa in the district of Said Abad on the outskirts of the city. He opened some windows to let the air flow through. Although he had aircon, he had found that if he opened windows at the front and rear of the house the air flowing through created a natural wind tunnel making it more refreshing. He started up the motor to pull back the pool covering and went and changed, throwing his bag on to the bed, he could unpack later; he needed a swim first. After ten lengths of the pool, he went through his ritual of prayers to Allah kneeling on a mat on the grass beside the pool. When he was in the West his prayers were done in secret. He avoided any contact with the local Muslim communities or Mosques, which he knew were under constant surveillance by the intelligence agencies in those countries, why take chances when you did not need to. He dressed in fresh Arab clothing and ate a cold dinner alone. He made one phone call to let his masters know he was back and arranged to meet the next day.

The next morning brought a clear blue sky with a slight breeze that once more flowed through the house. He loved the mornings here best. It made him feel alive and alert, ready for whatever the day would bring. Today he dressed in light casual slacks and a white short-sleeved open neck shirt and pulled on his favourite Italian leather moccasins. Collecting his wallet, mobile phone, and keys to his white Mercedes, he left the villa and drove the car east towards the centre of Tehran. Traffic was busy even for the late morning, but he had given himself plenty of time to arrive early for meetings, taking that time to check the area and your surroundings for enemy surveillance. In the centre of Iran there should be no enemy surveillance, but he had been fighting his enemies far too long to take chances. The CIA and Mossad were more than capable and could operate anywhere in the world where they believed danger to come from. He parked in a shopping centre multi-storey car park in the Panzdah e Khordad city centre area and made his way on foot through the centre entering and leaving some of the shops but not buying anything until a newsagents, where he bought the Tehran Times. By the time he had circled the café twice, the two men he had come to meet were already sitting outside drinking their coffee. The café was on the edge of the city's famous Grand Bazaar, and hundreds of people were milling around the shops and stalls, making it easy to get lost in a crowd, or hard to spot someone in the crowd; so the café location had both its good points and bad. As he approached he could see at least four bodyguards, two sitting at one of the tables close to his contacts and two standing a short distance away. None of the four made any attempt to conceal who they were. They were here to protect their masters, not act as secret agents.

'Good morning gentlemen how are we today?'

It always amazed the two men that the Arab would always be in his in Western mode from his clothing to his everyday language and greeting.

'Good morning my friend and may Allah be with you.'

The Arab noticed two things, first, that General Malek Hasheem Khomeini greeted him in English, and second, apart from the Islamic blessing, was that he called him friend but no name. The two men stood, and they both kissed him on the cheeks three times in the Arab

26

way. Both men were also dressed in the Western style, the General was taller at over six foot at least six inches taller than the man standing beside him who stood at five foot seven. According to the files in Mossad HQ in Tel Aviv he was Ibrahim Shallah, he was medium build but muscular, clean shaven with a slight scar under his lower lip which had been the closest he had come to an IDF bullet in the war against the Israeli Defence Forces in Gaza; he was the current leader of the PIJ. All three sat and ordered more of the strong coffee the café was famous for, with a side order of fresh water and some oranges for the sweetness. The reason they had met in a café and not in an office somewhere was at the request of the Arab. He did not trust meeting in government office buildings. Enemy intelligence agencies would always start with the offices of the States they were targeting, both for surveillance and the identification and recruitment of agents. For anyone watching, they would appear to be three businessmen discussing making money over a cup of coffee, rather than planning terrorist operations around the world. The General, even though he was dressed in civilian clothes, always had difficulty passing himself off as someone ordinary as he sat and stood in the fashion of a trained military man, ramrod straight. He also looked fierce with a heavy dark moustache and jet-black hair and with eyes to match he looked dangerous, not the kind of man you would pick a fight with. He was also on the files in King Saul Boulevard in Tel Aviv where Mossad records stated he was currently the Commander of the Clandestine Department of the Islamic Quads Force. He kept out of the media that so many of the Guards Generals were happy to be seen in and considered his job to be a secret one and always tried to live his life that way. With the coffee and oranges on the table they started to talk in general terms at first, both men inquiring how things went in Spain and how was the Arab's travels. The conversation business like, and matter of fact.

'You had a successful trip, making great press for our cause around the world,' said the PIJ leader.

'Yes, successful. The martyr will be in the arms of Allah now and the Western devils wondering what has happened,' replied Abdullah.

'Did you have any problems with your passports?' asked the General.

Iran had supplied the documents, training, and money for the Barcelona operation. The Western powers knew that the Iranian government supported many terrorist organisations with money, weapons, and training. Iran had become one of their main targets for surveillance and intelligence operations for that very reason.

'No problem at all. Having a Spanish passport, they just flagged me through. I felt comfortable just moving about their security which was very lax, even in a large city like Barcelona. They are not prepared for us.'

'I'm not so sure that will not be the situation in the future.' said the General, 'they'll be more prepared .'

'Abdullah, now that you are back, the General would like your help in something he has already set in motion.'

'How can I help, General?'

'My country, as you know, fully supports your actions in Gaza against Israel and throughout the world. We also support the Jihad as Israel is our enemy as it is yours. We can continue to carry out these smaller operations resulting in many deaths of the infidel. But, we feel, sometimes we must really hit them hard and make them listen. Since 9/11 the Western powers have become used to and accepting these small operations despite there being two wars in Iraq and Afghanistan. All we have really succeeded in doing is to bring down their wrath on those countries and increase the money they now pour into their security agencies which now direct their considerable attention and power towards ourselves. We need them to utterly understand that we will not be defeated, and we will bring the fight to their doorstep, not just the small villages of Iraq and Afghanistan, although we will still fight them there as well. We believe that 9/11 was such a great success that we must now follow the example of that success and move to a higher level of bringing the Jihad to their doorstep.'

The world knew the story of 9/11 when al-Qaeda terrorists had flown passenger jets into the Twin Towers in New York and the Pentagon Building killing over three thousand people.

'Your operation in Barcelona was just such a step but now we should move it up, move it forward.'

Abdullah began to feel a little of the intensity the General was trying to portray.

'Move it up?'

Now it was the turn of the PIJ leader to speak.

'My brother you must understand, Allah has a plan for you. There are other soldiers already on the move, your task will be to help them bring that plan to the Devil's door in London.

We cannot tell you everything now, but in the next few days I want you to visit our training camp where we train our European converts to the cause and chose for yourself soldiers of the Jihad who will aid you in this mission. When you've done that we will meet again. The Commander of the Camp has been told you will be coming and to give you everything you need.'

Abdullah knew the training camp the leader referred to. It was the same training camp where he had spotted a very committed woman from England named Margaret Brown. The Arab finished his coffee.

'Goodbye gentlemen until we meet again.'

'Inshallah,' said the General using the Arab word for 'if Allah wills it'.

Chapter 4

Jim Broad had filled his coffee cup and remained sitting at the conference table. Broad always respected the office of 'C' the head of MI6, so when Sir Ian Fraser sat opposite him, he would refer to him in one of three ways, Sir Ian, Sir, or Boss.

'Jim, we have a little problem which I think your SG9 team might be able to help us with.'

Broad sipped his coffee and waited for the chief to explain more. He knew if his Black Ops SG9 team were to be used it wouldn't be a little problem.

'I received a secure phone call this morning from Tel Aviv, to be precise Kurt Simon himself.'

Broad knew who Kurt Shimon was and of his legendary Kidon teams and their operations around the world.

'As a heads-up he tells me they have an ongoing operation against an Iranian and Hezbollah outfit which may involve some sort of explosive device moving from Tehran towards Europe possibly even London. Now their people are following a Quds Colonel with his Hezbollah bodyguards to Malta. The problem is they do not think this Malta team have the full components yet, and the whole device won't be brought together until it reaches its final destination, which as I say could be London. They don't want to jump on these people in Malta too soon, when they might not have anything on them letting anyone else get away.'

Broad was not happy where this was going.

'So, tell me, why are they telling us this exactly?'

Sir Ian smiled. He could always rely on Jim Broad to hold him to account, the one thing Broad was not was anybody's *yes man* and Fraser respected that.

'I think three reasons Jim. The first is they have seen how we dealt with the Islamic group in Manchester, the Israelis respect that sort of action. The second is they're worried that this group might slip through their fingers and end up in London blowing up half the city when they had them under control for a short period, and third, I think they know we already have an experienced asset in Malta.'

Broad could understand the logic of the first two.

'David Reece, he lives in Malta?'

'Exactly Jim, he lives there, he knows the ground so to speak, and he is our asset, fully equipped to get a handle on things and report back what's happening. Not only that, but he can also take action if necessary.'

'What information have Mossad provided; do we have the full picture?'

'Mossad believe the Iranian Colonel arriving in Malta either has access to or is in the process of moving a small amount of plutonium which has been manufactured in Iran. He has a small crew of

Hezbollah minders with him, and they're arriving on an Iranian merchant container ship which will dock in Valletta tomorrow night. Ships out of Iran are all well monitored since the Americans pushed up their sanctions because of the Iranian nuclear activity. Mossad were able to link into this coverage once they had some intelligence about the movements of this Colonel. They believe he is just moving the plutonium for a handover to another team who will continue with the operation to its conclusion. The Americans will use their satellite coverage wherever they can help. All we can do for now until we know much more, is get involved, so that we have the right information moving forward. Then we can better decide what we do next. That's why we need to get Reece close to the Mossad team, so that we have timely information, and we can decide what's in our best interests, not just those of the Israelis and Americans.'

'Why don't Mossad just bump off this Colonel, they did so in Malta once before?'

'They don't have enough information as to the full plans of the Iranian government and this Colonel. He is also being protected by at least four Hezbollah terrorists, making a shoot-out in downtown Malta out of the question. We need more information, Jim. The Prime Minister out of respect for our links with Malta, will, if necessary, let the Maltese government know if we need to move forward to a kill scenario. For the moment, our job is to gather information and identify more of this team and then as a last resort and only if necessary, move on them.'

'So, what do I tell Reece?'

'Just what we've been talking about, that there is an ongoing Mossad operation in Malta, and he might be of help to them. I know you're worried about us exposing one of our secret assets, but if a device is heading for London, we need our people in there, making decisions on our behalf. In addition, I'm sending Matthew Simons, he is on his way to Heathrow now to catch the next available plane to Malta, with his Middle East knowledge and language expertise he'll back-up Mister Reece in whatever way he can.'

'Is he ground operationally trained?'

'He's done all the firearms, surveillance, and anti-ambush training as far as a desk officer can be trained, no on the ground experience, but his brain and what he has in it will compensate for any deficiencies.'

'I hope so. Hezbollah are a dangerous outfit to come up against in the best of times. So, what you're saying boss is that this is now an official SG9 operation, and I have control?'

'I am indeed Jim, it's over to you and your boy. Simons has been told to contact Reece and brief him on what we know. Contact Reece and let him know he is on his way and give him the details of the Mossad people so he can link up with them that's where we will start.'

Broad drank the rest of his coffee and stood to leave.

'I'll get back to my office and get things rolling and keep you updated.'

'Thank you, Jim.'

The rain outside had stopped, and a weak sun had started to break through the clouds as Broad got into the back of his car.

34

'Where to, sir?' asked his driver.

At first Jim Broad was deep in thought and had not heard the question, then replied when the driver asked the same question again. 'The office please, Brian.'

The office of SG9 the most secret unit of MI6 also known as the Department was a non-descript building inside the perimeter of London City airport. As the car moved out of the car park Brian could see in his rear-view mirror that his boss was lost in deep thought and there would be little or no conversation during this journey.

Chapter 5

David Reece turned in the bed and looked at the face of Mary McAuley as she lay with eyes closed breathing slowly and quietly. The morning sun was shining through the linen curtains bringing a new day into the room and their lives. Mary slowly opened her dark brown eyes and she smiled at the face of the man lying beside her.

'Good morning sleepyhead,' said Reece.

'Good morning, have you been watching me long?'

'Long enough to realise how really beautiful you are when you're sleeping.'

Mary sat up, the thin sheet falling away to reveal her naked body. Reece turned on his back placing his arms behind his head. Reece was also naked, and Mary thought how strong he was sleeping or awake, but she didn't tell him that. She could see the five-inch ragged white scar on his right shoulder where the splinters from a bullet had entered his body. He had told her some of the story, how he had been involved in a shoot-out with an IRA gunman. He never complained about it, even though she knew he was in pain in those times when the metal moved in his shoulder, then he would let out a small groan or stretch his arm for some relief. If it were bad, he would take some pain relief tablets and the pain would soon settle down. She rolled over and sat astride him, his manhood now between her legs. Looking down at him she could see his clear blue eyes which always seemed to get darker when they made love. His hands held her hips and she could feel the firmness as he entered her, as their bodies now moved in sequence both looking into each other's eyes, no words being said.

The buzzing of his smartphone interrupted the moment. They both tried to ignore it, but it continued breaking into their thoughts. Mary stopped first and turning off him lay flat on her back.

'You're going to have to answer that.'

Reece was already reaching for the phone beside the bed, his mood in the moment broken. Whoever was calling at this time of the day better have a very good reason. When he answered the voice of his boss made him sit up and pull the sheet around him.

'David, I'm glad I caught you. I hope I didn't disturb you at anything?' said Broad.

Not for the first time Reece felt his boss had cameras watching his every move.

'No, just about to have breakfast. What's up?'

'Good, are you still in your home location?'

Reece noticed his boss was being secure with his words, not using the word 'Malta' meant he was being extra careful, even though the phone Reece was using had a secure encryption. Broad was obviously worried in case someone was listening to their conversation.

'Yes, I'm still at home.'

'We have a situation which might need your skills, at the very least an on-the-spot assessment, that's why I'm calling you. Our Israeli friends are in your city and running a little show that could have end repercussions for us at home. I want you to link up with them today.'

Again, Reece noted how his boss had told him that Mossad were working an operation in Valletta without specifically saying so. He knew Broad was old-fashioned when it came to talking over the phone even encrypted ones.

'I'm sending you Matthew Simons this afternoon and he'll be able to help you with the connection to our friends and bring you up to date. I'll send you a name and where they're staying. This person will be expecting you this evening and will be able to tell you what they know. You have my number call me if you need anything.'

The call ended without goodbyes.

Mary had sat up. Pulling the sheets around her, watching Reece throughout the call and noticed how his expression had changed from relaxed to one of deep thought as he put the phone back down on the bedside table.

'Work?'

'Yes, and it's come to visit.'

'What do you mean?'

'I have to pick one of our people up from the airport this evening. That was the boss, he's sending me the details.'

Right on cue his phone buzzed on the table. Reece read the message.

'It looks like our little holiday is over for now and we might have a guest staying over tonight. Let us go for a walk and some breakfast with a strong coffee and I'll explain what I know.'

Even though this woman had at one time been an agent in the IRA working for Reece and now they were lovers, there was only so much he could tell her. Need-to-know was always the way of secret organisations and now, she didn't need to know. He knew she would understand even though she'd asked him to leave that world behind. He always remembered one of his instructors when he was on a course with MI5 telling the class of agent handlers, 'The thing about keeping secrets, it's a lot easier if you don't know them in the first place. It's a need-to-know business.'

After they'd worked together in Manchester saving the life of the British Prime Minister in the process, she still felt she was an outsider in that part of his world, and she didn't like it, she felt there was that one part of him he would always have to keep hidden from her.

'OK, give me fifteen minutes to pull something on and brighten up my face.'

'There's nothing wrong with your face, or your body for that matter. Maybe we can pick up later where we were before that call rudely interrupted us.' He smiled.

They walked hand in hand along the promenade of the Qawra seafront to his favourite little café on the headland overlooking the Mediterranean Sea as it splashed over the rocks of St Paul's Bay. The early December sun was up and although there was a small breeze it was warm enough for the T-shirts and shorts, they both wore.

With the coffee and croissants ordered, they sat looking out at the view. Reece had selected Malta and this special place to retire to after the danger of his days in the Special Branch of the RUC police force in Northern Ireland. That was before Jim Broad had caught up with him and invited him to come work for him at SG9. Reece had weighed up his options to retire at the young age of thirty-seven or work a little longer doing the job he loved and the one he knew he was good at. When he had told Broad that he intended to live in Malta, he had no problem with him living there as it was only about three hours flying time to London and the same for many of the main cities in the Middle East and Europe where Reece would be operating.

'Can you tell me what's happening,' she asked.

Reece knew the question would come and he was prepared for it.

'There's not much to tell now, London are sending a guy I know who will tell me more. I must pick him up at the airport this afternoon and then we are going to meet with some people in Valletta. Now you know as much as I do. At least the work for now is here in Malta. You can be sure I'm not happy having to work in my own back yard.'

'If I know your boss that won't last long. You will be on the move wherever it takes you.'

He could see she was already worried. Anything involving his work with the prospect of them being apart hurt her and he knew this. Her

40

eyes avoided his gaze instead she looked at the waves crashing over the rocks at the entrance to the bay.

'Well, I'll keep the bed warm for when you get back.'

'That would be nice, but you better make up the spare. I think we'll have a guest to stay. As for keeping the bed warm, let's walk back slowly and see if it needs warming up now.'

'Calm down big boy, let me finish my breakfast first.' She laughed.

Chapter 6

The Islamic Jihad training camp was a good two-hour drive west of the Iranian Capital. After leaving the motorway, his drive continued along a dirty, dusty, bumpy track into the mountains through two small villages. The Arab enjoyed the drive in the open backed Discovery Jeep he used for such journeys. The wind in his face and hair was better than any car's air conditioning system, and he felt at one with the land around him which always reminded him of his Gaza homeland. As he went through the mountain villages, he could see the spotters in doorways, and some looking after the sheep in the fields. He knew all of them had been supplied with smartphones which they would be using to announce his journey as he got closer to the camp.

The camp had originally been a base for the Iranian Republican Guards Desert Warfare teams and covered two square miles, it had then been handed over to the various Islamic Jihad groups to help them with a location where, they could train their best recruits. Like any camp in the desert, the Portacabin huts and tents were mixed with a few concrete one-story buildings, everything the same sandy colour; the whole camp was surrounded by a fifteen-foot wire fence topped with razor wire. The Arab had trained there himself many years before where he was identified as someone special. He had his medical background, and he was clear why he had joined the cause, and why the West was the real enemy of Islam. His instructors noted how he not only picked up the skills of an exceptional assassin but also how he was able to talk to others, bringing them around to his theology and his plans for the future. He had taken two sharp bends in the road and when he came around the second, he could see the camp, just off the road to his left. He turned down the driveway to the entrance approaching the security barrier, where two men in desert fatigues and armed with Kalashnikov AK47 automatic rifles provided the security that had to be passed by anyone wanting access to the camp. He told the guard his name and that the commandant was expecting him. A quick check by radio and the guard told him he was to go to the first concrete building on the right where someone would meet him, and the barrier was lifted. As he drove through the entrance gate, some memories of his own training days came flooding back. At first, he remembered how the training was completely unexpected. The first few days were filled with how to keep clean in the camp, and how to make a bed properly military style. The recruits then filled out forms and were thoroughly questioned on their backgrounds and their reason for being there. It was nearly a week before they were given weapons to strip down and clean, before a basic firing test to start with, just to see how accurate they were. Evenings were always filled with prayers and religious instruction using the Quran. It was always emphasised they were the soldiers of the Jihad, the Holy War. They washed their own pots, pans, and plates, even though there was a kitchen separate from the recruits, they did their own cooking, cleaning up after they had eaten. As he parked in front of the first building on the right standing outside, with a big smile on his face, was Kalil who had been the base commander when he had trained here and still in charge. He stood around five foot eight, with broad shoulders a large nose above a thick black moustache with his standard black beret placed over his short black hair almost covering his dark brown eyes. His smile of welcome told the Arab all he needed to know; he was glad to see him. He would always remember Kalil as a strict commander but who had now turned into a friend.

As he got out of the Jeep Kalil embraced him and kissed him on the cheeks.

'As-Salaam-Alaikum.'

'Wa-Alaikum As-salaam,' replied the Arab.

Kalil stood back and looked the Arab up and down.

'They have been feeding you too much my friend.' He laughed 'they told us you were coming. Let us go inside, I have some of your favourite coffee ready.'

'That would be wonderful I'm only beginning to remember how hot it can be under your blue skies. Why is it so quiet?'

At almost the same time he asked his question he could hear a loud prolonged burst of gunfire which to his trained ear was that of AK47 rifles on fully automatic.

'As you can see Abdullah our firing ranges are still busy,' replied Kalil.

The Arab remembered back to his own weapon training on the same firing range at the other end of the camp. Many hours of weapon familiarity and use until he could lift any gun, fire it quickly and accurately; then break the weapon down into its working parts to clean and oil them for future use. As he was always told by the instructors a clean weapon is a good weapon.

'So that's where everyone is. By the sound of things, you are busy Kalil. I hope you're not wasting too much ammunition?'

'Don't worry my friend, just enough to get the job done as we always told you. Since your day we have split the camp into different training categories, weapons, explosives, religious teaching, and now how to work with nuclear weapons.'

'Nuclear?'

'Yes, the Ayatollahs are pushing ahead with the whole nuclear plan, so they want our fighters to know how to use it. We have a few young jihadis learning daily from two of our scientists who come down from the city. Now come in and tell me how I can help you.'

Entering the large ground floor of the building he noticed nothing much had changed since his own training days here. The walls which had been painted white a long time ago were now a dusty grey colour. Many posters of the Ayatollah adorned the walls, and they showed their age. There were two wooden chairs behind a desk on which stood a laptop and a printer. The two large windows were closed, each were fitted with air conditioning units that were circulating cool air around the office. He knew there were three rooms at the rear, a toilet, a briefing room which could seat around twenty people and a large cell block, which on occasion had been used to detain traitors to the Jihad.

Near one of the windows was a large couch and two large leather chairs. On the coffee table in front of the couch was a large coffee pot with two small cups some milk and a bowl of sugar.

'Come Abdullah take a seat; the coffee is ready. When our lookouts reported you were on your way, I warmed the water.'

The Arab sat in one of the leather chairs facing towards the window. Kalil poured the strong black coffee and went to a small fridge beside the desk to bring back a bottle of cold water. The Arab took the offered coffee cup and poured a little water into the coffee taking away some of the bitterness from the Arabian beans.

'Just as I remember it, so strong you could stand up in it.' He laughed.

Kalil added a little water to his own cup then a little milk.

'I have become fond of the sweetness the milk gives it. Now to business how can we help you? Tehran did not tell us anything, only that you would be coming, and we are to provide you with whatever you need, no questions asked. All I can think is that it must be very important if it is to involve the Arab the man we call 'mu'alim' which means both craftsman and teacher, so which one are you today my friend the craftsman or the teacher or maybe both?'

Abdullah sipped his coffee which was still a little bitter and a little hot so he would let it rest for a while.

'Your coffee is good as always my friend. I have been given a little job to do which requires someone to help me, someone of a particular kind. I am hoping you will have just such a person here, someone currently training for the Jihad with rough edges who needs a little smoothing by myself to be the help I need. It can be a man or woman, but they must be able to take orders and do what I say. They must also be intelligent and street smart, be able to smell trouble without seeing it, and capable of dealing with it.'

'You are right to come to me and I think we just might have one or two people who fit your requirements. I like to think all our people are special, but as you know some are more special than others. I have our top five people on file here and you can use the laptop to read up on them. I'm needed down at the firing range for an hour, so I'll leave you alone to read, and when I get back, we can discuss what you want to do.'

'Wonderful my friend, but can you leave me a fresh pot of your wonderful coffee to help me concentrate?'

When Kalil left, the Arab started reading the files on the laptop screen. He took his time, each file gave a little of what he was looking for, but in the end and after two pots of coffee, there were two separate piles of paper he had printed from the computer. He had been especially interested in where the people on file had come from; their age, their appearance, their special skills if they had any. He was looking for something the instructors hadn't picked up on, that something that made them special, and looking at a computer screen would only tell the basic story. He worked on the files one by one making notes as he went along. Two hours later he had two possible students; for that would be what they would now become, no matter what they had learned at the camp. If he selected either or both, he was the Teacher, and they would be his students, his apprentices, now he would need to see them and speak with them for himself.

When Kalil returned the Arab showed him the two files he had printed off.

'I need to speak to these two individually, are they still in the camp?'

'Ah, I see you pick the best fruit my friend. Yes, they are still here I will send for them now. Do you mind which one you see first?'

'No, just don't tell them who I am. When I speak with them, I'll do so alone. The less you know the better.'

Kalil nodded, then taking the radio from his belt he spoke a few words giving the instructions that the two students were to come to the office at once. Fifteen minutes later they could hear voices outside followed by a knock on the door.

Kalil stepped outside, then returned with a man dressed in desert clothing and desert boots. The Arab guessed he was in his mid-twenties and noticed how he walked across the room to where he sat watching him. The student was what would be described as of Middle Eastern appearance, with olive skin, dark brown eyes, and the beginnings of a beard, he was muscular at around five feet ten in height. So far exactly how he was described in the file on the desk in front of Abdullah.

'Please sit down,' said Abdullah as he pointed to the chair in front of the desk. Looking first through the file in front of him, the Arab then looked the man in the eyes.

'I've been reading your file and I know you speak English so please do. Do you know who I am?'

'No.'

Abdullah did not elaborate any further.

'It says in your file you originally come from London. Why are you here? I know the standard answers, but I want a truthful one. Why are you really here?'

The man across the table looked back into Abdullah's eyes and a slight smile appeared at the corner of his lips.

'Well…?' asked the Arab.

'I come from a strict Muslim family in Brixton and all my life white, mostly English and Irish men have asked me the same question. 'Why are you here?' This was even though I was born there, brought up as a child there, but just because I worshipped a different god and looked a different colour, they hated me, and I didn't even know them. I went to my local Mosque and, when I was older with some friends, I started to attend the Finsbury Mosque, mainly because it had a reputation for the kind of worship to Allah that I thought I needed.'

'And did it?'

'For a time, but then I saw that the preaching of the holy book was pretty much the same as I had heard before. Then one day a Mullah came to speak. He came from Iran, he was in England illegally, and he talked of Jihad and the need for young men and women to be prepared to fight for the faith. The thing that struck me was that those present were not the usual men, but it appeared to me a select few, who had been observed and invited to this talk. He said something that made me think, he said it did not matter how we fought the Jihad in foreign wars and countries, or on the streets where we lived, but either now or one day soon we would have to fight for our God, our families, our people. I realised then that in my whole life I'd been going through the motions of being a good Muslim but without really committing myself to what that meant.'

'What do you believe now?'

'I decided that I had to be true to myself and Allah, and step forward instead of leaving it to someone else or to future generations. Now is the time of Jihad, of Holy War, and as the Mullah said that day, now is the time for action to get involved, no matter how small or big, you can get involved. Stop leaving it to others, and if you honestly believe now is the time, then step forward. So, I stepped forward with a few others that day and asked how. I'd never been involved with the police or as far as I'm aware I've never been under their surveillance, so I left my home and made my way to Iran, with an introduction from the Mullah to some people in Tehran and here I am.'

He had been leaning forward across the desk in the chair to help get his point to this man asking the questions. Now he sat back, to await the next question from this strange man who seemed to have an air of authority about him that he had never seen before.

'I see from your file you've excelled in firearm training and are quite the marksman.'

'Yes, I seem to enjoy that the best, especially the rifle. Maybe, I think, it's because it can do more damage and I can imagine the damage I can inflict on those people who not only cursed me for the colour of my skin but cursed the God I serve.'

The Arab could see a flash of anger in the student's eyes as he spoke these last words.

'It's easy to imagine killing another, but a far different thing to do so. Do you really believe you could do it? Men, women, children, Christian, non-believers wherever you find them.'

The student knew from the question and the way it was asked that this man had killed in the name of Jihad and that he knew how to kill.

'I do not hate non-believers. I'm sorry for them; they do not know Allah the Holy One as I do. That is not their fault. But they have been killing my people in the name of their God and will continue to do so unless they are stopped. They have the opportunity to convert but if they ignore that opportunity then according to the Holy Word they must die, and if I am to be the instrument of Allah, then I believe I could do it.'

'So, you want to die for Allah?'

'I'd rather fight for him, but if it's the wish of my God that I should die, if that is his purpose, then so be it I will die.'

The Arab had seen and heard enough.

'When you came in, I asked if you knew who I was. Now, do you have any questions for me?'

'No, I've answered your questions and although I've not seen you here in the camp before I believe you are here for a reason, a purpose, and if I'm to learn who you are or what that purpose is, you will tell me if I need to know.'

This was the answer the Arab was hoping for, and the file on the desk had indicated he had made the right choice when asking that the student should be brought to the office.

'Your name in your file is Mohammad Latif is that correct, your true name?'

'Yes, that is the one given to me by my father when I was born and the one on the passport I travelled with through Turkey and to Tehran. I did not want to risk being stopped with a false passport.'

'Where do your family think you are now?'

'When I went to the London School of Economics I lost touch with my family, living in student accommodation. When I finished my degree, it was then I decided to come here. As far as I know no one knows I'm here.'

'You might think that my friend, but the British Secret Service MI6, will notice your passport shows you've left the country flying to Turkey and you've not returned. Your passport will be highlighted for such a return where you would be detained for questioning. They may even be making enquiries about you as we speak, but they'll soon let it drop as you do not have a background that has been brought to their attention before, which is good. From this day on I will be your teacher and you will know me as such, that will be my name to you. Tomorrow you will leave here, and you will be brought to accommodation in Tehran where we will talk further. You will not speak of this meeting to anyone. Under my teaching and command, you will take part in a special mission for Allah. You will be given a new identity and passport and the skills you've been training for will be put to good use soon. Do you understand all this?'

Mohammad nodded, then stood then for some reason, he felt he should bow slightly before leaving the office.

The door to the office opened once more, this time it was Kalil.

'Are you ready for the girl?'

'Give me five minutes then send her in.'

'Was he what you are looking for?'

The Arab knew Kalil couldn't help himself asking, even though he would know it was wrong to do so.

'He will be leaving you tomorrow and he cannot talk about what we discussed so do not ask him my friend. After I've spoken to this woman, we will have another cup of coffee and I'll tell you what you need to know - no more no less. This you understand.... yes?'

Kalil smiled. He knew he had just been rebuked in the nicest way for asking questions when he should have listened instead of speaking. He turned and went outside to find the next student.

When she entered the office, the Arab realised the file on the table in front of him did not do her justice. Her photo showed eyes that were tired and wary of the world. Maybe because the photo was black and white the true deep darkness of her brown eyes did not show

53

through. He knew from the file she was only twenty-five, but the world had treated her badly according to the written words, but he wanted to hear everything about her from her own lips. She wore the traditional headscarf of eastern Islamic women covering her hair and most of her face and when Abdullah invited her to sit and to remove the scarf, he could see the surprise in her eyes as she obeyed the command without protest. Islamic women were not used to being without headdress when in the company of a strange man, however since being at the camp she had begun to expect the unexpected and to obey commands.

Abdullah smiled a smile of understanding, and this seemed to reassure her as she smiled back. She removed the headscarf to let her lush dark brown hair fall to almost cover her face but not enough to cover the three-inch scar on her left cheek, Abdullah noticed both.

'Please relax, Shama, you are not in trouble, and even if you were, from what I've read in your file you could deal with any danger if you had too. Yes, I've read your file and I know a little about you, your past, and why you are here. But I would rather hear from your own lips the answer to my questions.'

'Who are you, and why should I answer any questions?' she replied sitting straight backed in the chair. He noticed how her breasts pressed outwardly upwards against the brown linen shirt.

Again, the Arab smiled and spoke softly.

'For now, please think of me as your teacher and just simply call me Teacher. This is not some interrogation test or exam for your training. As I said, all I want to know for now is, what is not in the file and the real you, so please relax and help me out if you can.'

Now the woman nodded her agreement.

'Thank you. Can we start with a little bit about your background? I know you are from Baghdad and your family sent you here for your protection. The file does not clearly state why you need protection, maybe you can explain?'

Abdullah knew by her hesitation that talking of her past might cause her pain, he waited, letting her take her time to let her tell her story her way.

'I know you speak your native Arabic, French, and English, so if you could answer in English that would be helpful.' Abdullah wanted to see how good her English was. He was surprised just how good when she began to speak.

'My father was a teacher of languages at Baghdad University. He taught me different languages for as long as I can remember, some I remembered better than others and this helped me when I applied to be a nurse at the city hospital.'

'You are only twenty-five so you must have worked hard?'

'Another thing my parents taught me; you can be whatever you want to be if you work hard enough. I studied clinical medicine dealing with everyday illness and I loved my work.'

'And you had to give it all up because you killed a man?'

'I killed an animal.' She spat out the words with the flash of hate mixed with anger in her eyes.

'Please forgive me but I need to know why. All it says in your file is that you killed a man, so you had to escape Baghdad. What really happened?'

He waited as she took her time to answer, she moved from side to side in the chair and stared at the floor, before lifting her head to look him in the eyes. She began to speak slowly at first, getting faster the more her memory came back to her.

'As I said I was a nurse in the hospital, and I dealt with many kinds of injury. I had been seeing one of the junior doctors for a few months. With Asher, it was nothing serious, but I liked him, he was kind and my parents approved. Unknown to me he had been secretly treating injured Hezbollah coming back from Syria. I did not know he was under surveillance by the security police, not until one day they came to arrest him at the hospital. The police inspector leading the arrest was a well-known brute. We had treated many of his poor victims, from beatings to knife wounds, inflicted by him in the cells at the central police station.'

'What was his name?'

'Kamil Burgah,' before continuing she licked her lips and took a deep breath as if there was a bad taste in her mouth.

'When he came to arrest my Asher, he beat him badly while his thugs held him up so he could punch him freely without Asher being able to defend himself. I tried to intervene, but Burgah slapped me on the face knocking me off my feet and before I could get to my feet, they had already taken him. When I went home, I told my parents what happened. My father told me not to get involved, as he knew of this Burgah, and how dangerous he could be. I was not happy, so I decided the next day I would go to the station and ask about Asher.'

'You disobeyed your parents,' the Arab was interested to hear how far she would go to disobey a direct order.

'I know. I did not want to, but I thought it would do no harm to go to the station and ask about Asher; I had feelings for him, I cared for him.'

'What happened next?'

'Burgah took me to his office. The bastard was smiling when he told me that unfortunately Asher had been shot dead while trying to escape. My head was spinning, I couldn't believe it, I did not believe it. He just sat there smiling not caring, then he came around the desk and locked the door to the office. He told me his men knew not to disturb him when his door was locked. He looked at me as if I were a piece of juicy meat he wanted to eat. He asked me why I cared about this Asher, the traitor to Iraq. Was it because he was good in bed, and did my parents know I was a whore who slept around? Now I was too angry for words, I stood and tried to slap him across the face, but he grabbed my hand and forced me backwards across his desk. He was a big man overweight, and his breath smelt of stale tobacco. He pushed his full weight down on me and when I fell across the desk my hand found a long letter opener. I lifted it and tried to stab him, but he grabbed my hand and twisted it behind my back turning me around, and pushing me face down into the desk, he leant over me, and I could feel his whole body pressing down on me.'

The Arab could see the pain in her eyes as she tried to continue. Once again, he spoke softly.

'I know this memory is difficult for you, but you need to get it out, to tell me everything to cleanse your soul and spirit. I do not judge you.'

Again, she took a deep breath before speaking, looking around the room then at the files on the desk before letting her eyes rest on the face of the Arab. She wanted to get everything out into the open and for once in a long time for some reason she believed in this man in front of her. There was something about him she felt she could trust.

'I could feel him thrust his body against mine. I'd never been with a man before, but I knew what he was doing. To put it in simple terms, he was inside me raping me, and calling me bitch and whore as he did it. I closed my eyes and gritted my teeth trying to think of Asher, my family anything other than what was happening. Soon it was over, I heard him breathe deeply and speak the words, 'Yes, yes, you bitch yes.' But it was not over. As he stood, he sliced the sharp paper opener across my cheek. From being raped to feeling the pain and blood pour from my face I stood in shock. He threw the paper opener on the desk and told me to get out and if he ever saw me again, he would give me twice as bad, pass me around his men and mark the other cheek, as you would brand a cow. Then he made his mistake. He turned his back to me to unlock the door. He obviously thought that his little whore had had enough and would want out of there, but he was surprised when I said is that all you have big boy, can we do it face to face next time? The one thing about being a nurse that he should have remembered was that we know exactly where the human heart is in the body, no matter if it's a good or evil one. I moved in close to him and I could see his eyes light up with surprise at what he thought I was going to do with him, but they were even more surprised when I shoved the paper knife deep into his heart the blade all the way into the handle. He tried to cry out, but I held my hand over his mouth as he fell to the floor dead in seconds.'

'Why did you kill him? Why not report him?'

'Who would believe my word against him? He made me feel scared, dirty, and he could blame me for inciting him to rape me? I could have been stoned to death, and he would have made sure that is how a Sharia Court would have found it against me. I thought about this afterwards; but not at the time, the anger in me just burst, yet I felt totally under control and justified. Since then, I have thought about it …. I know he got a quicker, cleaner death than the one I would give him now. Being a nurse, I knew how to test myself for infection or pregnancy and I was clear of both.'

She had answered a question he had been thinking about.

As she told her story Abdullah watched her face closely. He could see the strain the memory was bringing to her. A tear settled at the side of her eyes.

'Let us stop there for a moment,' said Abdullah.

'Let us have some of Kalil's fine coffee, then we can continue in a few moments.'

All she could do was try to smile and nod her agreement.

'Just black and strong for me,' she said.

'The way I like it,' he said as he filled the two small cups.

He thought he would change the subject of the conversation for a little while. The hot sun outside had started to go down on the hills in the distant horizon and the room had more shadow and had cooled slightly.

'How long have you been in the camp?' he asked even though he knew the answer from her file.

'Three weeks.'

'And from what I've read you're a good student. Is there anything you enjoy more than any other in your training?'

As she sipped the hot coffee slowly, she lifted her eyes to look at him to answer.

'I enjoy it all, and I understand how each part fits together to get the best out of me. But if I was to say one thing, I enjoy more than any other, it would be the comradeship, how I've found people like myself who want something different for ourselves, and if that means we must fight for it, to kill for it, to die for it, then I will be ready and more prepared for the future with what I'm learning here.'

The answer he heard was spoken with clarity and passion. These were exactly the things he was looking for in his students. He had heard enough to stop the interview there and then, but he wanted to hear the full story to be completely sure and to let her totally unburden herself to him so that she would feel a comradeship with him, as with no other.

'Can we get back to your journey, the one that has brought you here? What happened after you killed this bastard as you called him? How did you escape; you were in a police station in the middle of Baghdad after all, how did you get to here?'

There was that deep breath again before she started speaking. The wounds and memories still strong. He sat further back in his chair and watched her face once more taking the strain of thought.

'He was dead on the floor without a sound, but with a lot of blood - much of it over me. My mind seemed to be clear and calm possibly from my years of training and being told to slow down and concentrate when I dealt with people in pain or when they had died. I remembered he had told me he always locked his door when he was with people like me, and his staff knew not to disturb him. Even though, I knew I wouldn't have much time. Using tissues from his desk I wiped the blood off my dress, blouse, and hands as best I could, but the stain was still there, so I used a simple trick, I put my clothes on inside out. People don't look to see if you've dressed backwards and with the time I had it seemed the best thing to do.

I took his key and left, locking his door from the outside to give me more time. I walked through the building and straight home, and no one stopped me or seemed to notice. My parents were shocked and at first they wanted to go to the authorities and complain about Burgah and what he had done and the situation he had put me in, but my father eventually realised the danger we were all in if I stayed in Baghdad.'

'I can understand that. Apart from him being a policeman did he have other connections?'

'Connections?' She laughed 'You could say that. He was known throughout Baghdad as the jumper, as he moved seamlessly from one faction to another from Saddam's Ba'ath Party through his security police, to the Americans as an interpreter and torturer, to a job as the city's chief political hunter, and all along the way he made himself a small fortune. He was hated by the people of the city, and that included his own police officers who were genuine law enforcers.'

'It sounds like you did the country a favour. Please, tell me more of how you've come to be here?'

'That's simple. My father's brother is a member of Katib Hezbollah in Iraq, so within the hour my uncle drove me in his Jeep, and using roads he knew, he smuggled me to a small town across the border, the people there brought me here. I'd told my uncle and my parents I wanted to be a soldier of Jihad. Now I'm here answering questions from a strange man.'

She sat back in her chair her story told or so she thought.

'What happened to your parents when the authorities came looking for you which I'm sure they did?'

'Yes, they came and took my parents in for questioning but all they could tell them was that they did not know where I was, which was the truth. As I said there was no love for Burgah, so they were released, and they've not been bothered since.'

The Arab was satisfied. He closed the file, stood, and slowly walked around the desk sitting on it in front of her. Looking down he could see up close that despite the white scar on her tanned skin she was indeed beautiful with eyes that could persuade many a man to do what she asked and that was exactly what the Arab would need from her.

'Thank you for taking the time to tell me your story it has been of great help to me. I may have a mission for you to undertake are you ready to do that without question?'

'Yes.'

'Good. This will be your last night here. Tomorrow Kalil will bring you to another location. I will be there. You will be given a new identity and from now on you will know me as Teacher. You will speak to no one about this do you understand?'

'Yes.'

'Good, until tomorrow then. When you leave please ask Kalil to come in.'

He watched her as she walked to the door and the way she moved brought stirrings of his own basic animal passion. Many Arab men would look at her with disgust because of their deep-seated religious beliefs, but Abdullah only saw a brave woman who would be useful in his fight against the real enemies - Israel and the West.

The Arab instructed Kalil to have both students brought to his villa for three the next day. He instructed him not to ask them any questions and would only tell him they were needed for a mission of great importance. One day soon he'll hear of it and know that he played a part in training his people well for the Jihad and Allah. They parted once more as friends and soldiers in the war to come.

Chapter 7

The main international airport in Malta is busy throughout the year, but especially busy at the height of the tourist season from July to the end of September when the temperature on the island can start to fall and some heavy rainstorms from Africa can bring the island to a halt. When Reece had arrived at the airport, the sun was still warm and the clouds small and white. The arrivals area was still busy but not that busy, making it easy for Reece to pick out Matthew Simons as he came through the customs screens and into the exit area. Reece had sat in on some of Simons talks on the Middle East, its politics, wars, and terrorist organisations. He had a lot of time for Simons and respected the easy way he spoke to get his subject across, taking time after his talks to stay and answer any further questions from his class. Reece had been one of those who stayed and living in Malta not far from the North African coast, he had asked Simons specifically about the risk of terrorist attacks on the island. He had smiled when he replied that they were unlikely but not impossible. Islamic terrorist groups were always targeting the many holiday destinations frequented by British tourists who they considered soft targets for extreme large-scale violence such as the attack on the tourist beach and hotel in Tunisia in the tourist resort of Port El Kantaoui. Thirty-eight tourists, thirty of whom were British, were killed by one gunman. The one thing Reece knew from his life of fighting terrorism wherever he had worked was never to let your guard down and trust no one.

'Matthew how are you?' asked Reece.

'Hi David, it's great to see you. A bit flustered to tell you the truth. I've had little time to breathe since this morning. I was glad the flight took three and a half hours; it's given me time to capture my thoughts and read the files I have for you.'

'Well, let's get going, my car's outside. We can talk on the way to my place, and you can tell me all about why you're here and how I'm going to be involved. You know the boss he likes to surprise me.'

As they drove from the airport Simons told Reece the reason he was here and what London wanted Reece to do.

'I have the files on my laptop which we can download when we get to your place, but basically we will know a lot more when we meet up with our Israeli friends later.'

The sun was almost gone and with it the heat of the day.

'Have you been to Malta before?'

'No this is my first time. I believe it's a beautiful island.'

'If we get the time, I would love to show you around.'

'Time might be a problem, David. I googled Malta on the way over, so I know a little of the history, but if we get free of work, I would love to take you up on your offer and look over the place; it looks fascinating.'

'It is. I love the mixture of all the different Mediterranean cultures from the east to the west, but as usual work gets in the way.'

'Is Mary at your place?'

It did not surprise Reece that Simons knew about Mary. The operation they'd worked on in Manchester and the connection between her and Reece was well known in the top circles of MI6 and the Department.

'Yes, she's back at the villa. She only knows that I'm picking someone up but not who or why.'

Reece knew the need-to-know aspect of his work was always paramount to getting the job done and staying alive.

'I'm not worried about that David. In fact, I'm looking forward to meeting her. I believe she is a stunning beauty.' He smiled.

'She's my stunning beauty you remember that.' laughed Reece.

The rest of the drive was in silence as Reece concentrated on the traffic which was busier than usual for that time of day, and Simons continued to look out at the architecture as they drove, passing under the walls of Mdina, the Silent City to their left and the Dome of Mosta Church in the distance, on their right. Malta traffic still moved on the same side of the roads as in England, but some of the local population drove as if they were in the crowded streets of Rome or London, cutting each other up, always looking for the short cut and sounding their horn loudly if they had to overtake a slower driver. It took Reece another forty-five minutes before he was able to park outside the Villa Joseph in Qawra.

'I can see why you don't want to live in London, it's beautiful here,' said Simons as they entered the gardens of the villa.

'You should see it on a really sunny day.'

'Maybe I will one day.'

Mary was in the front room reading a book when they entered.

'Mary, I would like you to meet Matthew, a friend from the office,' said Reece.

'Pleased to meet you, Matthew. Did you have a good trip?'

Simons, for the moment, couldn't speak. He was transfixed by the woman in front of him.

'Ohhh...pleased to meet you. Yes, thank you it was quiet, no bumps.' He smiled.

'I haven't made any dinner as I don't know what you want to do, Joseph?'

Simons looked at Reece with his eyebrows raised in question.

'It's OK, Matthew. She likes to call me by my code name. In fact, she insists on it. No, sorry we only have time for a quick drink and a chat then we must go out again. I'm afraid you'll be eating alone tonight but I hope we'll be back in time for a nightcap.'

'No problem. Matthew come with me, and I'll show you your room.'

'David, where do you want me to set-up my laptop so you can get a look at what I've brought?'

'Over there on the dining table then go with Mary and I'll fix us a few drinks. What's your poison?'

'Scotch and ice if you, have it?'

'No Scotch here, only the best Irish, Bushmills, OK?'

'Perfect.'

Reece went to the kitchen to get the drinks while Simons left the laptop on the table and followed Mary with his bag to his room.

Two Bushmills later, while Mary continued her reading in the bedroom, Reece gave a breakdown of the issue ahead.

'So, basically London wants us to work with Mossad to keep an eye on this Iranian and a couple of Hezbollah thugs. Find out what they're up to and if necessary, bump them off if it gets too sticky?'

'Well, let's hope it doesn't get too sticky, I don't fancy shoot-outs no matter what the odds.'

'Tell me Matthew, with your knowledge of how these buggers work, what's your gut telling you? My experience is from your everyday Irish cowboy. These Arabs scare the hell out of me.'

'And so they should. They're not just Arabs, as you call them. They come from many groups, religions, and on the odd occasion single people who just hate the West and their false gods. To them, and they honestly believe this, anyone who does not worship the one true God Allah, are infidels; devils who need to be converted or killed. To tell you the truth, the West hasn't helped with its many years of interference in the Middle and Far East, Iraq, Afghanistan, Syria, Libya. Yes, you and I know some of the interference was needed, but much of it was a mistake, now the birds are coming home to roost. Just as you saw in Manchester, when the Islamic side was willing to work with the Irish side to get the job done and again with 9/11 in the States and 7th July in London, they've decided to take us on wherever they can. The gloves are off, and the West has had to take off theirs in response, resulting in the Black Ops organisations such as the Department and you. These people will never stop I'm afraid until they kill us all and get their own version of an Islamic world whatever that will be.'

'Or unless we kill them first. I know what you're saying. I've seen these people up close, and they don't want to talk, to negotiate, they're willing to kill themselves to get the job done. Let's get moving, you wait outside by the car, I'll just say goodbye to Mary. We can grab something to eat on the way, there is a pizza takeaway at the end of the road we can eat in the car.'

Chapter 8

They ate as Reece drove into Valletta, the evening traffic light on the coast road that took them past St Julian's Bay and skirting the Harbour at Sliema, around the Yacht Basin and on into the city itself. Simons watched the beauty of Malta unfold with so many different sights to see, he again had appreciated why Reece preferred to live here instead of London.

'Have you ever worked with Mossad before David?'

'Just on the periphery once. I don't know if you remember when Colonel Ghaddafi shipped the Provos tons of weapons in the eighties and one of the ships, the Eksund, was stopped by the French with one thousand AK47 rifles, over fifty ground to air missiles and two tonnes of Semtex?'

'Yes, I remember the one that didn't get away.'

'Correct, it was believed afterwards that two similar ships had already got through. The Eksund was being monitored by Mossad, and RUC Special Branch had been informed to expect another shipment of weapons and an increase in attacks because of that information. The French who have always been sympathetic to the Arabs and wanted more cheap oil from Ghaddafi jumped on the ship first, releasing those involved within a short time. Of course, the British, Israelis, and the Americans, who all knew about the ship, were unhappy to say the least. My part as a Special Branch officer was to deal with the aftermath of these weapons getting through resulting in hundreds of dead. I've always respected the fact that Mossad face the same enemies and dangers that we have and that was one occasion when they wanted us to get these bastards as much as we did.'

'Well, these bastards as you call them have something that is far more dangerous than all the weapons in those ships, so let's hope this time your connection with Mossad will be more successful.'

Reece knew his way through the one-way system through the centre of Valletta City. Soon they were pulling into the car park near the ancient city walls and the five-star Grand Excelsior Hotel.

'Well Matthew, it looks like Mossad have a bigger expense account than SG9.'

Reece knew something of the hotel. It was a five-star experience throughout with stunning views from the Tiki Bar and Restaurant overlooking the Marsamxett Harbour and the historic Fort Manoel, with the entrance to the harbour and the Mediterranean Sea in the distance. When Mary had first come to Malta with Reece, they'd spent an amazing afternoon relaxing in the sun on the terrace after a wonderful lunch while drinking their second bottle of white wine.

Reece asked the receptionist to try the room of Mr Stressor and to tell him Mr Reece was waiting in reception for him. He waited while the receptionist called the room and she confirmed that Mister Stressor was on his way down.

They took a seat at a table in the large reception area and waited. Five minutes later one of the lift doors opened and a man and woman walked towards where Reece and Simons were sitting. Reece noticed by the way they dressed and walked that they fitted right into the type of client the hotel preferred; people with class, both were the appearance of good health itself, fit and tanned. The woman wore jewellery to complement the white linen dress with a single string of white pearls around her neck.

Both men stood as the man reached out his hand.

'Mister Reece?'

Reece shook the offered hand.

'It's David and this is Matthew.'

'Both Jewish names from the Bible,' said the woman 'and if it's first names I'm Anna and this is Palo.'

'Both names, not from the Bible,' smiled Reece.

'Please let's sit here. It will be quieter than the other areas of the hotel,' said Palo.

As they sat facing each other Reece thought how beautiful the woman was, and how if she was, as he had been told by Simons, a member of the famous Mossad Kidon teams, how deadly she could be.

It was the woman who took the lead.

'We all know something of why we are here. You know our background and we yours. It's why we are here that matters,

72

basically because that's what our masters want us to do. As time is of importance I'll get right to the point. We know that a ship carrying an Iranian Colonel will dock in Malta tomorrow evening. Our masters want us to watch him and find out what he is up to for now, nothing more nothing less. At least that is our understanding. Do you feel that is correct?'

'That's our understanding too,' said Reece.

'I'm sorry we didn't ask if you wanted something to drink?' asked Palo.

Reece had been waiting. He knew the prices and if Mossad was footing the bill, he would be happy to have a drink.

'Thank you, a Bushmills Whiskey, on ice,' said Reece who knew the hotel was one of the few places on the island that served his favourite tipple.

'Same again,' said Simons.

Palo called a waiter and ordered the two whiskies and a bottle of Chardonnay Wine with two glasses.

'Tel Aviv was impressed with how you dealt with that threat in Manchester,' said Anna.

'It was a team job, and we lost a few friends.'

'I think the innocent people who walk the streets of this world don't realise we are at war every day,' said Palo.

'I'm inclined to agree with you there Palo,' said Matthew, 'and for every one of these terrorists we kill, two more pop up. It's going to be a long war. As we are only four will that be enough to cover what you want to do?'

'For now, Matthew, I think we will have enough. If we are working together, I expect our masters will want daily updates. I'm sure if we need to increase what we need; like you, we can get extra resources here quickly.' Again, it was the woman who spoke, taking the lead in the conversation.

Reece had something to add to the discussion.

'The one thing we found in Northern Ireland; the more we killed the experienced guys, then those who stepped into the dead men's shoes were not of the same calibre, making it easier for us to close them down when they tried to carry out their operations. Cut the head off the snake and the body dies.'

'There's a difference David,' said Anna, 'the Irish terrorist knows there is a risk of being caught or killed but he always hopes to escape. The people we will be dealing with here and some of those you dealt with in Manchester do not care. To them it is an honour to die as a martyr for Allah. They don't worry about being caught which makes them more difficult to deal with.'

The waiter interrupted the conversation when he arrived with the drinks.

Reece raised his glass, 'Cheers.'

Both Israelis raised their glasses and spoke in unison. 'L'Chaim, to Life.'

'Do you have much information of this Colonel and what he is up to, and why he is coming here?' asked Reece.

Again, it was Anna who spoke.

'Not much more than you have already. I understand our boss has been in touch with your boss and a full file on Colonel Ali Shafi of the Quads Unit of the Iranian Republican Guard is available to us all. He is the head of the Security at one of their nuclear development sites. Another one that they deny having. From our information he is on his way here on an Iranian cargo ship; carrying, we believe, a small amount of plutonium for what purpose we are unsure. We do not know if he is going to use it himself or give it to or sell it to someone else. Malta has no strategic attraction or purpose for Iran so we believe he may pass the plutonium on to someone here, or the ship with him and his package will sail further to another port. In the meantime, it's our job to observe and report.'

Reece swirled the ice cubes around the glass. Looking at both Mossad agents he took another sip of the whiskey before he spoke.

'I presume you have all we need for tomorrow. Up-to-date photos of our target. The details of the ship, when it will arrive, and where it will dock in Valletta, it's a big harbour.'

This time Palo answered.

'Yes David, we have all those answers. The ship is expected around 6 p.m. Can I suggest we exchange phone numbers to keep in touch and we can send you all those details? Like you, no doubt, we all have encrypted phones so the details being passed won't interfere with our security or yours. We have contacted one of our people who lives on the island, and they've already supplied us with two cars and radio equipment we can use. They will also supply us with the details of a building close to where the ship will dock. A building we can observe safely from. We understand that as you live here in Malta you may know your way around fairly well, so that will be of great help if we need to follow this man.'

'I don't know every nook and cranny, but I have a basic knowledge of Malta. Do you have maps?'

'Yes, we have good maps,' replied Palo, 'the type used by tourists as we find they highlight important places of interest better.'

'Good, have you weapons?' Reece asked.

'From tomorrow we will have them,' answered Anna.

'Good. I understand that this Colonel will have some Hezbollah minders with him and if things go tits up, we need to be able to get out of trouble,' said Reece.

'Tits up?' asked Anna with an inquisitive smile.

'It means if things start to go wrong or there's danger, we will also be armed,' said Reece.

'What are the local security forces and police like, are they inclined to get in the way?' asked Anna.

'The biggest danger is the police.' said Reece, 'It's not a big island so they don't miss much, and as we are out of the tourist season their problems are few leaving them free to catch-up on their own holidays and paperwork. I do not see them as a problem. There is a small naval unit based here in Valletta which concentrates more on smuggling from Africa and Sicily; again, this should not be a problem. There is a small military unit based inland. They do a lot of training in the other European countries with a small contingent on ceremonial duties. Again, with this being out of the tourist season, this is only on a couple of occasions. All have access to weapons, but in all my time here, I've never heard of a single shooting. Unless we are stupid enough to bring attention to ourselves, we should have no problems.'

'What if we have to use our weapons?' asked Palo.

'Let's hope that won't be necessary, but my training, and I am sure your training, is to shoot to kill when threatened. When I was undercover in Northern Ireland, two British soldiers in civilian dress accidentally drove their car into a place where a republican funeral was taking place; both were armed but tried to fire their guns in the air to keep the crowd back. Unfortunately, this did not work, they were overwhelmed, captured, beaten, and shot dead. I saw the whole thing afterwards as it was videoed from an army helicopter above the scene. It was not something I'll ever forget. After that any of us working that war made a promise to ourselves that if we were in a similar situation we would shoot to kill. We would rather face a twelve-man jury of our peers than be carried by six men to our grave.'

'I couldn't agree more David,' said Anna.

'Would you like another drink?' asked Palo.

Reece downed what was left in his glass.

'No thank you. I think we should all get an early night; we could have a few busy days ahead of us. Excellent, let us meet back here tomorrow at 3 p.m. and work from there. For tonight we will update London as I'm sure you will do the same for Tel Aviv.'

Standing they all shook hands.

'Until tomorrow then,' said Maria.

'Until tomorrow,' said Reece.

As they walked back to the car Reece could only think about the female Mossad agent and how her body moved in that white dress showing every curve when the slight breeze had caught it as she'd walked from the lift towards him. He loved Mary but he knew like all women she would want to know what the other women in your life looked like and how you felt about them. He would have to lie about Anna's beauty, but then he was good at lying.

Mary was still up when they got back. Simons went to his room to update London on the meeting with the Mossad agents, while Mary poured them all a glass of red wine.

At this time of year when the sun went down it could be cold, especially when you lived in a house on the shore of the Mediterranean Sea, when the winter storms could bring a strong wind directly off the top of the waves onto the shore.

'How did your meeting go?'

'It went OK, but I think it will mean more work for a few days for myself and Matthew so you might be on your own for a while.'

'What's it all about Joseph. Will you be in danger?'

'I can't tell you too much, the less you know about these things the better, but this I can tell you, it's basically a watching job. We will be working with other people to gather information for our bosses to keep them happy.'

'These other people you will be working with. Does it include a woman?'

There it was! The question he knew would come. Mary could read him like a book when it came to his job, and she knew if he was going to be working on a watching brief then there would always be the possibility that there would be a female operative working with him.

'Yes, one of the other team is a woman operator, why?'

'Oh, I don't know, just instinct, I think. It's hard enough for me not knowing what you're doing all the time and I understand. The secrecy, the need to know, you've always explained but I know when you must work closely with others sometimes there will be a woman and I suppose I'm a wee bit jealous that it's not going to be me by your side. What's she like? Is she beautiful, no, don't tell me I'd rather not know? But is she beautiful Joseph?'

Reece smiled and taking her in his arms kissed her.

'You never have to worry about another woman beautiful or not, she is there like me to do a job, no more no less. I love you Mary, no one will ever be able to take your place.'

Now it was her turn to smile, and she poured a little more wine.

'Right answer, Mister Reece.'

Simons came out of his bedroom.

'I hope one of those glasses is for me?'

'Of course, help yourself,' said Mary.

'Great I needed that,' said Simons as he took a large swig from his glass, 'London updated, and we are to go ahead as agreed at the meeting but keep them informed.'

'By the sound of things, you're both going to be busy tomorrow, so I suggest we finish this bottle of wine and get an early night.'

'Matthew and I have a few things to discuss but it won't take long.'

'Then I bid you both goodnight, but don't stay up too late. Are we still walking up to the café in the morning?'

'Yes, and Matthew too if he wants to join us.'

'No thanks. I've had a long day and I'll need a lie-in if you don't mind guys.'

'Just me and you then Mary.'

Chapter 9

The Arab, as was his usual routine, began his day as the sun was rising, leaving the villa for a three-mile run then ten lengths of the pool before a simple breakfast of bread and fruit washed down with two cups of strong coffee. After a quick shower he drove to the Grand Bazaar in the city and once again met with the General of the Quads Overseas Operations outside the same café where they'd met before. This time they were alone and as far as he could see the General's bodyguards were keeping a low profile because they were nowhere in sight. The Arab told the General he had found the two students he needed for the next part of the operation. He also requested that he provide two new passports, giving him the details that were required, he would send him the photos later. The General described what the operation needed and how he should proceed. He knew the Arab would proceed as he would see it, and that the details he had given to him would only be used as the outline. The meeting lasted just over an hour. At the end of their conversation the Arab now knew the target and was pleased as he drove back to the villa that he had recruited the right people to complete the operation with success. As he left the café he did not notice the dust covered blue

Toyota Hiace van further down the street. If he had, he would have noticed that the rear windows were black one-way reflective glass. The kind of glass that would protect the two Mossad agents inside, who could take their photos without being seen. Their target for the morning had been the Quads General. The man he had met with was unknown to them, and they had no idea that the batch of photos they transferred later that day would raise so much interest at Mossad HQ in downtown Tel Aviv.

Kalil brought the two students to the villa, not trusting the task of such an important assignment to anyone else, he appreciated that as the operation would be led by the Arab, the fewer people who knew of it the better. He did not stay long and after a coffee left for the city where he had business to see to, before returning to the training camp. The Arab showed the students to their rooms which were a great improvement on the tents and Porta cabins they had been staying in during their training. He told them to shower and change into fresh clothes to get rid of the desert sand, then meet with him on the open terrace where the cool breeze was blowing gently through the olive trees that surrounded the property.

One hour later the two students sat beside each other facing the Teacher who had a large file on the table between them.

'We will eat later. But first I'm sure you're both curious about a couple of things. First, why did I choose you and second, what are we going to do? So, do you have any questions?'

Both remained silent.

'I'll start with the first question which in a way answers the second. You both have the skills I'll need if we are to complete our mission. You both know how to use weapons and communications. You both know something of the use of nuclear weapons. More importantly, you are both committed to the cause even if your reasons for being here are different. But most of all to me you're still fresh, still with much to learn, skills that only I can teach you. I've been given a mission that consists of three parts. This is your first lesson, security, for your own part in the plan, you will work alone. You may have to kill someone to complete your part. Are you willing to do that if you have to, or if I ask you to?'

Both students nodded.

'Even if the person you have to kill is to your knowledge a good Muslim?'

Both students looked at each other before nodding once more.

'Good, because there may be a time or a reason when you will have to kill someone Muslim, Christian whoever. You must always continue to believe in the reasons you've joined this Holy War. The same reasons why I've chosen you. The Jihad is more important than our lives. If it is to succeed, we must always believe that. As I told you yesterday, you're the students, and I'm the Teacher. For this operation you will be working in Europe under my command and with different identities. We are finished for now, so you may go to your rooms to pray and rest. Before you do, I need to take your photos for your new passports. We will talk more around dinner this evening when I'm sure you will have many questions which is only natural.'

The students never said a word and having posed for their photos taken on the Teacher's camera phone, retired to their rooms while he forwarded their pictures to the General.

The empty plates after dinner on the veranda showed the students enjoyed eating something better than the training camp food. The evening breeze was blowing gently through the trees surrounding the villa. The Arab, who liked to cook, had made the meal. The conversation included how the students felt about their training, world events, and the news of the day. The Arab spoke with a quiet voice, a voice that both students listened to with concentration, neither wanting to miss anything being said by the Teacher.

'I've chosen you both for an important operation. You each have in your own way a particular set of skills that Allah needs. You both speak English and from now on that is the only language we will use between us; here, now and wherever you are when you leave here on your tasks which I'll explain to you each in turn alone. The part you will each play will involve your own individual skills. At the start of the operation, you will be working on your own, but like the jigsaw, if you're successful, we will all come together at the last part to complete our mission. Therefore, I'll brief you alone. The less each of you know about the full jigsaw, the safer our security will be. When we each complete our parts and we come together at the end game, only then will you understand why this has to be this way.'

'Are we to sacrifice ourselves for the sake of Allah?' asked Shama.

The Arab could see no fear in her eyes nor hear fear in her voice when she asked the question. He could sense she did not fear death and he respected her even more for being brave enough to ask it.

'No, my child I know you both have dedicated your lives to the cause of Islamic Jihad. You both knew from the start that there would always be the possibility to give your life to that cause, to be a sacrifice to Allah if needed. The operation I will describe to you both will not require you to give that sacrifice, but to send hundreds of the enemies of Allah to hell and if the operation goes well to live, where you will be known among the soldiers of Allah, as one of his great heroes. If you do die during that operation then you will be among the greatest of the Martyrs and will pass easily into paradise to sit at the feet of Allah and hear him call your name. For now, you will rest tonight. With the early morning we will run, swim, and keep fit; then your education for the operation will begin, when I'll teach each of you what is expected. We do not have much time and there is much for you to learn and understand, so be awake with the sunrise and ready for the day and to fight as a soldier of Allah and Jihad. Inshallah, the future is in God's hands so until tomorrow, relax. This evening take a walk, enjoy the night sky, we will talk in the morning.'

Chapter 10

Jim Broad had spent the morning at his desk reading through the many intelligence reports from his SG9 agents around the world and the other files from MI6, MI5, and GCHQ, that linked into his own team's operations on the ground. Broad always tried to be in the office for 7am to get ahead of things before the day brought its own problems. He read for the fourth time the update from Matthew Simons, telling him what was happening in Malta and the meeting with the Mossad agents. The circulation notes at the top of the page showed the restricted readers who would have access to these reports, the Prime Minister, Sir Martin Bryant, the head of MI6, MI5, and Broad. The need to know strictly restricted to these few. Only they knew who and what SG9 were. Their job to find and eliminate those terrorists threatening the UK. It had taken Broad the full hour he allowed each day to satisfy himself that he had read enough, and to feel he was fully up to date with what was going on in the world he inhabited. The red-light button on his desk phone started flashing indicating that Sir Ian Fraser was on the secure line.

'Good morning Jim, how's things?'

'Not bad Sir Ian. What's up?'

'I suppose you're up to date with today's reports and the Malta operation?'

'Yes, just finished reading them it looks like our people have a grip on things down there.'

'Yes, but something has come in this morning which might interest you and have some influence on what your team in Malta are doing. Could you meet me at my office in an hour for a chat, I don't like spending too much time on these things.'

Broad knew of 'C' and his old-fashioned methods where he preferred to see people's faces over a table rather than a voice on the phone.

'Yes, that's not a problem see you in one hour.'

'Good man, see you then.'

Putting the phone down, Broad lifted the Malta file one more time to make sure he had all the answers for his meeting with Sir Ian, then buzzed his secretary to arrange for his driver to have the car ready in ten minutes. London traffic was light and even though he was early for his meeting, Sir Ian had Broad brought into the office as soon as he arrived forty-five minutes after leaving his own.

'Have you read the overnight reports?' asked Fraser.

It was a question where Fraser already knew the answer. He knew Jim Broad was a creature of habit and was always in the office early just to make sure he could answer questions when they came. Fraser felt it was only good manners to ask his Black Ops Chief such a question.

'Yes, I think I'm up to date.'

This answer let Fraser know that Broad had read the reports but that he was aware that there was something he did not know, and that was why the summons to the office of 'C' instead of a chat over a secure line.

'I see our people have met up with the Mossad crew,' said Fraser smiling.

Seeing his boss smile when asking a question was a rare thing and it helped Broad relax. Whatever it was that Fraser was going to tell him it was not going to be trouble.

'Yes. Everything is looking good, and I expect them to get back to us later today after they do some work with the two Mossad agents.'

'It's early days and I want you to know that Sir Martin Bryant has been in touch with me, to say that if we need anything, he can contact the British High Commissioner in Malta to get it for us, no questions asked.'

'I'm not too happy with any involvement from civil servants, even Bryant or High Commissioners,' answered Broad.

'Don't worry, Jim. I told him the same thing while thanking him at the same time. Apparently, the High Commissioner is an old university chum of his, and, according to him, understands the need-to-know philosophy. But we should always keep contacts like these sweet. Do not burn our bridges as it were. But why I really asked you here concerns a call I had this morning which may have some bearing on what is happening in Malta. The call was from Kurt Shimon in Tel Aviv. It would appear they have an ongoing operation in Iran during which their agents photographed a meeting between a high-ranking Quads officer and another man, who from their files, they've subsequently identified as our friend the Arab.'

Fraser pushed a file across the desk to Broad before continuing.

'As you can see Jim the photos are excellent and better than anything we have on file here, so I suggest we get them out there to our people on the ground as soon as. I suspect knowing how Mossad operate, these pictures do not tell the full story, so we need to suspect everything we are being told. I like Kurt Shimon, but I don't love him. He's in the same business as us protecting his country and, like us, we have some secrets we don't tell everybody and that includes our friends.'

'You mean the CIA?'

'I mean everybody, but especially the CIA. Their big problem since 9/11, is any information they get they react on, and most of the time they react too quickly by sending in the heavy cavalry or just hitting everything with a drone. We are a bit more subtle. Let us find out what the bastards are up to first before we blow up half a city block just to get one guy.'

'Mossad haven't held back from doing just that in the past,' said Broad.

'I know that only too well, so let's keep some of our cards close to our chest as well. Like you, I read a report; but it only tells half the story. I want you to talk to Reece before he meets up with these Mossad people today. Send him the photos but tell him to keep them to himself and Simons. I want to see if their people have the same photos and if they share them with us. Tel Aviv will presume we will give them to our people in Malta, but I want to see if they've given them to their own people. There may be something going on here that Shimon doesn't want us to know, the full picture may be hidden, so let us play it slowly and let us see if they have any more cards up their sleeve.'

'I hope they aren't playing games. These people we are dealing with don't play for fun, they play for real.'

'I see in the report that the plan for today is to sit and watch, to try to work out what this Iranian is up to. Have you any thoughts on what might happen next?'

'It's a wait and see game, but if he comes ashore with anything that looks like a bomb or a weapon, between our guys and the Mossad team, we should be able to handle it.'

'You mean take him out?'

'If we need to, but he'll have those Hezbollah bodyguards, so let us hope it won't come to that. Reece is experienced enough and knows the land in Malta, so he'll make sure the Israelis know the score. We will work with them if the threat concerns both our countries, but we will not be taking orders from them. If we consider that threat needs to be eliminated, we will work alone if we need to.'

Sir Ian stood and walked to the large window overlooking the Thames. Broad could see he was deep in thought and waited to allow those thoughts to surface.

'Right Jim. You get back to your office and update Reece on the way forward. I have a meeting with the PM in Downing Street at ten and I will do likewise. The Arab is the terrorist poster boy and with this

Quads Colonel arriving in Malta most likely working with him, they're up to something big. If we can nip it in the bud before it gets too far all the better, but for the moment we don't have enough of the picture to do that, so tell Reece what we need. After I have seen the PM, I'll give Tel Aviv a call to see if I can push them for more information on what they think this meeting between The Arab and the Quads General in Tehran was all about.'

Broad sent the photos to Reece then called him.

'Good morning David. I thought you would like something juicy to start your day, a nice photo of our friend the Arab. Do you like it?'

'It's better than the one Matthew brought. So, do we still think there is some connection between him and our Iranian friend here?'

'We do, especially as he was meeting with an Iranian Quads General. 'C' thinks so as well. He is briefing the Prime Minister as we speak. We want you to be wary of our Mossad friends let them tell you the story of the meeting and the photos. Don't let them know you're aware of them yet. Have you everything you need?'

'Yes, for now.'

'If you run into any problems with the locals, the British High Commissioner to Malta is an old school buddy of Sir Martin Bryant. I don't know if he would be of any use but horses for courses when needed. His name is Sir Julian Richardson Smith. Good luck today, we can catch-up later.'

Bryant keeping his finger in the pie, thought Reece. Only if really needed was an understatement.

'Mary. Are you ready for our walk I need to do some serious thinking and the fresh air will help?'

You know me, I'm always ready.' She smiled.

Chapter 11

After a run, a swim, and a light breakfast the Arab spoke to Shama first, now his student with the new name of Yasmin, at the table on the veranda. The male student Mohammad now Hassan having gone for a shower after his run.

'You are now Yasmin. Your previous life is gone. It was but a preparation for the life you're now going to live, the life of a soldier of the Jihad. You have already been told it will be a hard life, one of danger and test. Your new passport and documents will arrive today. Tomorrow you will fly from here to Rome, then from Rome to Malta, where you will meet with an Iranian Colonel who will pass to you a small package. You will then return to the airport and take a flight to London. There you will receive details of a safe house where you will stay until I come for you. Do you understand all this, what I say?'

'Yes, will I be supplied with a weapon?'

'Only when you get to London, you're training on how to use many different weapons will always be useful to you.

'I know it might not be what you expected to do on your first mission but the meeting in Malta and your transporting to London of the package you will be given, is vital to the success of our plan. That is why I asked you both yesterday if you could kill a Muslim. You must always remember you will be alone, and the Colonel will have Hezbollah bodyguards who are not your mission. The Arab spent the next hour describing in detail the part Yasmin had to play if the mission was to be a success. Your job is to collect the item and get to London safely. Have you any questions?'

'I'm to be alone until I get to London?'

'Yes, as I've said, this part of the operation is for you alone; an important part of the final jigsaw when we all meet again in London. You will be supplied with your documents, money, and a phone with only two numbers, mine and your fellow student Hassan. You can call me at any time but do not call Hassan until you are in London. The less we say over a phone the more secure we will be. Hassan will be waiting for you when you get to London. Let him know when you've landed.'

'Will I be able to recognise this Iranian, will I have the information I need?'

He could see she was worried and needed some reassurance.

'Do not worry Yasmin you will be given all the information you will need plus a photo before you leave. I have every confidence in you and the Iranian will be expecting you but will not know what you will be doing.'

'This package I have to pick up from him and transport to London, will it be easy to get through airport security?'

'Yes, it will look like a normal small walking stick and will be made of lead which does not give off any sign of what it really is; a small amount of weapons grade plutonium which on its own won't constitute a device. You will need to walk slowly with it as if you have a leg injury and you will be able to carry it on-board the aircraft and place it in the overhead locker during the flight. I don't anticipate any problems.'

'Thank you for placing your trust in me, I will not let you down.'

'Allah will be with you; you have nothing to fear so rest now and prepare yourself for tomorrow and the mission ahead. When you return to your room, please ask Hassan to come here.'

The Arab poured himself another cup of coffee before sitting back at the table. He felt the cooling breeze as it travelled through the branches of the trees and could smell the orange blossoms that surrounded the villa. Hassan refused the coffee when he sat opposite the Arab.

'How are you today Hassan,' the Arab asked in English.

'I'm fine thank you. I've had my run, my swim and a good breakfast so I'm ready for the day.'

'Good, we need to get to work, now the operation has started. I've briefed Yasmin on her part which eventually will take her to London. You will fly to Paris in two days from now. Then I want you to take the Eurostar to London and contact our friend in London. You will then meet with Yasmin who, if things go to plan will already be in London. She will text you to let you know she has arrived.

Tomorrow you will be given your papers and passport with any information you will need.

'Your part of the plan when you get to London will be to find rented accommodation with the help of a trusted friend who already lives there. His details will be in the papers I will give you. I'll give you a phone with only mine and Yasmin's number. I am number one and Yasmin two in the phone's address book, they will be the only numbers you will need, and the phone won't be used for anything else not even to call for an Uber or a pizza, do you understand?'

Hassan nodded.

'When you get to London text me one word, *arrived*. Once you text me, I will move from here to London. You will wait with Yasmin until I arrive. Have you any questions.'

'No, I'm sure the papers I have to read will explain more of my mission.'

'Inshallah, read them well, you will destroy them after you have done so. Memorise what you need, and I will see you in London.'

When Hassan had returned to his room the Arab found a quiet place in his garden and kneeling on the soft grass, he knew he had chosen his students well, he bowed and prayed to Allah for success.

Chapter 12

Mary recognised the signs; Joseph had been quiet after his phone call with London. He had still been silent as they walked to their café on the Qawra seafront for the usual coffee. It was a bit colder this morning, even though the sun was up, so they dressed for the day, each with hooded fleece and long cotton trousers. Reece wore his favorite black baseball cap with the flag of Malta badge.

'You're quiet, Joseph. Are you OK?'

He stopped walking and turned towards the sea and stopped to lean on the rail that ran alongside the path.

'You know, I love this place. Our morning walk, the sea, the air, and I never want that to change. It is our bolt hole from all the horrors of the world, some of that world we've lived in. But I always hoped that it would leave us alone here. Now the bastards have come here, and I must do something about it. I'm worried that if something goes down here, then our little peaceful, happy world will be finished forever.'

She wanted to hug him tight. To hold him and protect him from his world, but she knew she could only do so much, and she felt the hurt he was feeling.

'Don't worry Joseph they can try to get us, but we are stronger together than they will ever be. Remember what I told you many years ago when you worried about things, they can't make you pregnant.'

He laughed at her remembering something she'd taught him that he had passed on to others. There are always worse things in the world, if you only deal with the ones you must face, it's enough to be going on with. He put his arms around her and pulling her close he whispered in her ear, 'Thank you for being here with me, I love you.'

'I love you too Joseph and I'll love you even more if you buy me a warm cup of coffee I'm freezing.'

'You're right let's get on with the day.'

After the coffee and the walk, they returned to the villa to find Matthew Simons working on his laptop.

'Did you enjoy your walk?'

'Yes, thank you,' said Mary, 'have you had any breakfast?'

'I stole some of your lovely Maltese bread, it's delicious.'

'You're welcome to whatever you need. I'm off for a shower to let you two talk and plan your day,' she said with a smile.

'You have a keeper there David.'

'You don't need to tell me. That's one thing in my life I can be sure of. Now are you up to date with the latest from London?'

'Yes, I've downloaded everything for you to go through at your leisure, but I think you probably know everything anyway. What do you think will happen today?'

'We work to the schedule and plan already agreed with our two Mossad friends, but we take everything they say and do with a pinch of salt, we can't fully trust them. Like us they have a hidden agenda of protecting their own country. I don't fault them for that but let's keep our guard up when we meet them later.'

'The new photo of the Arab gives us a head start if he appears. Do you think he will?'

'I'm not sure. His kind keep their heads down until the last minute. But, if he does show himself, he had better be prepared to die, because if the Kidon don't get him we will.'

'Don't you think we could capture him; he would be a great catch for our people to work on?'

'I don't think he would be willing to come along peacefully. I'm just saying that if we do see him, we need to be prepared for someone to die, and after Manchester I don't want it to be one of ours.'

Simons knew about the shoot-out with Sean Costello and Sharon Lyndsey, The White Widow, in Manchester; when one of the SG9 agents, April Grey had been shot dead by Lyndsey who had then escaped. In the subsequent confrontation Reece had shot and killed Costello before he could kill any more people. He also had heard the story in the secret world, how Reece and another SG9 agent had tracked down Lyndsey and her two bodyguards to Egypt and shot all three dead.

'What about weapons? Do we have them?'

Reece went to the set of drawers in the dining room and took out a handgun.

'Are you familiar with firearms?'

'I've done all the usual courses and drills, but I'm a desk jockey. I fire words from a computer not a gun.'

Reece placed the gun on the table and started to break it down into its component parts; then taking a small piece of cloth and a jar of gun oil from the same drawer, started to clean each part of the weapon, the stock, the barrel, and the spring. This took a few minutes then he expertly assembled the gun and placed it on the table in front of Simons the fully loaded magazine beside it. He then unloaded the magazine one bullet at a time and left it on the table beside the fifteen bullets and did the same with the spare magazine.

'I've had this gun since my Special Branch days it has never let me down. A clean weapon will never let you down. Removing the bullets now and again will let the spring in the magazine rest so when you need it to do its job, it's unlikely to jam. As a government agent I have an International Firearms Licence which allows me to transport the gun over most borders if it's not assembled in its killing capacity. But as you can see, I've assembled this baby so many times I can do it easily and quickly even in the dark. I know the Department like more modern Glock pistols without the safety catch, but Smith and Wesson will do for me with one round in the breech and fourteen rounds nine mill parabellum in the mag. Fifteen in the spare for good measure. Today as it's basically a sit and watch and report back gig, I suggest you do without a weapon. We have the name of the High Commissioner on Malta, and we can get one if we need to. I think our Mossad friends would be able to get us one if we need one, trust me on that. Embassies and Consulates always have weapons available in case of an attack on their buildings, but we do not want civil servants getting their nose in the game, that's when things can really go wrong. Take it from me I know what I'm talking about, there's been times when I would seriously consider shooting one of them instead of a terrorist. From their little worlds they can do more damage than an idealist with a gun.'

'I'm happy with that. As I say, I'm just a desk jockey but I'm also OK to sit, watch, and report. If we must follow on foot or in vehicles then I can do that. I'm only too glad that they drive on the same side of the road as we do at home.'

'I don't think the Iranian crew will be looking for a shoot-out but if anything does go down, you take cover, and leave it to me and our Mossad buddies. A fight is the last thing I want here. I live here and hope to do so for a long time.'

Mary came back into the room, her hair still wet. Even though it was long she preferred to let it dry naturally, the heat in Malta usually taking care of the drying process quickly. Even though this time of year it was cooler it was still warm enough to get the job done.

'You two still chattering?'

'We have finished for now, so a fresh pot of coffee would be good if you're going to the kitchen,' said Reece.

'Watch it you, what did your last slave die off?' She smiled.

'Answering back,' laughed Reece.

'When will you be going into the city?' she asked.

'After lunch about two.'

101

'Any chance of a lift? You can drop me off near the bus station. I fancy a walk round the town and a look in the market.'
'Yes, no problem, but it depends on how good your coffee is slave.'

After dropping Mary off in the city, Reece parked up close to the hotel and with Simons, waited once more in the reception area for the two Mossad agents.

The reception area was busy with what appeared to be a bunch of new arrivals booking in. This was one of Reece's favourite pastimes to watch people and try to guess who they were, and where were they from. Then break down in his head what kind of business they worked in, it was his way of keeping his surveillance skills in tune.

When the lift door opened for what seemed the tenth time and the two Israelis walked out, he spotted them easily through the crowd of residents setting out for the afternoon in the city, or just going through for a late lunch in the hotel restaurant.

Standing to greet them Reece couldn't help but notice once again how beautiful Anna looked; now dressed in a blue polo shirt and tight-fitting jeans that seemed to enhance her full figure. She wore her dark hair in a long ponytail, and he was sure the leather bag that hung heavily from her shoulder carried more than just make-up. Following behind her, Palo wore his brown open necked shirt loosely around the waist of his linen trousers covering no doubt, as Reece did, the holster and pistol that agents always carried in the draw position. The Beretta .22 pistol was the favourite of Mossad, used many times in their operations and political assassinations around the world. Easily concealed, the .22 ammo gave off a reduced sound yet was deadly at close quarters. No James Bond shoulder holster for anyone who was trained properly in the game they played on the streets of the world.

'Good afternoon,' said Anna.

'Good afternoon. Are we ready for the day?' replied Reece.

'Always David. We have the details of where the ship carrying our friend will dock and we've arranged for an empty apartment overlooking the pier to observe from,' said Anna.

'You have been busy. Have you any other update for us?' asked Reece.

'Let us order a pot of coffee and sit and discuss our plan for today,' said Palo.

When the coffee had been poured Anna spread out a small tourist map of Valletta and the Grand Harbour. For anyone observing them they were just four tourists planning their day.

Pointing to the map Anna proceeded to show Reece and Simons where they needed to be for the ship's arrival.

'As you might know, David, I've visited the island on many occasions, but always as a tourist. This is my first time to look at everything through the eyes of an agent. I have good memories of the people and this city, so like yourself I'm familiar with the streets and the surrounding buildings and harbour.'

Reece only nodded and looked back to the map.

LIGHT OF THE SUN

Anna pointed out the route from the hotel to the apartment overlooking the Harbour and the pier where the expected ship would be docking.

'That's about a mile from here,' said Reece.

'You do have a car, don't you?' said Anna.

'Yes, and I suggest we move it close to the harbour in case they use one. The traffic system around the city is mostly one way, so even if they do use a car, they won't be difficult to follow.'

'We can't afford to lose them, Mr Reece,' said Palo.

Reece looked at Simons and smiled before replying.

'No, Palo that would never do. Don't worry it's an island, they'll have difficulty getting off it without us knowing.'

Anna spoke again as she produced a file from her bag and handed round a photo.

'This is the latest photo we have of our Iranian.'

Reece and Simons both noticed that it was not the latest one of the Arab.

'This is our target Colonel Ali Shafi of the Iranian Republican Guards Quads Unit. As you are aware, our intelligence indicates he'll be carrying an item to hand over to a yet unknown person and our job is to identify that person then await further instructions from our masters.'

Reece could see that Anna oversaw the Mossad side of this operation; Palo sat observing both the SG9 agents as Anna spoke. The photo was in colour which Reece appreciated, black and white was OK, but it never really showed the person as they were; the

104

suntanned skin, the eyes, the colour of the beard. Anna had not shown them the up-to-date photo of the Arab, they were holding back on full disclosure and that suited Reece. Why bring something into the game unless you're sure it's going to play a part, what part the Arab might play, if any, was still not known.

'Have you everything you need if we leave for your apartment now?' asked Reece.

'Yes. I have the address and the keys. I'm assured it is stocked with all our needs and I have two handsets for communications in my bag here. Shall we go?'

Reece finished his coffee and led the way to the car. The address wasn't hard to find. Reece had to park two streets away as there was no parking permitted on the main road. Across from the apartment was the Grand Harbour with the pier close against the road allowing only for loading and unloading.

The apartment was typical of the old harbour. The three floors had once been a dockside warehouse with a large, blue, wooden door with two windows showing to the front and with a small balcony on the two first floor rooms. Reece and Simons remained on the first floor while the two Mossad agents checked out the rest of the building. All the windows had wood shutters, that when opened could be fixed back against the outside walls with a metal hook. The shutters on the windows that Reece now looked through had already been hooked back and despite not having been cleaned in some time there was a clear view of the harbour pier across the main road. The pier for the moment was empty, while in the harbour beyond, shipping moved in and out from the Mediterranean Sea. The room consisted of a few large chairs, a table with four wooden chairs and in the back corner a small kitchen with a fridge and cooker, a kettle, a microwave, and all the paraphernalia a small family would need. Anna and Palo returned from their inspection. Both looked out the front window observing the same scene Reece and Simons had just observed.

'Well, what do you think David?' she asked.

'I've been in worse places.'

'There's two single beds on the next floor if we need to get some sleep.'

Anna took out her file once more and placed it on the table.

'I suggest we get comfortable and use our time to familiarise ourselves with all the information we have. The ship which is called the Qom is expected to dock around 5 p.m. and our satellites are confirming it's on schedule. It is basically a small container ship sailing between ports in the Mediterranean dropping off and picking up foreign cars. As we already know Shafi is coming to meet up with a contact to pass on what we believe is a small amount of plutonium, which has been manufactured in Iran against the wishes of the international community. Our job is to identify that contact and await further instructions. He will be protected by his Hezbollah bodyguard friends; at least four of them.'

'I'm still a little confused,' said Simons. 'Why Malta, why here?'

This time it was Palo who answered.

'Malta has always been close to Africa and the Middle East by its proximity to these countries. Hezbollah and Islamic Jihad have always done the dirty work for Iran, and we know in the past they have had some support here in Malta from a few who are not active but willing to provide somewhere for the terrorist masters and their operators to rest up between operations. The Islamic Jihad know this island as one where the security is weak and not likely to interfere with them. Another reason why Colonel Shafi will meet the contact here, believe it or not, is that he has a fear of flying and this ship voyage suits his purpose to carry out his side of the plan away from the prying eyes and ears of the CIA and our own services. Malta also has good travel links with the rest of Europe allowing his contact to move quickly from one place to another.'

Once more Anna reached into her bag and took out two Motorola wireless handsets.

'These are set to a secure frequency just for our use, so keep them on button number two at all times. They are fully charged, and we can recharge them here using that standard plug and cable beside the kettle.'

Reece had noticed the cable when he was checking out the room.

'How do you want to cover this,' asked Reece, 'we can't all sit looking out the window?'

Anna smiled and once more Reece noticed how beautiful this woman was. *If Mary could see her now*, thought Reece, *she would be worried*. But Reece decided to put on his professional head as he always did in this sort of situation.

'I'm sure we don't have to teach you anything when it comes to surveillance in any operation. We know about Manchester, how you and your team tracked the terrorists and dealt with them,' she replied. 'Then you must also know we lost some people there. People who meant a lot to me. We also know how the Kidon operate and your professionalism in dealing with your enemies. I always think of surveillance in percentages, 90 per cent filled with adrenaline and concentration, 5 per cent boredom and 5 per cent terror, keep thinking that way and we will be OK. So, I suggest we cover this from two fronts. Once the ship docks, we each take turns in the car with one of the radios. The person in the car ready to drive out here on the main road and pick one of us up if our target uses a car or taxi. Two of us can observe from here with the other radio and one of us can rest. If he leaves on foot then we have three of us here who can follow. If it drags out, we can all switch places at intervals, so we all get a chance to rest. What happens after that, is down to the target. Whatever he does will dictate what we do.'

'Exactly as we would do it David, but hopefully not so much terror,' said Anna.

'As we've all been briefed and shown this Colonel's file, I think we need to consider the dangers here,' said Simons.

'The dangers, can you be more specific?' asked Anna.

Reece nodded for Matthew to continue, and he looked back to Anna and Palo to see if they reacted in anyway.

'The file and the intelligence we have shows us that this Colonel has a lot to do with the Iranian secret nuclear programme. The information that he may have travelled from Iran with a small amount of plutonium which he intends to hand over to a yet unknown person with connections to an Islamic terrorist cell can mean two things. One, this has been sanctioned by the Iranian leadership and two if I have any experience on how they work they intend it to be used by this terrorist cell in a deniable operation against the West.'

'I think we are all in agreement so far Matthew, so what happens now?' asked Anna.

'If he hands over the plutonium successfully that is his job completed, we let him go home. But in what form is the plutonium, how will he deliver it, and can we confirm he has it? There are so many questions that need answers.'

Again, it was Anna who spoke as she reached into her bag once more and produced a handheld device similar in appearance and size to that of an electric stunning device.

'You have answered your own questions. This little device has been invented by our boffins as you would call them. It can be carried discreetly, and it will register if plutonium is within a ten-meter radius. Yes, I can see you are thinking that means we will have to get close to this Iranian or his contact to confirm the presence of the plutonium. This is where our close surveillance comes in. It will have to be accurate and done in a way where we don't expose ourselves.'

Anna took out one more small package from her bag.

'These are ears mics, all fully charged and linked up to each other. When in your ear they will pick up the radios and we can speak discreetly.

'I suggest we use these when we are following or close to the target. Do you know how to use them?'

'Of course,' replied Reece.

'Can I suggest we keep the call signs simple,' said Anna.

'I'll be Alpha One, Palo Two, David Three, and Matthew Four. Are we all OK with that?'

They all nodded in return and proceeded to place the devices in their ears.

'You seem to have it covered,' said Reece, 'Can I suggest we relax for a bit before this ship docks, then Matthew or Palo can take the car and park up ready to pick us up if needed? I do not think this Iranian will want to hang about too long with a package of nuclear poison. He will want to hand it over and get out of here as quickly as possible. For all we know this could all be done by tomorrow; then we can all go home and get back to living our lives again.'

Anna smiled. 'We will be lucky if it's that easy. Let us hope so. The ship should be docking in the next few hours. I think we are ready, let us see where this Colonel leads us.'

Chapter 13

Before the Qom, with its cargo of cars and the Iranian Colonel and his Hezbollah minders, had entered through the entrance to the Grand Harbour at Malta, the Arab had watched as his two students were picked up by Kalil and transported to the Imam Khomeini International Airport in Tehran. Now the plan he had agreed with the Iranian General in the Bazaar was underway, he felt more relaxed; the wheels were moving. His own part in the plan would begin in two days and he was ready.

Hassan had the easier journey to begin with, a direct flight to Paris. The airport security in France was extremely tight, and for one moment he thought his documents wouldn't stand up, the only luggage he had was a shoulder backpack. He would spend no more than two days in Paris as a tourist before moving on to London. He only stayed one night in a city centre hotel. He found he didn't like Paris; it was too decadent, too noisy. The next day before catching the Euro Star from the Gare du Nord train station to London St Pancras, he followed the briefing from the Arab, wiping all fingerprints in his hotel room before making his way to catch the afternoon train. Travelling this way was to avoid the far stricter security at the British airports. It was the first time he had used the Eurostar, and even though the journey took two hours and fifteen minutes, at speeds of up to 186 mph, he was able to enjoy the whole trip feeling more relaxed than he had done for months.

The Arab had been right. The security at both stations was relaxed and Hassan, still using the excellent false documents he carried, passed through the checks without problem. Following his instructions, he caught a taxi outside St Pancras and told the driver to take him to the home of Arsenal Football Club and the Emirates stadium in North London. The driver was a Chelsea fan, so Hassan was glad to have a conversation about the past successes of the two clubs, as his knowledge of the current teams was little. He paid the driver and walked up the steep steps at the front of the stadium, then a complete circumference of the whole building bringing him to the statue of Thierry Henry the famous Arsenal footballer. He sat down next to the statue and took his time observing his surroundings. Hassan then spent the next hour walking through the streets and roads using the anti-surveillance techniques he had been taught while in Iran. To the experienced eye he knew these would be spotted as basic, but nevertheless he would do his best to try to ensure he was alone in his travels. Although it was dry, and the sky was grey, he could feel the cold more than usual. He had been away too long in the warmth of the Middle East, and he had forgotten how different the climate was in England. He stopped to put on a sweater under his coat then found a coffee shop on the main Rock Street within walking distance of the Finsbury Park Mosque off St Thomas Road, his next destination for the day. As he settled down to a coffee and a sandwich, he felt good that he had almost completed the first part of his plan and he was happy that he was not under surveillance. The Arab would be pleased with his student, but he had warned Hassan that when he approached the Mosque, he would be under British anti-terrorist surveillance, as the Mosque had a history of involvement in the cause of the Islamic Jihad. He told Hassan to wear his shemagh scarf over his face on the roads approaching the Mosque until he was inside the building and again when he was leaving. He had timed his walk around the area and now a visit to a café to ensure that the time of day would see the sun start to go down and the light start to fall, making it more difficult for any observer to be certain about faces and descriptions.

When he left the café, he pulled the black and white shemagh from his backpack, putting it on, he made sure it covered most of his face with only his brown eyes showing and satisfied after one more full visual sweep of the road, he walked in the direction he wanted to go getting closer to the Mosque. In that area of the city, which had a large Muslim community, full face coverings were not unusual. Twenty minutes later he turned into St Thomas Road. He had gone over the maps with his teacher many times and now he was pleased that he had been a good student. His teacher would also be pleased, that not only had he listened, but he had put into practice what he had been taught. As he walked towards the building he watched for the spots where, if he were to carry out surveillance on the Mosque, he would place people to monitor the coming and going, recording vehicles and people. He knew it would be difficult for security agencies to operate in the vicinity of the Mosque as local people were mostly attendees and would expose any such surveillance if spotted. The building itself was not a distinctive construction; with a central Minaret and side windows which made the red bricked building look, from the outside, like a small block of apartments. The Mosque had a particularly significant history in the Islamic world. It had been a hotbed of insurrection and intrigue in promotion and support for the various Islamic causes and groups around the world. The British government, who had been monitoring the activities at the Mosque for many years, and its then Imam, a radical preacher Abu Hamza al-Masri, put pressure on the trustees to have the Mosque closed following an anti-terrorist raid. Although it was reopened in 2005, the British security services still considered it a place of interest in the war against the world terrorist threat. He knew from his own time in London that the building was more than adequate for what it needed to do, spreading the word of the one true faith. Hassan kept up his anti-surveillance and the only thing that aroused his suspicion was a Transit van at the top of St Thomas Road. The van at first glance appeared empty but was positioned in such a way that anyone in the back of the van could observe out of the rear windows, which were blacked out giving them a clear view of anyone walking down the road but not entering the building which was to the side of the van. Hassan walked past the van, paying it no specific attention, up the steps and entered through the main Mosque doors which opened to his touch. In the main entrance hall, he removed his shoes and stood to face a young man who approached him from a side room.

'Can I help you?'

'I'm here to speak with the Imam Mohammed AAyan. He is expecting me.'

'Who shall I say?'

'Tell him the one he has been expecting from the East.'

The young man appeared puzzled at the answer but replied 'Please wait here,' before going through the two large doors in the centre of the hallway.

Hassan dropped his backpack on the floor and keeping his face covered waited for only a few minutes before the large doors were opened once more. This time the man facing him was familiar to him from the media pictures he had seen.

Mohammed AAyan stood just over six-foot-tall with a long grey beard that still showed some of the black it had once been. His build was bulky, fat mixed with muscle, he was wearing a full-length shirt with a brown three-quarter length waistcoat. Half of his large face seemed to be covered by what Hassan could only think were cheap, black, thick lens NHS glasses.

'So, my brother you have come from the East. If so, you have a message for me,' he said through a smile that showed a full set of perfect teeth.

Hassan looked around for others but there was no one else.

'We are alone my brother; you can speak freely.'

'Our friend in Iran sends his best wishes and says the time has arrived for you to help him.'

AAyan reached out his arms and placing them around Hassan's shoulders with one arm and picking up the backpack with the other guided him to the side room the young man had originally came out of.

'I've been waiting for this day. Let us relax in here.' He showed the way to a small, empty office containing two large leather armchairs, a smart flat screen TV on a stand in the corner and a large prayer mat. There were no pictures on the cream-coloured walls only a large mirror.

As they both sat AAyan spoke again.

'Do not worry brother. Here we can talk freely. I have this room swept for electronic devices every morning.'

'Thank you for seeing me. I have a message here,' said Hassan as he removed a memory-stick from the zipped pocket in his jacket.

AAyan took the device and inserted it into the side socket on the TV, which he switched on. Taking the remote he found the information he needed and pressed play.

Almost immediately the face of the Arab appeared on the screen and his voice in English was loud and clear.

'My brother, thank you for helping us in the name of the one true god that is Allah. My brother Hassan who carries this message is just the first of what will be many soldiers in this war around the world against the enemies of our people. He has his mission for now, the details of which you do not need to know. This will not only protect him and those who come after him, but you also. As they say, what you do not know you cannot tell. For now, he'll explain to you what help you can give. Please give that help with my appreciation. I'll be in touch in person very soon. Allah Akbar, Allah Akbar.'

The screen went blank, the voice and picture gone.

'So, Hassan can I get you some tea, some coffee?'

'No thank you. I've been travelling all day and I need to rest. This is where I need your help.'

'Whatever you need in the name of Allah I will help.'

'For now, two things. Somewhere to stay that will accommodate up to four people safely.'

'And the second.'

'A secure burner phone number where I can reach you at any time.'

AAyan stood and moving to the mirror he pulled it from one side to reveal it was attached to the wall by a set of hinges. Opening a cavity behind it he removed a small Nokia mobile phone. And some keys and a piece of typed paper. Then closing the cavity and swinging the mirror back in place it became what it was minutes before, just a mirror.

Hassan was a little surprised and noticed that AAyan was smiling when he sat back in the chair once more.

'As you can see, we too have our secrets.'

'Indeed,' replied Hassan.

'These are the keys for just such a safe place, a flat on the Edgware Road. It's an apartment on two floors above a barber shop, the details and the secure number for this phone are on the document. I'll keep the phone on me from now on. I suggest you study them and destroy the paper when you're sure you know the address and the number. Now, be careful when you leave. I'm sure you noticed the Transit van across the road. It belongs to the British Security Services, and they'll have taken your photo when you came in.'

'I wore my face covering.'

'Good. Do the same when you leave. I do not think their finance is able to stretch to have a permanent surveillance team to cover this building, but we cannot be totally sure, so take whatever precautions you can when you leave. Use the Underground whenever you can as they struggle to follow our people through that system.'

Hassan stood to leave.

'Thank you for your help. I'm sure we will be in touch.'

'In the name of the one true God that is Allah, may you be safe and successful in your mission in his name.'

'Inshallah, God wills it.'

Hassan pulled the scarf up over his face, pulled his shoes back on and turning left out of the Mosque door, he walked with his head up appearing to pay no attention to anything around him. If anyone had taken his photograph, they would get nothing from it to identify him, and the casual way he walked wouldn't give anyone, who was not surveillance trained cause for concern. He walked to the main Finsbury Tube station and as far as he was concerned, today was a rest day for the anti-terrorist surveillance teams; he was satisfied he was alone.

Chapter 14

It was almost 5 p.m. exactly when the Iranian merchant vessel the Qom, started its docking procedure alongside the pier in Valletta's Grand Harbour. Reece watched through the high-powered binoculars that were perched on the tripod just back from the window. The ship was in a lot better condition than he had imagined. Showing very little rust, it looked like it had just slipped off the runners. *A newly built vessel, it must have had a full paint job recently*, he thought. He could see what looked like cars on the deck covered in waterproof tarpaulin to protect them from the salt water. On the same deck men were going through the business of getting the ship alongside the dock and secure. Ropes were thrown to men on the dock where they were pulled over the metal and concrete bollards securing the ship to the dockside. Within minutes the whole process of docking was complete. Palo and Anna who, were standing behind him could see the smoke that had been coming from the black funnel on the ship reduce until there was no more mixing with the still blue sky.

'It looks like there are cabins just under the bridge,' said Reece.

'I think we have some time yet. They will have to have the gangway pulled in and I'm sure the local customs people will have to check the manifest before our friend can leave the ship,' Anna replied.

Palo, who had watched the ship come into dock, now walked to the kitchen, and switched on the kettle.

'We have plenty of time for a coffee then.' He placed three cups on the table.

'Sounds good, make mine black,' said Reece.

'Do you think Matthew will be all right?' asked Anna.

Reece knew the one-way street he was parked up in. It was a slight hill, and he would be parked facing down towards the harbour and the sea. Reece picked up the radio.

'Alpha four, come in, over.'

He replied almost immediately.

'Here, over.'

'Good man you're awake. Just to update you our package carrier has arrived. We would guess nothing more for at least an hour, are you OK?'

'Yes, no problem, I'm in a quiet spot nothing much going on, happy to stay here.'

'Great will keep you updated, over and out.'

Reece looked once more at the blown-up picture of the Iranian Colonel.

'He should be easy to spot. There won't be a large crowd of passengers coming off at the same time, and if he has a couple of minders as we expect then we will be able to identify them too,' said Reece.

'Let us hope so. I always love it when they make things just that little simpler for me,' said Anna.

Palo brought the coffee and Reece took it and sat in one of the chairs allowing Palo to take over the binoculars.

Anna sat down in another chair.

'What about your woman David, is she all right after Manchester?'

Anna was letting him know they knew all about Manchester and the SG9 operation, but he wasn't going to be her best friend just yet.

'She's fine.'

'Sorry, I didn't mean to pry; just interested from a woman's perspective.'

'Then you will know how she feels. Having been involved in this stuff yourself it's not nice and she is the bravest woman I know.'

'She must be. That is why I asked if she was all right. By the sound of it she is indeed a strong woman. Maybe I can meet her sometime.'

'Once this is over, I don't see why not. I'm sure she would like to meet you as well.'

Reece could only try to imagine the conversation there would be between these two beautiful women both now important parts of his life.

'What about you Anna? What is it like for a woman from Israel in this game? Your life must have been like mine and the women I've worked with, especially on the streets of Northern Ireland.'

'Similar? I would say from what I've seen of your war in Ireland terribly similar. Northern Ireland has a terrorist problem just like Israel, where fanatics want to kill you every day and the country is bordered by a country that gives safe ground to those same terrorists to operate.'

'There the similarity ends. Where we both have terrorist groups who want to kill us and wipe us off the face of the earth, the ones in my country don't want to commit suicide.'

'Ah, but there you're wrong. What about the ten hunger strikers. They committed suicide.'

Reece smiled at this attempt to drag him into a discussion that was seeking to learn more about him and his own wars.

'That's why we are here to try to stop more killings. Realistically that is why I do this. My own problem is that every time we kill one more of theirs, two more jump out of the trenches to take their place. When does the killing stop?'

Now it was Anna's turn to smile.

'That has been the question since man first stood on the earth. There is a story that a man was sitting on a bench beside Jesus, and he asked him, if you are truly God then why do you allow war, disasters, famine, and man killing man? Jesus replied, I was about to ask you the same question. You see David there'll always be these kinds of people and there'll always be those like us who are willing to put our head above the parapet and try to stop them.'

'For now, I will agree with you. But I know the time will come for myself, when I will want to leave the front line, leave it up to someone else. I just hope that when that time comes, I won't have enemies who are not willing to let me have a peaceful life.'

'As you say, let us hope that when that time comes, there'll still be people like us willing to stand between them and you.'

'I think I'll stretch my legs and see if Matthew is OK, he's parked two streets away and I'll still have the ship in view when I'm walking. Anything happens shout out.'

'You can be sure of it. But we should be all right for at least an hour allowing time for the custom check of the ship's contents and crew manifest.'

The first thing Reece noticed when he left the front door of the apartment was the temperature drop. The sun had started to go down and the air was fresh with a slight breeze coming in off the sea. He was glad he could stretch his legs and clear his head. Even though none of them smoked, the apartment was stuffy with the windows closed, no air was circulating inside.

Matthew Simons saw Reece turn the corner into the street. With the sun starting to go down, the streetlights were coming on and his view was just as good as when the sun was high in the sky. Reece climbed into the seat beside Simons.

'All quiet so far. Now with the ship docked we will have to wait and see what happens.'

'I know that. Do you think I'm stupid?' asked Simons.

'No don't be daft. I'm only here because I needed a breath of fresh air and I missed you.' Reece smiled.

Simons laughed.

'Well, that's all right then, I missed you too. Have our Israeli brother and sister got anything more for us?'

'No. Everything as it was. If the Iranian comes off the ship and gets into a car, you, pick us up and we follow. If he comes out on foot, we follow, and you catch-up. Let's hope he won't keep us waiting too long, I would like to sleep in my own bed tonight.'

'At least you will have the lovely Mary to cuddle up too. I've been thinking; he is here to meet someone and between our friends in the apartment and our own people we don't know who. If we are lucky and we do spot his contact, what then? Do we close them both down or try to follow both?'

'I don't think we have the resources to follow them both. We are doing this on a shoestring as it is. It seems when it comes to our Mossad and SG9 masters, it will always be down to money, and we are expendable and someone to blame if things go wrong. In this game if you remember to look after yourself and trust only yourself you will be all right. We know the Iranian is here to pass something on, so when he does that, we follow the receiver and wait for further instructions. Ours is not to reason why.'

'I know ours is but to do and die. It's the die bit I'm not too fond of.'

'And on that happy thought I'll get back to our Mossad friends. Is there anything you need?'

'No, I'm OK, thanks. If I do, I'll give you a shout. Nobody seems to be paying me any attention, so I'll just read my copy of The Malta Times once more and wait to see what happens, keep safe.'

Reece let himself back into the apartment and found Palo still sat at the window checking things through the binoculars. Anna was sitting at the kitchen table with another cup of coffee in front of her.

'Is Matthew OK?'

'Yes, no problem, probably a little bored like us, but OK. Nothing new then?'

'No but the coffee's fresh.'

Reece poured himself a cup keeping it black. He sat at the table facing Anna. He looked at his watch.

'I don't think it will be long now before we see some movement. The customs check will be short provided all the paperwork is in order, and I'm sure it will be, they won't want to bring any unnecessary notice to themselves.'

'I agree. We are ready. We can't do anything until they move, but we're ready.'

At almost the same time the Air Malta flight from Rome was landing at Malta's main airport. A young attractive woman passed through customs without any problem and taking a taxi from outside the arrivals building, she asked the driver to take her to the Casa Ellul hotel in Valletta, but first to stop off at a good souvenir shop on the way.

Chapter 15

Reece decided it was time to check in with Mary, God knows when he would get a chance again. She answered his call on the second ring.

'Hello sexy.'

'What if I had you on speaker,' laughed Reece.

'Then you would still be sexy, but I know there's other things I would rather have you on.'

'Enough of that I'm trying to do a job here.'

'So why are you calling me then and getting me to think I should put something nice on if you're coming home?'

'Not yet but hold that thought. I'll let you know when I'm on my way and you get into that something nice for me to help you out of. That is why I'm calling to update you. There's nothing happening here yet so, yes, I might be a little late.'

'Spoil-sport I'll just have to start without you then.'

'Don't you dare, I'll need all of you when I get back. Don't worry about food we can pick up something here.'

'OK but take care. I love you.'

'I love you too.'

When Reece cancelled the call, he looked across the room to see Anna smiling back at him. Realising he was blushing; he could only smile back.

'Don't worry David, we all need someone some time.'

At the same time Yasmin was arriving at the Casa Ellul Boutique hotel in the centre of the city of Valletta. The receptionist noted the details of the British passport that contained her picture and gave her name as Carletta Maguire from Catford just outside London. The Arab had booked all her travel arrangements and accommodation in this suite only hotel. Suite number five overlooked the narrow street outside. The rooms that faced this way all had the small iron balconies with a window door that opened inwards. When she opened the doors, the iron protecting rails left the balcony just wide enough for the width of her feet to stand on. The open doors let a cool breeze into the room. There was the usual air conditioning unit on the wall, but it needed to build up the cooling fan after she'd switched it on. Lying on her back on the large four poster bed she realised she was tired. Yasmin took out the burner phone she'd been given and switched it on for the first time since leaving the Arab and Tehran. When the signal showed she could send her message she found the number that had been coded in and sent the words, *I am here room 5 Maguire*. Then lying back on the bed, she fell into a quick all enclosing sleep.

At the docks, Anna had taken over the binoculars and raising her hand she spoke to Reece and Palo without taking her eyes away from them.

'Guys. I think we are on.'

Both men went to the window standing behind her to look out. They hadn't switched on the lights as the sun had gone down, three people being illuminated looking out of a window was just not normal.

Reece could see three men coming down the ship's walkway but, without the benefit of the binoculars, he couldn't see their faces, but Anna could.

'It's definitely him, Shafi with two minders either side of him; both look the part, staying close, heads moving from side to side to see what they can. Shafi is using a walking stick which is strange, there is no mention of him needing one in the files. Here, have a look.'

Reece and Palo took turns to watching the men walk through the docks to the security hut at the entrance gate; then through and onto the main road, turning left and away from where they watched. Shafi looked just like his photo in the file. The two men walking each side of him but a step behind both had the look of young fit Arabs, each with a close shaved dark beard. If he were to describe them Reece would have said they were identical twins and only their jackets were different. One wore a denim coat while the other was wearing what appeared from the distance to be cheap imitation leather. Shafi from his bearing, sharp dark suit and open necked white shirt, emanated power.

'It looks like they're staying on foot and going in the opposite direction to Alpha Four,' said Reece, 'Let's move.'

'Palo, I'll stay with David on this side of the street to follow them into the city if they cross the road. You follow on their side and if they stop, we all pass by them to get ahead and turn back if needed I presume, you're armed David?'

'Aren't we all!' he replied.

As they left the apartment Reece called Simons to let him know they were on the move.

'Stay where you are for now, they might jump into a vehicle yet.'

'Understood,' replied Simons.

When they left the front door of the apartment the three targets were about 200 yards ahead of them still walking away from the docks.

Reece could see Shafi looking down at the screen of the mobile phone he was holding, then stop and speak to the two men following. All three then crossed the road to be on the same side as Reece and Anna. Even though they looked in the direction of Reece, they were paying attention to the oncoming traffic in the road while crossing. They then turned away from the watching pair and walked on with their backs to them. Reece noticed that each time Shafi looked at the screen he placed the walking stick he was carrying under his arm so he could work the screen with both hands.

'He's using the Sat Nav on his mobile. He is following it to a destination,' said Reece into his mic so the whole team heard at once.

'Roger that,' came the reply from Palo and Matthew. Anna just nodded her agreement having spotted the same thing herself.

'Why do you think they're walking?' asked Anna.

'For a number of reasons, I think,' replied Reece, 'They would know any taxi driver would be sure to remember picking up three Arabs from the docks and where he dropped them off. Then they have been cooped up on a ship for a while so they would like to stretch their legs and get some air. But I think the main reason is they will be taking their time and checking for surveillance following them. If they spot us, three things could happen, they could confront us, but they wouldn't be sure how many we are, so that is unlikely. If they do spot us, they might continue with their operation and try to lose us. Or three, they call the whole thing off, return to base and declare they have a spy in their ranks, all three of which will be bad for us so let's be careful.'

As Reece followed, he knew he would have to use all the trade skills he had been taught by MI5 on the streets of London many years ago and had used successfully to stay alive in Northern Ireland and most lately on the streets of Manchester; where in the end, he had to eliminate another terrorist. He was also thinking of Mary McAuley by his side on those streets, the woman he loved, when he thought of her he was glad she wasn't here now. He had put her in enough danger in her life, even though he knew she would give anything to be by his side instead of Anna the Mossad agent.

'They are turning into a side street,' said Anna breaking into his thoughts.

'I know the street, they'll be walking up a steep hill towards the city centre there's not much cover for us, no hotels just a few shops and the street will be quiet at this time,' said Reece.

'Alpha Four from Alpha Three come in, over.'

Simons replied to Reece immediately. 'Roger Alpha Three?'

'Our friends are walking towards the centre of the city, although they're taking the long way about it. Look up San Paul and Sant Orsla streets. Go there and find yourself a parking space. Don't know where they'll be going to ground yet, but that will get you closer to us, over.'

'Roger Alpha Three I'm on my way.'

'You do know your way round here David,' said Anna.

'Old habit. I'm sure like me when you did your surveillance training, they gave you a patch of a city to learn every nook and cranny, every street, every bus stop, taxi rank and subway station. They drilled it into you, so you didn't get lost up a dead-end alleyway. When I first moved here, I made a point of walking every inch of these streets and sat in a lot of cafes to watch the world go by. I still don't know every nook and cranny, but I think I know enough, at least I think I know more than the people we are following.'

'You're not giving away any secrets David, that's exactly as we are taught. Alpha Two let's keep this distance they seem to know where they are going.'

Palo waved from across the road and continued walking at the same pace as Reece and Anna.

131

The three men continued their walk, and Reece could see that they were relaxed by the way they kept walking straight ahead, not looking around, confident that they were in a city where no one knew them. The city was now a mixture of office workers going home and people going out for an early dinner in one of the many restaurants or perusing the tourist shops and buildings that were still open. Although the sun had gone down the evening was cool, but not cold; the street lights now bright against the dark blue sky. Once more the three men stopped while Shafi studied his mobile phone screen. Pointing, he said something to the men before they turned right into the next street.

'All call signs they've gone into San Pawl Street. Alpha Four be aware when you go into that area,' said Reece.

'Roger Alpha Three,' replied Simons.

The three men continued along San Pawl Street, then turned left into the next street.

'OK, everyone that's them into San Gann Street,' said Reece.

Palo and Simons replied 'Roger.'

Reece turned to Anna. 'I know this street. It leads up towards the centre and there are more shops and restaurants with a small Boutique hotel near the middle on the left as we go up.'

'Maybe that's where they're heading for?' said Anna.

'One of us must be psychic Anna, that's exactly where they're going.'

The three men had gone into the only hotel on the street. The last man of the trio, the one in the leather jacket, stopped for a moment to look up and down the street.

Reece was confident they were far enough back for comfort and not raising any suspicion. Appearing satisfied, the man had turned and entered the hotel.

'Alpha Four we have them at the Casa Ellul Hotel on San Gann Street. Can you park up nearby?' said Reece.

'No problem. I'm just round the corner in San Pawl Street,' replied Simons.

'What do you want to do now?' Reece asked Anna.

'Do you know this hotel?'

'Yes, it's a slightly upmarket one with a small reception area and a cocktail bar to the left when you go in. The rooms or suites as they're called are on three floors around an inside courtyard where they place some chairs and tables for dinner. There is a fountain in the centre of the courtyard with a statue of Heracles at the back end. I think there are only about twelve suites. It's called a boutique hotel because it's small but expensive.'

'You seem to know it fairly well. Have you stayed there?'

'No. I took Mary to dinner there once because the chef had a reputation for good food. The meal was nice but a bit too expensive for my liking. I hate it when chefs try to show off giving you microscopic portions which they call cuisine by using a special name of their own. I like the food to fill the plate. We didn't go back. As I said if we go in there and they're still in reception they'll clock us and that will make it difficult to follow them in the future; they might remember our faces.'

'We don't have a choice, David. We don't know who they might be meeting in there. I need to get close with the little device in my bag which might give us an indication if they have the plutonium with them.'

'I can't argue with that, and a man and a woman together will register less interest than one of us on our own.'

Anna spoke into her mic.

'Alpha Three and I will go into the hotel and find out what we can. Everyone else stay alert if we need you to come running.'

The affirmative replies from Palo and Simons came back.

'OK, David let's go and sample a cocktail, shall we?'

Colonel Ali Shafi was confident that, so far, his mission was safe, and he was now where he should be at this time. He did not need to approach the reception desk which at that moment was unmanned. He knew the room number and stopping to tell his two minders to wait, he turned to the stairs on the right of the reception with an arrow notice on the wall pointing up which said Suites 1 to 5 first floor. As he was talking to his minders, he noticed behind them, a man and woman coming in through the revolving doors: the couple continued past the men and into the cocktail bar. There was nothing special about them as they appeared to be smiling into each other's eyes and holding hands. He did not pay much attention to the man, but he did notice the woman, she was exceptionally beautiful, if only he had the time. *A couple very much in love*, he thought before he started to climb the stairs.

Reece and Anna were lucky, there was only one table which gave a view of the reception area, and it was free. Anna sat at the table, her back to the reception. Reece sat opposite Anna looking over her shoulder. Anna lifted her bag onto the table, looked inside and then at Reece.

'No alarm signal, nothing showing, he doesn't have the plutonium with him.'

'Provided your little device is working properly.'

'Let's hope so.'

A waiter came to the table.

'Can I get you something to drink?'

'Can I have a Bloody Mary,' said Reece.

'Make that two,' said Anna.

When the waiter left Anna looked at Reece once more.

'I think I heard him tell his men the room number. He said five. What are they doing now?'

'Sitting in reception,' said Reece looking over her shoulder.

'When the drinks come, I'll go to the little girl's room and update Palo and Matthew. Then we sit and enjoy our drinks for a while.'

The drinks arrived and Anna took her walk.

Reece watched the men without letting his eyes fall on them for too long. He could see they looked fit and were pretending like him, to be natural without drawing attention to themselves.

Reece pressed his elbow against his side and could feel the hard metal of the Smith and Wesson reassuring at his waist. He could also feel a slight stab of pain in his right shoulder the shrapnel from the wound received in that shoot-out with Sean Costello years before.

Ali Shafi knocked lightly on the door which after a few seconds was opened by Yasmin. She was always a light sleeper and the time she'd slept had rejuvenated her strength, she felt ready for the next part of her mission.

'Yasmin, I am the Colonel.'

It was the agreed approach, the one the Arab had told her, and she gave her reply.

'I am the daughter of Allah.'

'As-Salaam Alaikum, Yasmin.'

'Wa'alaikum salaam, Colonel,' replied Yasmin.

Introductions over, she opened the door and waved him into the suite.

'You have a nice place here. Will you be staying long?'

She knew his mission brief would only take him as far as where he stood now.

'Not long. You have the package for me?'

He noticed by her tone that she did not want to take any longer to complete the handover than she had to. *A pity,* he thought. She was quite pretty, and he would have liked to get to know her more intimately if they had the time. As a Colonel in the Republican Guard, he was used to getting his own way, giving orders that were obeyed instantly and having his way with women even though he was supposed to be faithful to his wife. He smiled as he remembered an old saying. 'There's no such thing as a married man a hundred miles from home.'

'The package as you call it you may already know, this is it.' He held out the walking stick in both hands like a Samurai handing over his sword. She took it from him and immediately she could feel that it was heavier than she expected.

'You notice the weight, I'm sure. That's because the outer shell is made of a special form of lead.'

She noticed that apart from the weight, the walking stick looked like it was made of silver with Arabic engraving on the outside.

He held out his hands once more and she placed the stick back in them.

'You are right, the outer casing is, as I say lead but, covered by sterling silver and the engraving you also noticed is very special too.'

'What does it say?'

'The Light of the Sun.'

'What does it mean?'

He walked over to the bed and beckoned her to follow him. Laying the walking stick on the bed he started to unscrew the silver knob at the top.

'As you can see you unscrew the top clockwise, this is opposite to the normal anti-clockwise as a simple security measure should anyone try to see if they can open it. Inside the hollow tube wrapped in another material to protect you is the weapons grade plutonium which if used in the way we want will answer your last question, it will light up the sky with The Light of the Sun. The lead of the outer shell and the material inside will protect against the x-ray machines and explosive detectors at airports and security checks from finding the plutonium. Is it your job to deliver the walking stick to its destination?'

'That is none of your concern. We each have our own part to play in this operation and to protect its security we only need to know our own part, no more.' she replied sharply using the words of the Teacher.

Again, the Iranian Colonel felt as if she'd slapped him across the face and he wasn't happy. *Maybe this woman needed a lesson,* he thought. Throwing the walking stick on the bed he pulled her two arms down by her side then pulled her in close to his body and tried to kiss her on the lips. To his surprise she didn't resist instead putting her arms around him, returning his kiss with her lips for a longer time than he expected. He relaxed his grip and when she pulled back from him he was surprised once more that when she stood in front of him, she was holding his gun in her hands. She'd removed the weapon easily from his shoulder holster when his attention was elsewhere. Now it was aimed at the centre of his chest.

'What are you doing?' he asked.

'A certain gentleman tried to force himself on me once before and I had to let him know his approach was not welcome.'

'That was not my intention. I thought you would like some company to help relieve the stress of your part in this operation.'

She smiled as she noticed the sweat on his forehead and the nervousness in his words. Suddenly he realised who he was dealing with, not the timid little woman he expected.

'I know about stress, and I agree. Maybe we should relax a bit to complete our part in the mission. At least let us lie on the bed and get comfortable.'

'I don't think I could relax with you pointing my gun at me.'

'It's a German Glock isn't it, with one in the chamber I presume.'

He just nodded never taking his eyes off the gun in her hand.

Waving him to lie down on the bed she moved to the opposite side.

'Now let's lie down and relax and to help I'll put the gun under the pillow until we are finished, then you can have it and be on your way no more to be said.'

'It will take a lot of foreplay to help me relax after this,' he said before lying down. She bent forward slowly slipping her gun hand under the pillow. This relaxed the Colonel seeing the gun placed out of sight and the fact that his two minders knew where he was helped reassure him.

Kneeling on the bed Yasmin placed her legs astride him and once more leant forward to kiss him. She could feel his manhood start to go stiff between them and his arms searching for her waist closing his eyes in response to her lips. At the same time, she stretched her right hand under the pillow and bringing out the gun she lifted a pillow with her left placed it over his face. The sound in the room was loud to her ears but she knew the pillow had deadened it to anyone outside. She left the scorched pillow in place, while the dark

139

red blood spread slowly below it, then placed the gun on top of the body and pulled the duvet over it covering it up so it would look like someone sleeping there. Looking down at the form on the bed, she now remembered her final briefing from the Arab at his poolside in Tehran.

'When you receive the package, you will kill the Colonel. He is an enemy of the holy Jihad and a spy for our great enemy that is Israel.'

She had not questioned his instructions, if the Colonel was such a spy, then he should die. She was a soldier of the Jihad and that was her mission to kill the enemy no matter who and where she found them. She had been wondering how she was going to do it and once again in her lifetime due to the arrogance of a man, the weapon had been provided.

Quickly collecting her things in her backpack and checking she had no spots of blood on her clothes, she slid the walking stick down the inside of her jeans. When she walked, she was unable to bend her leg so she would pretend she had a slight limp. She would only have to do this until she was far away from the hotel. Placing a Do Not Disturb sign on the outside of the suite door handle, she took the stairs to the ground floor and reception. Leaving her key at the empty reception desk she walked past the two men sitting beside each other and without making eye contact walked out of the hotel to find a taxi from the stand at the end of the street.

'Malta airport please,' said Yasmin as she threw her backpack onto the rear seat then took her time to sit behind the driver and stretch the leg with the walking stick across the seat.

Anna sat back down at the table.

'Anything happen while I was away?' she asked.

'Not much, our two boys ordered coffee and a young woman left the hotel. What about the guys?'

'I updated them and told them to meet up somewhere near the hotel where they can observe the front door. Palo had already found a café with tables outside it with such a view and Matthew is going to meet up with him. Did the young woman leave the hotel because the coffee's bad?' Smiled Anna.

'She didn't seem to want to wait around to find out.'

'Shall we order another one while we wait? We don't know how long we will be here?'

'Good idea I like my Bloody Mary spicy and this one is exactly right. But we will have to take it slowly we need to keep our heads alert for this.'

'You're right let's make them Virgin Marys without the vodka. We will have to use our imagination instead.'

'Yuck. It will have to be good to imagine a Bloody Mary without vodka but let's go for it.'

Chapter 16

Having received the text from Hassan that he had arrived safely in London, the Arab closed his villa and left his car at the airport before catching a flight to Rome, then a connecting flight to London Heathrow. The new false British and European Union passport he was using identified him as Doctor Ali Hussein Mohammad. His cover story was that he was a pediatrician at Guys Hospital in London. The documents and the cover story put together by the Iranian Quds Covert Operations Directorate were of the highest quality. The one thing the Arab was sure of was that the British always respect their police and their doctors without question. As he had expected, the documents and his experience in using false papers allowed him to pass through airport security with ease. The fact that he only had a small cabin bag made the experience even easier. When he had landed at Heathrow, he took the Heathrow Express to Paddington Station in central London then, after a quick text message exchange with Hassan, took a taxi from the station to Edgware Road where, when he knocked on the door, it was opened by Hassan. *The mission is progressing to plan*, he thought, *each playing their part as he had asked.* At the same time Yasmin had arrived in her taxi at

Malta airport. She made her way to the ladies' room and inside a cubicle she removed the walking stick from her jeans. Now she could bend her leg and using the stick as it was meant to be used walked to the departures desk to book in for her flight to London with Malta Airlines. If everything went well, she would be in London by midnight.

Back in the boutique hotel in Valletta, Reece tried to keep the conversation casual, smiling across at Anna each time one of the men in reception started to look around checking his surroundings.

'These Virgin Bloody Marys don't taste all that bad.' He tried to smile once more as he took a sip.

Anna could only laugh. 'They are terrible, and you're not a very good liar, Mister Reece.'

Reece laughed back.

'You're right, it's terrible. Our friends are looking a little nervous. Maybe it's the coffee?'

'Shafi is upstairs meeting someone we don't know maybe handing over the package. When he leaves, we will know the handover may have taken place. Hopefully, he walks out with the contact.'

'I hope it's soon. I don't think I could drink too many of these,' said Reece, holding up the glass that was now almost empty.

Palo and Matthew were into their second pot of coffee and getting to know each other while watching the front door of the hotel which gave them a good view of anyone coming or going. In the last hour, the only one leaving was a woman on her own, carrying a rucksack and walking with a limp. She was wearing some sort of scarf pulled in tight over her head. Looking round she spotted the taxi stand and left in one of them. Since then, there had been no one in or out. The evening stars were coming out. Although the temperature had dropped it was still warm enough to sit outside and the few tables that there were, were increasingly being taken up by the customers of the night. Those same customers of the night were also filling up the streets, making an atmosphere of the flowing life of Malta, with locals, tourists and business owners coming and going.

'I've never been to Malta before, but from what I've seen I would like to come back as a tourist sometime,' said Matthew.

'I've never been here myself. In a way it reminds me of Jerusalem, the buildings; the history involving the Mediterranean. Have you ever been to Jerusalem?'

'No, I'm sorry to say I haven't. That's another place for my list.'

'If you ever go there let me know and maybe we can meet up. I'll show you around the sites the tourists do not get to see, the ones protected by the security and the IDF, sacred sites to the Jewish people if you really like history.'

'I'll do the same if you're ever in London.'

'It's a deal. You never know, what happens here might see us both in London and Jerusalem sooner than we think.'

Inside the hotel, Reece had continued to watch the men over Anna's shoulder. He noticed they were getting more agitated, looking at their watches talking quickly to each other. The one in the leather coat had got up and walked back and forth while at the same time looking up at the lights on the lift numbers and then the stairs for movement. They had been there for almost two hours.

'I hate this waiting for something to happen,' said Anna.

'Especially when we can't drink real alcohol. We will give it another thirty minutes then we can swap places with the guys at the café. These two are beginning to look like cats on a hot tin roof,' said Reece.

'They must be like us. Starting to wonder what is taking so long. It's a waiting game for everyone but I think a change of scenery for us is a good idea.'

'I'll take a quick trip to the steps outside and let the boys know what we're thinking can you cover here?' asked Anna.

'Yes, no problem but avoid eye contact when you walk by them.'

'Of course, darling, I don't want to make you jealous.'

'I'm not worried about me, it's them I don't want getting ideas,' smiled Reece.

True to her word Anna walked straight past the two men without looking in their direction. Reece noticed the two men paid no attention to the woman but continued in close conversation with each other still looking at their watches and then at the stairs where they last saw their boss two hours ago. From years of interviewing terrorists across a desk Reece could see from the men's body language they were planning to do something soon.

Anna had returned and sat in front of Reece once more when the men made their move.

'I don't think we will have to wait much longer. Our friend in the leather coat just went up the stairs and his buddy is standing by the front door,' said Reece.

Anna spoke quietly into her mic to update Palo and Simons.

Ten minutes later Reece watched as leather coat came back down the stairs and whispered to his partner to which his partner asked a question. Leather coat shook his head in the negative. Both men then went up the stairs together. Although they did not seem to be in a hurry or panic Reece could see the concern on both their faces.

'Somethings wrong. They don't seem happy. I'll follow them you stay here. They have seen you twice and we've been sitting here for some time. If they spot me, they might think we are residents, but I think it's time to get a little closer. Tell Palo and Matthew to take up position outside and be ready for action if we need it.'

'OK David but take care. Our handover friend might not be here yet and that's causing them confusion.'

Reece passed the reception desk and noticing there was a young girl behind the desk he turned left, taking the stairs two at a time. Each floor of the hotel had closed glass fire doors giving a view of the long corridor leading to the suites. Reece could see the first floor was empty as he reached the second, he could hear loud knocking. Slowing down he took care to look through the glass doors in time to see both the Arab bodyguards shoulder charge the door which on the third charge they broke through. Reece turned and made his way back down to sit beside Anna, who had now turned her chair to face the reception area.

'I think we may have a problem,' said Reece.

'What's happening?'

'Our friends had to break down a door to a suite on the second floor. They are in there now so I think we will be seeing them soon with or without their boss.'

Twenty minutes later his prediction came true. Both bodyguards came back down the stairs this time a little faster than when they went up and left the hotel.

'Alpha Two and Alpha Four try to follow our two friends and see where they go. We are checking up on their boss,' said Reece into his mic.

'Roger that,' replied Palo, 'we have them, they seem to be heading back the way they came.'

'Anna, you stay here and cover my back if anyone else goes up the stairs '

'What are you going to do?'

'We have to know what's going on up there. The way those two left tells me there is something wrong. We need to act now.'

'Just so you know: I hear anything that sounds like trouble, I'm coming up gun blazing.'

'Just make sure you're aiming at the bad guys,' smiled Reece.

Reece passed the reception desk which was empty again and took the stairs two at a time once more. He had noticed there only seemed to be one CCTV camera and that was facing the reception desk. There didn't appear to be any on the stairs or in the corridors leading to the suites. Reaching the empty second floor, Reece walked slowly until he was standing outside the door to suite number five. He had intended to listen at the door, but he could see that despite the DO NOT DISTURB sign which still hung from the handle, the door frame was splintered, and the damaged lock set back from the closed position leaving the door slightly open. Reece pulled out the Smith and Wesson and gently pushing the door with the barrel, he slipped off the safety catch, ready to fire quickly if he needed to.

The lights were on and, with the gun in the fire v shaped position, with his arms straight he swept from left to right and focused on what he could now see was the body of Shafi lying face up on the bed. He didn't need to check if he was dead. Shafi's eyes were open looking at the ceiling and it was clear that a bullet had passed through the centre of his head, just above them. The bathroom, like the bedroom was clear.

Looking around he could see the bloody pillow with the scorched hole lying on the floor. He searched the pockets, and checked drawers and the room, making sure to leave no prints, he used his handkerchief to touch the surfaces. There was nothing to find or any more to be gained by staying and he returned to the bar where Anna watched him as he sat at the table her expression full of questions.

'We need to move. I'll explain as we go,' said Reece standing.

Outside the hotel Reece told Anna what he had found, and he passed on the information to Palo and Matthew as they walked back towards the harbour.

'What the fuck's going on here? I don't believe the bodyguards killed him. That's probably why they left so quickly. They need to get back to the ship and report home.'

'I agree,' said Anna, what do you think happened?'

'If the bodyguards didn't do, it then it could only have been the courier he was supposed to meet. I can tell you this, whoever did it was a professional, someone with training. And whoever they were, they were gone before the bodyguards broke into the room.'

'Then who?'

'I saw a woman leave the hotel. She was limping slightly and wore a scarf. She passed by the bodyguards without looking at them which, now that I think about it; is exactly what we would have done in her place.'

'Again, I ask if she was the contact why kill him?'

'I think that's a question for people on a bigger paygrade than us,' said Reece.

Reece spoke into his radio.

'Alpha Four, did you see the woman who came out of the hotel before the bodyguards left?'

'Yes,' replied Simons. 'She passed us on the other side of the street and got into a taxi.'

'Alfa Three?' It was Matthew Simons again.

'Go ahead, Alfa Four,' replied Reece.

'Our two friends are back on-board ship.'

'Roger that. Both of you go back to the apartment we will meet you there.'

'So, we go back to the apartment for a catch-up?' Said Anna.

'We need to contact our bosses, tell them what's happened and what we think needs to be done next.'

Chapter 17

Two hours later the four agents had gone over the operation so far and Anna and Reece had both updated their bosses. In the case of Anna to the Director of the Mossad Kidon Units Kurt Shimon in Tel Aviv and for Reece it was Jim Broad, Director of Operations SG9 in London. Both agents had spoken to their relevant bosses in separate rooms away from the hearing of the others.

'How did it go for you?' Reece asked Anna when she came back into the front room.

'Not bad, he seemed to take it very well. Then I don't think anyone can read Kurt Shimon when he's about to blow his top. How was it for you?'

'Jim Broad is going to get 'C' to phone the British High Commissioner to ask him to discreetly find out what the Malta Police find out. If I know anything, someone with a name like Julian Richardson Smith does not do discreet; they're more like a bull in a China shop but will always make sure to protect their asses making sure the shit falls on someone else.'

'I presume when your boss uses the Old Boys' network, they make sure this Julian won't know about us?'

'Correct. We disappear into the sunset or sunrise, as it will be coming up next. In the meantime, I think our bodyguard friends will stay on that ship awaiting instructions from Tehran. We also must assume that our lady friend who left the hotel and took the taxi is our courier and killer and headed straight for the airport. Why she killed him we have yet to discover. The last we saw her was over four hours ago so if flights were on time and I've checked on flights out of Malta dot com they are, then she could already be in London. Our technical people at GCHQ in Cheltenham are checking CCTV and manifests for passengers leaving Malta and landing in London for that timeframe. My boss wants me back in London as soon as possible. Matthew is to stay here and keep an eye on our friends on the ship and if necessary be available to link up with the High Commissioner and local security forces.'

'My boss told me I have to stay with you, so it looks like I'm going to London. Palo will stay here with Matthew as back-up.'

Matthew Simons, who had been watching the people coming and going through the harbour and on the ship through the binoculars, raised his hand in acknowledgement. Palo, who had been listening into the conversation, nodded in agreement. The lights in the room had been dulled to reduce Simon's silhouette at the window making the room seem secretive to the conversation it could hear, if, rooms heard secrets.

'I've been thinking about how the woman walked to the taxi,' said Palo, 'She seemed to be limping or had some form of stiffness in her leg. Do you suppose she had the walking stick down her trouser leg?'

'That's a good bet, especially if she's the courier and assassin. I saw no sign of the stick when I was in the hotel suite,' said Reece.

'But you did see Shafi with his face blown away,' said Matthew.

'Yes, and we still don't know why and that's the problem. There's something else going on here that we don't know about. Maybe we will know more when we get to London. There is plenty of stuff in the fridge, so I suggest you take turns at the window while the other gets some rest. Anna and I will take the car back to her hotel and my house to pick up our bags and on the way, I'll get London to book us on the first flight out. They probably won't notice they have a dead body in suite five until the morning cleaning. I left the DO NOT DISTURB sign on the door and closed it the best I could when I left. Matthew if that ship sails with our two friends on it, let our people know then act on their instructions.'

Reece and Anna left collecting her bag from her hotel room then Reece brought them to his villa at Saint Paul's Bay. Mary was still up and after introductions Reece left Mary and Anna to get to know each other when he went for a quick shower.

Within a short time, Mary realised she liked this woman and had nothing to fear when it came to Reece. Anna told her of her life in Israel and how she loved her country without adding anything about her work for Mossad. She spoke more like a travel agent making Mary respond by telling her of her own home country in Ireland. Mary made a pot of coffee, and they were just sitting down to a cup when Reece returned from his shower. He was carrying a small rucksack which Mary recognised as his quick travel bag for travel at short notice.

'Only time for a quick coffee I'm afraid. I've booked us out of Malta on the last flight tonight. It's going to Paris, but we can jump on the Eurostar which will get us into London for six tomorrow morning. The first direct flight to London from Malta doesn't leave until ten thirty in the morning and I thought this will help us get ahead of the game. A game we are already behind on.'

Reece could see by the expression on her face Mary wasn't happy. Anna could also see Mary's face and excused herself for the bathroom.

'Mary, you know I don't want to involve you in this. I don't want to leave you here, but you know the business I'm in and I can only tell you it's not going too well now and that's why we need to get to London as soon as possible. I want you to stay here and wait for Matthew who will need to pick up his stuff. If he needs to fly back to London, why don't you jump on the same flight, and we can spend some time in Belfast when this is over. You're always saying you want to catch-up with your mother.'

This seemed to pacify Mary, she nodded and smiled.

'Good save, I would love that. You know I worry because I love you, so wherever you are and whatever you're doing it's important you stay safe for me.'

Anna who had caught the last bit of the conversation when she walked back into the room, said nothing but smiled at seeing the concern Reece had for the woman he loved.

'Mary, the flight leaves just after 1 am so we will need you to drop us off at the airport. I love you too and don't worry I intend to stay safe.'

'No problem, I'll get my coat.'

Chapter 18

The flight from Malta landed in London just after midnight and as she didn't have to wait on any hold luggage Yasmin found no obstruction going through the Terminal building. Following the lanes marked Arrivals EU she soon found herself passing through passport control where the officer behind the desk paid no special attention other than looking at her walking stick as she limped through. Outside the arrivals building she got into a black cab; the kind well known in London. She asked the driver to drop her off at the bottom of Edgware Road across from Hyde Park. When she'd sent the Teacher a text that she'd arrived, he had replied with the address she was going to. When she'd been with him at his villa in Iran, he had told her to get dropped off at the end of the road or street she was travelling to, and never to give the driver the exact address or to be dropped off outside. She was then to walk to the address looking for security forces who might be observing her or the address. In the taxi she soon relaxed in the seat, noticing two things, the large number of similar taxis leaving the airport and the drop in temperature which was a lot colder than the air in Malta. Forty minutes later she was knocking on the door of the apartment on Edgware Road, which was quickly opened by Hassan.

'Good evening,' said Hassan speaking in English as they'd been told by the Teacher.

'Good night I think at this time of the day,' replied Yasmin smiling.

Both embraced as if they'd not seen each other for years. Anyone watching at this time of night would think that they were friends or lovers. Hassan closed the door, took the rucksack off Yasmin's back and led her up a flight of stairs to the first floor above the barber shop and the street.

He pointed to a door on the right down a long corridor, which had stairs on the left leading up to what could only be another floor in the apartment. 'The Teacher is waiting for you through that door.' Yasmin walked to the door still in limping mode with the walking stick in her right hand. The room was well lit, bright with a set of wall lights and a ceiling light all switched on. The Teacher sat in a large soft chair facing the door with his back to the window that looked out onto Edgware Road, if the curtains were open.

'My child it is wonderful to see you once more,' said the Arab standing to greet her with a hug and kissing her on each side of her face. 'How was your journey? Tell me everything while Hassan makes us some tea.'

For the next hour during which Hassan joined them Yasmin told the Arab everything that had happened to her on her journey from Iran through Malta and then on to London. He made her go over her meeting and killing of Shafi three times, taking the walking stick from her as she spoke. Screwing the top of the stick clockwise he took off the knob and turning it upside down he let the contents, three long sticks covered in a thick plastic type of material slide out onto the couch. The Arab, satisfied, put on a pair of surgical gloves and slid the black sticks back into the walking stick screwing the knob back on. He took off the gloves and placed them in the bin in the kitchen.

'Do you think the bodyguards will remember you?' asked the Arab.

'No, I had my scarf pulled up and walked straight past them without eye contact.'

'Did you see or suspect anyone else on your journey?'

'No, I saw no one or suspected anything unusual.'

This satisfied the Arab as he stood once more. 'You will be tired. Both of you have done well and the first part of your mission has now been completed. You will both be staying here for the rest of the plan. I will be staying elsewhere, and you do not need to know where that is, it is not important. I'll return tomorrow morning and we will discuss the next part of our plan. In the meantime, rest, keep the walking stick here and you will know more tomorrow. In the morning make sure you pray to Allah that he will bless our mission.'

The flight to Paris and the train journey into London had gone well arriving on time at St Pancras just after 6 a.m. Reece had received a text from Jim Broad telling him that he should bring Anna to the MI6 HQ at Vauxhall Bridge for a 1 p.m. debrief and meeting. For now, he had booked them into apartments in Pimlico where they should get some rest. The Churchill Serviced Apartments in Pimlico were just as it said on the tin as far as Security Service Personnel staying and working in London were concerned. The stylish apartments were watched over by several ex-military personnel to ensure safety for the people using them. The smartly dressed concierge reminded Reece of a para regimental sergeant major he once knew in his days fighting the terrorist war in Northern Ireland. Built like a brick wall Reece was sure he could still jump out of a plane and hit the ground running if he had too.

'Good morning, Mr Reece, my name is Johnson. We have been told to expect you both. Here is your key, you're in apartment two on the first floor. The apartment has two bedrooms with a kitchen and bathroom ready for your use. If there's anything else you need just let me know.'

'Thank you, Johnson, to tell you the truth we are both knackered, and I know I need sleep, so if you could give us a wake-up call at twelve that would be great. I'm not confident I'll hear my own alarm.'

'No problem, Mr Reece, will do.'

Reece wasn't exaggerating. Anna went for a shower while he headed straight for one of the bedrooms where without taking his clothes off, he was asleep within seconds of his head hitting the pillow. Anna showered quickly and like Reece although the water jet had freshened her, she was asleep in the other bedroom ten minutes after Reece.

COBRA stands for Cabinet Office Briefing Room-A and is the

British Government's briefing and meeting room when there is a crisis in the country. Different Government Ministers covering their own departments can chair the meetings usually with experts in the relevant issue that brings the committee together to deal with the crisis of the day. The meetings are usually called in times of great need. At 8 am. While Reece and Anna were catching up on their sleep in Pimlico, just such a meeting was taking place in the Cabinet Office Building at 70, Whitehall, just behind 10 Downing Street. The room was windowless, with one large central table surrounded by brown leather commuter type chairs. In front of each chair was a small computer screen and on the wall was a large screen visible to all sitting around the table. The room was the British equivalent to the more famous American Situation Room in the White House. Chairing the meeting and seated in the middle chair on one side of the table, was the Prime Minister, Peter Brookfield. Present were his senior advisers in the fields of Intelligence and Anti-Terrorism. From MI6, Sir Ian Fraser, known to those present as 'C'; from MI5 Caroline Aspinall; from the Metropolitan Police Commissioner, Sir Stuart Stevens, and his Deputy Commissioner in Charge of the Anti-Terrorist Squad, Helen Francis. There were three other people who because of their rank and expertise were attending to ensure the PM was getting the best advice possible before he made any decisions. Suzanne Hughes MP, the Home Secretary; Sir Martin Bryant, Chair of the Intelligence Committee; and General Sir John Richardson, British Armed Forces Chief of Staff. For this meeting there was to be no civil servant present as notes did not need to be taken. This was a briefing and discussion meeting only. Any follow up or actions resulting from the meeting would be passed on to the various departments by the people present to carry out the final agreement made by those at the meeting. The PM opened the meeting by asking if everyone present had read the small file each had been given to bring them up to date with the issue before them. Everyone indicated they had, and he continued.

'Good. You will now be aware of where we are with this operation which I have sanctioned. Unless I'm mistaken 'C', we don't know where the plutonium, or the people that have it, are now?'

Everyone looked to where Sir Ian Fraser, sat opposite the PM, and waited for his reply.

'As everyone will see from the short report in front of them Prime Minister, we've been working with our friends in the Israeli Secret Service Mossad on this matter. From our end, we've identified the Barcelona Suicide Bomber as a onetime British Citizen and her connections to a Jihad terrorist known as the Arab, who attended university in this country before becoming the high-ranking terrorist master he now is. Intelligence received mostly from Mossad has indicated that the target for the use of this plutonium attack is somewhere in Europe most likely here in the UK.'

Although all those around the table were highly experienced in their own fields, some of them still took a deep breath as they thought of the serious threat that these words brought home to them.

'So, what you're saying Prime Minister, is that for now we don't know where these people are and there is an imminent threat of a terrorist attack in this country possibly here in London using a dirty bomb?' It was the Suzanne Hughes the Home Secretary asking the question.

'I think the question you're asking is correct in its assumption at this time Home Secretary,' replied Brookfield.

 Feeling the tension in the room Sir Ian continued.

'In a joint operation with Mossad our own people have been working to track down the terrorist cell involved. The trail led to Malta where we believe there was a handover of the plutonium by an Iranian Quads Colonel to a member of the cell. This Colonel was, we believe then murdered by this terrorist, who we believe, from our people there, to be a woman. We don't know at this time why they killed him. From further checks it's thought she may have taken a flight into this country shortly afterwards.'

'But how did she get the plutonium through the airport's security checks?' it was Martin Bryant who asked the question. Sir Ian knew someone would ask.

'As anyone who works in the security business knows there are ways and means. Our scanners should show such items up, but with modern technology, ways can sometimes be found to circumvent our systems, as we have seen in the past with the shoe bomber and the bomber who nearly blew himself and a plane out of the sky when one went off in his underwear. Our people did see the Colonel arrive for his meeting in the Malta hotel with a silver walking stick, which they couldn't find after he was killed. We believe the woman, who may now be in London, was the assassin; and that she brought the walking stick with her into this country. We believe this walking stick contains the plutonium.'

'What are your people doing now Sir Ian?' asked the Prime Minister.

'We have been working closely with Mossad during this operation, and my head of operations Jim Broad will be briefing me further today and I will of course bring you up to date then. We are asking for the CCTV and passenger details of the flight from Malta to London which we think the woman used. Our agents on the ground were able to see what she was wearing and it's possible she did not have time to change clothes before her flight. We have agents in Malta watching the Iranian ship and the Hezbollah bodyguards on-board in case they go back into the city of Valletta. I would suggest that you contact our Commissioner in Malta to ask their security and police to help us track down this woman by releasing any information they get while investigating the Colonel's murder, and the woman's movements afterwards. This will include access to the hotel and airport CCTV and records. I also have GCHQ at Cheltenham checking their systems and our access to CCTV at the London airports, looking for a woman with a distinctive walking stick who might fit our target's description. This will also require the help of our police, anti-terrorist people and MI5, especially anything they're getting from their agents and technical sources. Information, however small, is vital. I have a specialist, Matthew Simons. He's the head of our Middle East desk who is currently in Malta, and I've instructed him to return immediately and link in with all the agencies including those at this table to co-ordinate all the information we generate.'

'Of course, Sir Ian. As your people are already aware, I think you should take the lead in this country for now. Everyone here will give you whatever support you require. Going around the room does anyone else have anything they would like to add?'

'I think it's too early to comment now Prime Minister,' it was Sir Martin Bryant who answered on behalf of those there. 'The one thing I would like an answer to as soon as possible is, why was this Iranian Colonel killed? Is there something else going on that we are not aware of? How do we get these answers? We all know how Mossad operate. They've killed their enemies in Malta before. Are they at their work once more, and if anything goes wrong, would they leave us as the Patsy picking up the pieces? The Home Secretary will also have to consider if we should raise the current threat level now.'

'That is something to think about and I'm sure 'C' is on to it as well.' answered Peter Brookfield.

Sir Ian Fraser was waiting for something like this from Martin Bryant. Always the politician lining up someone to blame if things hit the fan. It was time to produce his ace up his sleeve.

'Correct Prime Minister. I can only answer Sir Martin with what I've already told everyone here, that this is an ongoing joint operation with Mossad. I think raising the threat level at this time might tip off our terrorists, and that might even bring an attack earlier than they planned if it's not already underway. Upgrading the level will bring questions from the press, the people, and fellow politicians, which could cause panic in the population. Without the intelligence Mossad have given us already, I do not think we would even be aware of much of what we do have. I can tell everyone here that I've been contacted by Kurt Shimon the Director of the Mossad Kidon agents. He tells me he is currently on his way to London as we speak, and he has asked to meet me at Vauxhall Cross this afternoon. I don't think he would be coming to London unless he has something of importance to tell us and he wants to be here when we progress this operation.'

Peter Brookfield looked around the room before he replied.

'I hope he has something for us. Because without a lucky break, as far as I can see, we might reach a situation where we will have to bring in severe restrictions on movements and increase searches. The people of this country will not be happy with that. Get out there and find these people as a matter of urgency. I do not want to see any leaks in the press that would cause panic and maybe tip the hand of the terrorists to change their plans whatever they are. If I think we will need another meeting Sir Martin will let you know. In the meantime, everyone, any information, give it to Sir Ian and his team so that they can catch these people. Sir Martin and Sir Ian please stay behind for a minute. Everyone else let us get our people hunting.'

After the three men were left alone Peter Brookfield spoke to the two men in a slow deliberate quiet voice.

'I think you will both agree with me, that this is probably one of the most dangerous situations we have been in. The reason I wanted to speak to you alone was because, once again, we find our most secret team SG9 deeply involved, from Malta to here. What I need to ask you. Should we keep them involved, bearing in mind that their original remit for their formation is not only to track down these threats but to eliminate them? From what you tell us, Sir Ian, they've carried out their mission as far as it was briefed to them in Malta. What I'm asking, I suppose is, do you think the national resources we have will be adequate to do the job without them now?'

'I understand what you're asking Prime Minister. SG9 has taken this as far as they could in Malta. The murder of the Iranian has muddied the water and they were tasked to find out who was meeting him and identify the item they were collecting. It was hoped we could have intercepted that person with the plutonium before they even got to these shores, but because of that murder and the assessment that the woman did the killing, we've moved on somewhat from the initial remit. Our SG9, and the Mossad agents at this moment are the only people who might have an idea of what this woman looks like and, who we are looking for. For now, I would like to keep our people involved if only to keep tabs on Mossad operating on our turf, even though they will deny it, I wouldn't be inclined to believe them. They are determined to get their hands on the Arab, and the niceties of good manners on their side will not be respected I'm sorry to say, probably because we would do the same in their place. I'll report back after my meeting with Kurt Shimon when I hope to have more information. The fact he is coming here personally means he not only is bringing something important to the table, but he wants to shoe himself into an operation on our soil involving his people.'

'All the more reason we should retain control Prime Minister,' said Bryant.

'OK. For now, we keep SG9 involved, but I want to be kept informed every step of the way, understood?'

'Yes, Prime Minister,' both men replied in unison feeling they sounded like a well-known pair of Civil Service Mandarins in a sitcom.

Chapter 19

Reece had slept deeply without dreams. He was awake before the wake-up call from Johnson but still replied with a 'Thank you,' when the phone had buzzed. Awake, he felt fully recovered from the exertions of the last forty-eight hours. Anna had heard the buzz of the phone and shouted from her room that she was awake. An hour later both agents were sitting in the outer office of the head of MI6 at Vauxhall Cross. To Reece, this office looked like so many more he had seen in government departments, modern furniture with the added flat screen computer screen on the steel desk. The secretary sitting behind it also looked like she'd come from a standard production line, white crisp blouse, dark pinstriped skirt, and black rimmed glasses. Reece thought her quite attractive for a woman who looked over fifty. She had asked them to take a seat as 'C' was busy now. She offered something to drink which both agents refused with a 'no thank you', then she returned to her typing.

'This is my first time here, what about you?' asked Anna.'

'A few times, and every time I came here the news was never good.'

'Well, the last time I spoke to my boss he wasn't happy so I'm ahead of you on that score.'

'At least you're one up on me. I've never been to Mossad Head Quarters. But when it comes to being told off, I've had some of those in the past, but I always think to myself, don't worry they can't make you pregnant.'

'Doesn't stop them trying,' smiled Anna.

The intercom on the secretary's desk buzzed. Pressing a button on the top of her desk, they heard the deadlock on the door open to the office of the head of MI6 release.

'You may go in now,' she said in her clipped educated voice.

The office was as Reece remembered it from the first time, when he was recruited by 'C' and Jim Broad into the Black Ops team that was SG9. Back then he realised he had been searching for a purpose in life, especially one where he could use the skill he had been trained in and used fighting the terrorist war in Northern Ireland all those years ago.

The same desk that had been used by every 'C'. Legend had it that it was the one used by Nelson on the Victory. The desk was clear of any files or documents, the only items being the tamper proof computer and a special desk communications console. Reece had been told the console allowed the director to speak securely with the Prime Minister as well as his equivalent in the CIA, Mossad and all the European Directors. In one corner stood the grandfather clock another item from a bygone age when the first head of MI6, Sir Mansfield Smith Cumming, who used the first initial surname to sign off all secret documents using green ink. The tradition stuck, every Director of MI6 afterwards used the prefix 'C', and the green ink tradition became protocol. Reece, when serving in the RUC Special Branch had always used the term Boss for his superiors. This was instilled into SB recruits so that an officer's rank was never spoken, protecting their identification as a police officer, especially in public, and in the undercover world they worked in. Reece rarely called Sir Ian Fraser 'C', using in the few times they met, the word Boss or Sir. The large bay window looking out over the Thames and London was fitted with windows that not only gave natural light but were bulletproof and made of a material that stopped audio or visual surveillance penetrating the room. Sitting at the large conference table, were three men. 'C' and Broad he knew, but the third man he did not know. Reece could see from the look of familiarity on Anna's face as she smiled but raised her eyebrows in question, that she did know the third man. Jim Broad stood to welcome them and gestured that they should join them at the table.

'Welcome David, welcome Anna,' said Broad. 'I think a quick introduction is needed for you both. Anna I'm James Broad one of the MI6 Covert Operations Directors.' Reece noted he made no mention of his department, SG9.

Pointing to the man at the end of the table that faced the bay window, Broad continued.

'This is Sir Ian Fraser, otherwise known in intelligence circles as 'C', the head of MI6 and of course you already know this man to my right, your own boss Kurt Shimon. For your information David he is the head of the Mossad Kidon teams.'

Both argents sat across from Broad and Shimon, wondering what was to come.

'I hope you were able to get some rest. I think you may be a little busy in the next few days,' said Sir Ian.

'Yes sir we did, thank you,' replied Reece.

'Good, then let us get on. Despite having the information that there was going to be a handover of terrorist materials in Malta we seem to have missed it. Instead, we lost the courier and discovered a murder. Not the greatest of operations, but from what we've learnt and discussed before you joined us it would appear none of these problems were down to how you carried out your part of the mission. I think Kurt can bring us up to date with some new information we were not aware of. It might help you understand a bit more about what happened in Malta.'

'Thank you, Sir Ian. It is good to meet you at last, Mr Reece. I've heard a lot about you. I hope you will forgive me but even Anna did not know what I'm about to tell you. The Iranian Colonel who was murdered was one of our agents. His own people would call him a spy or a traitor.'

Reece and Anna looked at each other, then around the table before looking once more at Kurt Shimon, who continued to speak.

'In a way, it was through Colonel Shafi that we first got on to what was developing in this terrorist plot. As head of security at one of the Iranian nuclear facilities he had been instructed by his masters in Iran to collect the plutonium and transport it and meet up with the courier in Malta. Anna, what you and David did in Malta was always going to be as good as the information you had at hand. The fact you were not aware of the information we had is not your fault. It was a matter of what you needed to know at the time, and I'd hoped that our dead agent Colonel Shafi would have given us the rest of the picture after his meeting with the courier. I would then have been able to brief you on the next part of your mission with a clearer picture of what was happening. We do not know at this time how our agent was blown or why they killed him without the torture that would be the norm for the Iranians and Hezbollah, but we will find out in the process of time. For now, we do not think your input to the mission has been exposed. We believe you are unknown to them at this time, although given by the fact they've killed Shafi, they must suspect we have some knowledge of their plans. I think the fact they appear to be continuing with their plans was deliberate. If we had had taken out the woman, the one we now suspect is the courier, then they would only have lost one member of what we believe is a bigger team. The other members of their team would regroup for a further operation; perhaps one we are not aware of. We believe this team is intact and will continue with its operation. It is now our job to find them and stop them. Now it looks like the target is here in the UK. I've told Sir Ian and our Prime Minister has told the British Prime Minister that Mossad are willing to work with the security forces in this country to help stop them.'

The room fell silent for a few seconds while Reece and Anna took in what they'd just heard. It was now time for Sir Ian Fraser to break that silence.

'As I told you when you joined us, we had already been briefed with the information you have just been given. I would think you might have some questions yourselves and the first question, I'm sure, will be what happens now? I'll hand over to Jim who is up to date. We've placed him in overall charge of the day to day running of this operation.'

Jim Broad had a pile of buff folders in front of him which he now passed around the table, keeping one for himself. Each folder had a large red X across the front with the words *OPERATION SEARCH* and *TOP SECRET* in capital letters across the top.

'I think the code name for this operation is very appropriate. This operation is now a country wide search.' said Broad standing to continue as if he was addressing a lecture hall.

Reece was laughing inside. Normally operation code names are selected by a computer so that they haven't been used before or the danger of being crossed over to another file. This name had either not been used before or had been deliberately selected by 'C' or Broad, who continued to speak, while at the same time reading from the folder in front of him. Everyone followed his voice while reading the words in their own folder.

'As of 10 a.m. this morning our two Hezbollah hoods have left Malta on the same vessel they sailed on into Valletta. We have instructed our two agents Matthew Simons and Palo to come to London on this afternoon's flight. When they get here, we've agreed they'll both run a combined operation desk at our rooms on the third floor, all information received will be fed through them. We have the resources of all the agencies at our disposal. All those agencies will be dropping everything else and concentrating their efforts solely on Operation Search. This will include the MI5 watchers, GCHQ at Cheltenham, the Met Anti-Terrorist Squad, and ourselves of course. David, I want you and Anna to work together on this. As you can see from the file, we still have little to go on, but we do believe this terrorist cell is here, somewhere in London. We do not think our girl in Malta hung around. We already have some feedback from Sir Julian Richardson Smith in Malta who has been speaking to his contacts in the Maltese government and police who are looking into the dead body of our Iranian Colonel. They inform him at this stage that they believe that he has been assassinated by the Israeli Secret Service, who I'm sorry to say Kurt, have form for this sort of thing previously in Malta.'

Reece could see a small smile at the side of Kurt Shimon's lips.

'Par for the course as you British would say,' replied the Mossad boss.

Broad nodded then continued with his report.

'Sir Julian was also able to tell us that a woman fitting our team's description booked into the same hotel room where the body was found and vanished without paying which we all know is a big no in the hotel trade.' It was Broad's turn to smile before continuing.

'The local police have been able to get the CCTV from the reception area of the hotel. They confirm through the local taxi drivers, that the woman went straight to the airport in one of their cars. Through his contacts and with a bit of persuasion from Sir Julian, who has told the local authorities the British government want to help in the search for the killer, he has been able to obtain the CCTV from the hotel and the airport security cameras.' Pointing to the opposite wall to where they were sitting Broad aimed the remote-control pen in his hand.

'If you would look at the screen the first video you will see is from the hotel.'

The video lasted about five minutes. Showing a young woman with Asian features with dark shoulder length hair. She appeared to know about the camera, keeping her head down the whole time, she was at the reception. They could see her talking to the receptionist but there was no audio. They watched as she handed over her passport which the receptionist appeared to scan with a scanner under the counter then handed it back with a key card before pointing to the stairs and lift. The video ended and Broad pressed another button on the pen.

The second time the video showed the woman carrying a small rucksack and walking with a limp. She was walking through the main doors and into the airport departures area of the building. After looking around, she walked to the ladies, where after a few minutes she reappeared, this time with a silver-coloured walking stick. Reece was not one hundred per cent sure, but he would have put a month's pay on it being the same one they had seen the Iranian Colonel walk into the hotel with, the one he couldn't find later. The woman on the video then booked in at the ticket desk before going through security, placing her rucksack and the walking stick through the security scanner before picking them up without problem on the other side. At the Departure Desk she had produced her passport, which had been scanned. The cameras, which had been in sweeping mode, picked her up moving through the airport and sitting a short time before moving through with other passengers to join her plane. Reece noticed she never lifted her head for a clear shot from the cameras. This woman knew what she was doing and wasn't going to make it easy for the security people who may be looking for her. The video screen went blank once more and Broad continued to speak.

'I'm sure you all noticed how she kept her head down and came out of the ladies with a walking stick, probably the one handed over by the Colonel, the one we believe contains the plutonium. How they've wrapped it we do not know yet, but however they've done it to get it past the airport security certainly works, because she was able to board a plane to London and we now believe she and her walking stick are somewhere in this country, most likely this city.'

Broad pressed the button once more and two full-frontal photos of the woman came onto the screen.

'These are the best photos we could get, but they are rather good. The one on the right is when she passed through the security search area at the airport. The one on the left is from her scanned passport. You will find copies of the photos in your file along with the details page of her passport.'

Reece looked down at the photo and tried to lock it into his brain.

'As you can see, even though Anna had the small Geiger counter and passed close to the Colonel when he had the walking stick in the hotel reception, it still didn't show any signal. We believe the

Iranians have in some-way found a covering for the plutonium that protects it from scanners,' said Kurt Shimon.

'Yes. On that we can agree. So, you can see we have a huge problem,' said Fraser, 'The plutonium is now in this country and our scanners are useless. We need to find these people fast and eliminate the threat from them and the plutonium. Do we have anything on her arrival in this country Jim?'

Broad pressed the button on the remote device again showing a red dot on the screen which he used to follow the woman as she walked through Arrivals at London airport. The video was like the one showing her leaving Malta but this time staring into a camera at the passport desk. The red dot then followed her outside the building for some distance before they could see she her climb into a black cab.

'As you can see, she arrived in London last night on the late flight from Malta and she still has the walking stick with her. We are currently trying to locate the taxi driver through the Met and MI5 but so far, we do not have any more information. We are also checking traffic cameras and APRN to try to track the taxi but nothing yet.'

Broad pressed the button once more and a screenshot of a passport came up.

'This is her passport document which is also in your folder. It shows her name as Carletta Maguire, twenty-five years old from Catford London. A quick check by the Met Anti-Terrorist Squad can confirm that a young lady of the same name lived there until two years ago when she appeared to travel to the Far East but did not return. There are two years left before the passport runs out. The photo looks like the real Carletta Maguire, but inquiries have confirmed it is not her. The passport has never been reported lost or stolen, so, I would worry about the real Carletta wherever she is. It would appear our lady who is similar in appearance is travelling on a false document, as we suspected. As of now she is our main target of interest. All resources are at our disposal. David if you could stay behind, I need to talk to you? For now, I believe Kurt has some information which he needs to update us with.'

Kurt Shimon stood as Broad sat back down at the table and walked over to stand in front of the wall screen.

'Thank you, Jim, and thank you Sir Ian for allowing us to help in this mission, which is critically just as important for us, as it is for you. As you've already heard Colonel Shafi, was indeed an agent of Mossad. Like you, we do not usually admit to who our agents are, dead or alive. Indeed, we have agents in the past, who have been captured and tortured before being executed publicly, hung from a crane in a square in an Arab town, just because we wouldn't admit they were one of ours. Shafi knew this when he became one of those agents. I have a quote in a frame on my office wall which keeps me going when I ask myself the question why am I doing this job? The quote from Golda Meir states, 'I understand the Arabs wanting to wipe us out, but do they really expect us to cooperate?' Golda is dead many years, but in my time, I've come to understand that these Arabs don't just want to wipe us out, but anyone who supports us as well. This operation involves our two countries and our separate intelligence agencies. If we are to defeat these people, we need to work closely together on this. It might not suit some in our political or civil services, but we are at the coal face as you would say. The niceties of politics are not available to us, so we fight a common enemy every day together or alone. You are aware of our main interest in this. One of our agents has been killed and we will find out how or who exposed him. We believe everything about this involves the one we call the Arab. In your folders you will have the information we have on him and two photos; the one which was taken at celebrations just after 9/11, and the other just at the start of all this when he was photographed by our agents in Tehran in the company of the Quads General. The reason I'm here today instead of talking via a conference call is that I have something more to bring to the table. Forgive me, Sir Ian, but I wanted to wait until we were all here as this was passed to me from our London Embassy this morning. Jim, could I borrow your remote for a second.'

Taking the remote Shimon took a small pen-stick out of his coat pocket and finding the slot at the side of the wall screen inserted the device and pressed the button. The screen lit up to show a photo of people sitting at a distance around what looked like a swimming pool with a building behind them. Shimon pressed another button and the photo zoomed to a close-up stronger focus showing two men and a woman sitting at a table by the pool outside what now appeared to be a villa. Using the red highlight button Shimon rested the light on each person in the photo.

'The same agents who took the photo of the meeting between The Arab and the Quads General outside the cafe in Tehran, followed the

Arab to the villa and at great risk were able to obtain this one photo. The first man is our friend the Arab; real name Abdullah Mohammad Safrah.' Highlighting the woman next to him he continued.

'This is the woman we've been speaking about; Shafi's killer and the courier of the plutonium into this country. The third man, we do not know. This photo was taken with a long-lens camera from some distance away. The villa just outside Tehran we believe belongs to the Arab and here we have him briefing his people. We again believe the briefing is for this mission in London.'

The photo showed the Arab and the woman from a frontal view, but the second man was side on, and they could tell that he was young, athletically built and dark skinned.

These photos are four days old and taken around the same time that Shafi was sailing down the Mediterranean towards Malta, so from the timeline we now have, we can safely assume that all three people in the photo at the villa are in this country.'

'Excuse me,' it was Reece who spoke, 'Considering how small the walking stick is and the Quads involvement why have the Iranians not just used the diplomatic bag and transferred it into this country without all this risk through Malta?'

Kurt Shimon looked at 'C' who nodded for him to answer Reece.

'A good question, Mr Reece, and one we asked ourselves when this whole mission came to our attention. I think we should look at a few important points. We think most importantly, the Iranian government have made a big thing of denying that they're working on any tactical nuclear weapons. They have denied access, as far as they can to the atomic energy inspectors, inspecting the locations, where we suspect they are creating the essential product to make such weapons. Because of this the West has come down hard on them with sanctions, leaving their own people suffering because of the Ayatollahs intransigent stance. If it was to come out that their officials were caught trying to use their diplomats to transport plutonium, then they fear those same suffering people would rise up and overthrow them. The Quads have always used the terrorist arm of Hezbollah and Islamic Jihad to do their dirty work. If such a terrorist was to be caught with such a weapon it's deniable. If they succeeded, then it suits Iran's purpose, namely, to damage the West, and in particular Israel, if they can. The people we have encountered so far are just such a terrorist arm and we know that the Arab has been involved not only with the Islamic Jihad but with the Iranians for some time. He is a willing partner and a dangerous opponent. This is the main reason why we are willing to work with anyone who is a target of this man to help catch him and his friends or eliminate them if necessary. Something I'm sure you have experience of yourself, Mister Reece, I hope that answers your question?'

It was Reece's turn to nod his agreement.

It was then the turn of Sir Ian Fraser to take back control of the meeting.

'Thank you, Kurt, everything is helpful if we are to stop these people in their tracks. As you can see, both our Prime Ministers have been briefed on this threat and both agree that we should work closely together on this. There are no state secrets at stake, just a threat from terrorists that both countries are aware of. That said, this operation because it's on British soil, will be led by MI6. The operations room to co-ordinate everything coming in and controlling reactions will be in this building. Matthew Simons will be the main conduit for the running of this operation from that control room. Everything will go through him. I expect him to be here in a few hours and ready to brief everyone on what we have at 5 pm today. Jim Broad will represent Kurt and myself at these briefings and report directly to us, so that we can then brief our Prime Ministers. Unless you have any questions, I suggest you go and make yourselves familiar with the set-up of the control room and collect what weapons and radio communications equipment you need from stores. We have laid on two BMW cars fitted with radios and tracking equipment in the underground garage. Does anyone have any questions?'

'If, as we expect, these three people are already in this country, what if they're ready to go now? What will we do?' asked Reece.

'A good question David,' replied Broad. 'We have put all our agencies on alert as far as we can, circulating the photos we have of our suspects. As everyone here will know, there are always many covert and surveillance operations ongoing in the capital at any one time. These can involve anything from counter terrorism to foreign spies and serious crime. We will divert some of the Watchers from the A4, MI5 and the Met Anti-Terrorist and Drug Squad teams from their own surveillance operations, to support the search for these people. The Met and the anti-terrorist team have extensive coverage of the city using a CCTV system with the ability for facial recognition, which will be monitored by a special team. On top of that, you have uniform police patrols who will be told to watch out for these people; not to approach, but to observe and inform us right away. Therefore, we need to have a strong control, with as much information as possible going through this building to prevent teams crashing into each other and causing more problems on the ground than the ones these terrorists will cause. We are not able to stop them if they were to go out this minute and carry out their attack, but with the information we are providing, these agencies can react quickly to such an attack, as they always can. The military have a Hazmat Nuclear and Biological Weapons teams at London barracks alongside our bomb disposal teams ready to move if needed. Our people at GCHQ and the Israeli equivalent are monitoring all calls between Iran and this country just in case our friends communicate with each other. Our next move is to get briefed up at 5 p.m. then get out there, find these people, and eliminate the threat. Anna, I know that Kurt wants to go to your Embassy to brief your ambassador, so if you could be back for five that would be great.'

Both Anna and Shimon stood to leave.

'As we are working together on this? I would like to have one of my people working in the control room with Matthew,' said Shimon.

'That will not be a problem your input will be greatly appreciated,' replied Fraser.

After the two Israelis left the room Broad and 'C' sat facing Reece across the conference table. Sir Ian leant across the table before he spoke directly to Reece.

'Now David, as I'm sure you know; this operation so far has not been going too well and we find ourselves in a dangerous situation where we have at least three high-powered terrorists in this country with plutonium for use in a dirty bomb. We all know the damage that would cause. I believe our Mossad friends have not been completely truthful with us. If they had been from the start, we could have nipped this whole thing in the bud. It is obvious they were depending on their dead agent to give them the heads up when to move. His death changed everything, it forced them to be more forthcoming with us. Pointing fingers now will get us nowhere, we are where we are. I'm saying this, because although we might appear to be working closely with Mossad, we should not trust them all the way. That's why anyone entering this building is scanned discreetly when they walk through the main doors. The scanners would pick up any bugging transmitters they would have on them if they wanted to leave one behind after their visit. Do not be in any doubt, we are in charge now. These people are in our country so we will run Operation Search our way, and if we can, we will deal with the terrorists in our own way, the way SG9 has been set-up for. Are you happy with that?'

'I agree as far as I'm concerned. I've told you in the past my reason for joining SG9 was for just this sort of situation. These people intend to kill us, our task is to kill them first. We have all seen the damage they are capable of. The only way they'll change is if we stop them and convince them this is not the way to progress their argument.' replied Reece.

Jim Broad stood up and stretched his legs, walking to the large window that looked out over the River Thames and London; raindrops were hitting the window. Turning back to face the men at the table he spoke once more.

'David, what this all boils down to now is, that we need to be as lucky as we were in Manchester. You were able to stop them then.'

Manchester was still fresh in his mind and always would be. The SG9 and SAS team had tracked down a terrorist cell which combined an Irish Republican sniper and Islamic fanatics.

'We had some luck, but we also had a good agent from the start which helped. This time, the agent has been killed and the bad guys are in the wind. And remember; in Manchester, although we stopped them killing the Prime Minister, we lost two of ours and a civilian.'

Now it was the turn of Sir Ian Fraser to join the conversation.

'Yes, but our experience tells us there is always the risk of losing some of our own. The case in Manchester being an example. But thanks to you and your team we stopped it being much worse and the whole cell including the woman leader who escaped to Egypt were eliminated.

In a way this operation is slightly similar. We are looking for these people, but this time we have a full-scale alert out there helping you, a lot more eyes and ears than you had in Manchester including, this time, Mossad. If you need anything more you will have it, but I want you to understand one thing; if you and your SG9 team do find these people and eliminate them; you're still a secret unit, which this country does not have or acknowledge. I know you understand this, but I'm reminding you. We have politicians who shit themselves that we have such people, who will always throw us to the wolves to protect their own skins if they have to.'

'You don't have to remind me Sir Ian. I remember how those politicians gave the terrorists everything they wanted in Northern Ireland, letting mass murderers out of prison after two years, and giving those on the run a free 'Get out of jail' card. The thing that makes me even more angry is that those same terrorists are now politicians with big salaries and big offices at Stormont, with chauffeur driven limos and bodyguards. Don't worry, when it comes to trust, then politicians are on a par with terrorists.'

Both Broad and 'C' smiled understanding.

'As Sir Ian just said David, anything you need. After this meeting, if you go to the control room you will find your colleagues from Manchester, Mr Cousins and Mr Harrison. You also have an SAS team at the London District Army Barracks waiting for your briefing as and when you need them. Their commander is also the same one you worked with in Manchester, Captain Middleton. And some more information I think you will be interested in; your lady is currently on route from Malta on the same flight as Matthew Simons and the Mossad agent you know as Palo. They should arrive in a couple of hours, and I've arranged for them to be picked up at the airport. I've booked a room for you at The Park Plaza Westminster Bridge Hotel so you can be with her later and get back here for the briefing at five. Tonight, the bill is on us. If you need it any longer, you're paying.'

Reece left the two men to their plans and when he walked through the outer office, he knew the secretary would be wondering why he was smiling.

Chapter 20

The windowless room was illuminated by light from a batch of screens. Two men sat in front of these screens, both using headsets to communicate to operators on the ground. The chat was familiar to the other occupants in the room, as they set up call signs, linking them to the control room and identifying each person they were communicating with and locating where each call sign was currently situated on the streets of London. Operation Search was underway.

Reece saw Joe Cousins and Steve Harrison as soon as he walked into the room. All three shook hands. 'Am I glad to see you guys,' said Reece.

'Malta seems to have been good to you,' said Harrison.

'If you think that Steve your eyesight's playing you up, you need a trip to the opticians.' laughed Reece.

'What's this all about?' asked Cousins.

Reece quickly brought them up to speed explaining the work with Mossad in Malta and the reason they were here today.

'Plutonium?' Henderson whistled softly to himself.

'Yes, and it's here somewhere in this country, most likely London.'

'Can I put in for my backdated leave now? For the first flight to somewhere sunny preferably,' asked Cousins.

'Afraid not Joe. Matthew Simons will have a more detailed brief, and hopefully an idea where these people might be when we get back here at five. In the meantime, get what you need from stores and catch-up on anything else that you can, and I'll see you both back here then.'

'I assume that includes weapons?' said Cousins.

Reece opened his Barbour jacket exposing his Smith and Wesson 59 resting in the holster.

'We can be sure the people we will be hunting will be armed so get what you need from the armoury. There are two BMWs ready for us down in the car park I'll take one, you two can have the other.'

Reece listened into the communications traffic coming and going through the airwaves, much of it familiar to him from his own days when working undercover in Northern Ireland when looking for a dangerous foe, always to be ready for the unexpected. *Nothing changes*, he thought, *the opposition might change but the threats were still the same.*

'Red Four to control in position three, over.'

One of the operators at the computer console touched the screen which displayed a digital map of London, a small red dot began to flash on and off showing exactly where Red Four was at that moment in time.

'Roger Red Four I have you,' replied the desk operator. Reece knew that in an operation this big, at least ten teams of eight would be spread out over the city, each covering a specific area. The teams would be colour coded to prevent confusion, White Team, Black Team, Red Team and so on. Each team would have a vehicle which could be a van, a black cab, or a motor bike; the rest of the team would be on foot. The teams would be a mixture of age with men and women from different ethnic backgrounds and skin colour.

His phone buzzed in his pocket. The screen showed a text message from Mary.

'See you soon, can't wait xxx'

Once again Reece was smiling as he headed for the lift. He picked up the BMW from the underground car park and drove out, joining the traffic over Vauxhall Bridge. Switching on the radio comms he could hear control continuing with its contacting teams in the city confirming their locations. Reece hated driving through London and would usually prefer to walk or use a taxi. The traffic was as always, busy and moved slowly. The good thing about the car he thought was that it had hidden blue flasher lights and a two-tone siren if he needed to move fast. He was sorely tempted to turn them on as he turned and drove slowly along the Thames embankment towards the Houses of Parliament but controlled the thought, for now.

The Park Plaza Westminster Bridge Hotel is located on the south bank of the Thames opposite the Houses of Parliament and Big Ben less than a five-minute walk from the London Eye. It was one of the hotels tourists preferred, with easy access to the historical buildings of church and government which, as Reece found when he entered his allocated room, he could see from the magnificent views across the Thames flowing three stories below. Reece threw his small bag onto the bed and checked out the minibar which was well stocked. The room had air conditioning with the usual large flat screen TV. The only whisky was Jamison, which would have to do for now. He made a mental note to buy a bottle of Bushmills as soon as he could find an off-licence. It would be an hour before Mary arrived, so he asked reception to give her a key to the room 303 when she arrived; he sent her a text with the number and that he would see her later for dinner. He knew Mary would make a beeline for the hotel pool so she would be totally relaxed when he got back from his next port of call, the London District Army Barracks. The army based there carry out responsibilities for everything within the M25 motorway corridor that surrounds London. Having worked closely with the SAS on operations in Northern Ireland and most recently in Manchester, Reece had great respect for the men who made up the most secret unit of the British Army. As he drove through the traffic his mind went back to those days in Northern Ireland when once every six months, he would travel to Hereford to brief the next incoming Squadron from 22 SAS coming to the Province to take over the task from the current one leaving after their six-month tour. In what was once Stirling Lines, named after the founder of the SAS, David Stirling, he would stay for a couple of days in the officer mess and drink heavily with the men before and after his briefing.

At the main entrance to London and the South of England's Army Head Quarters he presented his MI5 Security Services Pass. This document was used by all SG9 operators as it gave the correct amount of impressive credentials when operating on the British mainland. The document told those who inspected it, respect the person who presented it, ask no questions, mind your own business, and carry out the instructions when asked. When Reece said he was there to speak with a Captain in the SAS, no further questions were needed. The armed military sentry directed him to park at an office building close to the entrance then go inside where he would be directed to a waiting room while they located the officer.

The waiting room consisted of a row of four chairs and a large coffee table. Reece checked his phone while he waited, there were no messages. Ten minutes later the door opened and Captain Geoff Middleton, 22nd Special Air Service Regiment entered. The recognition between the two men would have been obvious to anyone watching. Reece stood and, taking the offered hand to shake it, he couldn't help but think again how fit and healthy this man looked and how strong his grip.

'Geoff, great to see you. You look great, I'm glad it's you.'

'I don't know if I could say the same, remembering the last time we worked together.'

Reece laughed. 'If there's going to be trouble, I can't think of anyone better to get me out of it.'

'What is this all about David, we got the shout at the Headshed and told to get here asap?'

Reece knew that Captain Geoff Middleton and his team would be permanently on call at the SAS Headquarters in Hereford or as the men referred to it, the Headshed, ready to move at a moment's notice to anywhere in the world to deal with any imminent threat.

'What do you know, what have they told you?'

It was Middleton's turn to smile.

'Come on David. You know we are like mushrooms, kept in the dark and fed full of shit. They tell us as little as they can. At least with you I know I'll get the truth. So, what's happening?'

'You're going to want to be sitting when I tell you.'

Reece pulled a chair to one side of the coffee table and sat to face Middleton sitting opposite.

'Seriously Geoff, what have you been told so far to save me repeating something you may already know?'

'The Headshed told us to get here asap with equipment to assault a building or take out a terrorist cell on the streets of London. I do not even know who the opposition are, or their firepower. I'm hoping you can tell me that.'

For the next half hour Reece brought Middleton up to date, taking him all the way from working with Mossad agents in Malta, to the present, where it was believed that the terrorist cell was somewhere in London in possession of plutonium ready to use as a dirty bomb.

'So, let me get this straight. You lost them. You don't know where they are, and we could all die at any moment?'

'Correct.'

'Then I can see why you sent for us. Find them, stop them and kill them, easy.'

'We know a few things about them and what at least two of them look like provided they don't use good disguises. We have every agency you could think of looking for them, including Mossad. We have all current ongoing operations; with the surveillance, bugs, and informants, being directed to provide any information they can towards Operation Search. Everything will be co-ordinated and run by one of our top MI6 Middle East experts through a control room at Vauxhall Cross. We have a full briefing there at five this afternoon. You should be there. The feelers for information went out this morning, and I'm hoping we will have something then. So, you should come, it will be fun, and you will get the opportunity to put your questions. In the meantime, bring your own team up to date. How many are there?'

'Counting me, ten with the option for more from the Headshed if I need them.'

'Until five then.'

Reece shook Middleton's hand. Once more the strong grip still there.

Chapter 21

'Did you sleep well?' asked Hassan.

Yasmin pushed her hair back from her face and with her hands folded it to the back of her head then using the elastic hair band, wrapped it into a ponytail.

'Yes, thank you. The bed was soft and cool. Is there anything to eat, I'm famished?'

Hassan smiled. He had not cooked anything for two reasons; he didn't want to make too much noise as he wanted to let her sleep, and the second reason was there was nothing much to cook anyway.

'There's nothing much in the fridge. If you can wait, there's a chip shop across the street and I can get us something?'

Looking through the window across Edgware Road Yasmin could see several shops but didn't have a clue which one was a chip shop.

'Chip shop, what's that?'

Hassan realised they probably didn't have any such thing as a chip shop where she came from.

'It's like a takeaway café that sells fried food like potatoes that are cut into small pieces and fish covered in batter.'

'The Teacher told us not to go out unnecessarily.'

Now it was Hassan's turn to look out the window.

'I think the Teacher would want us at our best for our mission. To be our best we need to be well fed and the chip shop is just across the street, so I'll not be going far, and I won't take long. There is some bread in the kitchen. Butter me two slices and get out the plates. Do you like salt and vinegar?'

No, she thought. She'd not tasted fish and chips before. She wouldn't risk it.

Hassan had been true to his word and came back with the fish and chips wrapped in paper within fifteen minutes of leaving the apartment.

Yasmin had to admit her food was delicious, but as she was hungry the new experience would have been the same with most foods.

They had just finished eating when they heard the downstairs front door open and close, and the footsteps coming up the stairs.

The Arab had booked into The Beaumont Hotel in Mayfair, and he could walk to the apartment but, as it was raining, he took a taxi to Hyde Park corner and walked the short distance from there. To anyone watching he looked every inch the businessman; wearing a dark three-piece suit, he walked fast to get out of the rain as quickly as he could, again this wouldn't stand out as everyone was walking at the same pace to avoid the same wet stuff. He had always hated the British weather and longed for the warm sun of the lands of Allah.

'Good morning children, blessings be upon you,' he said when entering the room.

Both Yasmin and Hassan stood for the teacher as children would in class.

'Did you sleep well my children?'

'Yes, very well,' said Hassan.

The Arab sat on the chair at the window and faced both of his students.

'What is that smell, have you been cooking?'

Both knew the teacher was no fool and a lie would be worse than the truth.

'We have eaten from the takeaway across the street. There was nothing for us in the fridge or kitchen. It only took me a few minutes to collect it and return here.'

The Arab was silent for at least two minutes. Both students sat on the couch and looked at each other and waited before the teacher spoke once more. He spoke softly and slowly making sure that both heard him and would understand every word.

'I'm sure you both know why I chose you for this mission. This mission is not just for me or a cause. You are the representatives of Allah on earth. It is him you represent and him you disappoint when you let your earthly needs come before his will, blessings be upon him. You do not just disappoint me, but you disappoint Allah and that is unforgiveable. But you and I know that man's flesh is weak, and the only way to be forgiven is to commit yourself to the will of Allah completely. His will demands your full obedience, and I as your teacher tell you to give that obedience to me now, totally, and maybe then we can complete our mission on earth in the name of the

LIGHT OF THE SUN

most holy. I'll not tell you this again. There will be no next time, or your mistake will get you killed by the enemy, and that mistake not only puts the mission in danger but might get me killed as well. So, understand, if we were to survive such a mistake be sure I will kill you myself and you will die in sin before the eyes of Allah. Do you understand. Do I make myself clear?'

Both students nodded, afraid to look into those dark eyes they both feared.

'I've stayed the night in a hotel near here and I see everything. From now, you only leave this building on my order, to do what I tell you. I'll pick up some groceries later.'

Again, both nodded without saying a word.

Now the Arab produced two London A–Z street map books from his pocket and handed one to each of his students.

'No more will be said. Yasmin, can you bring us coffee and I will tell you what you will do next in our mission?'

Five minutes later Yasmin had brought back the coffee and poured for everyone. The Arab took the book he had given to Yasmin and opened it.

'Yasmin. Here you will see I've circled the area of Trafalgar Square. I want you to go there this afternoon and get to know the area very well. Take your time and find the place where the tourists gather the most in numbers. Use your mobile to take photos. You can walk from here, that way you will be able to look for enemy security forces. Hassan and I will leave right away. We have other parts to complete for the mission. Use the British money you have if you need to. Do not worry, we have more. Do you have any questions?'

'Will I have a weapon?'

'It is good that you ask and are willing to have one. Hassan and I will be collecting our equipment and we will all meet here at seven tonight when you will know more. For now, you must act and be like a tourist. The police do not randomly stop people in this country, the British shout and scream if such liberties are taken. Hassan, when you were given the keys for here, there were three on the keyring, I took one last night. Give one to Yasmin so she can return here if we are still out, then get your coat and come with me. We all have each other's numbers in the phones, so we can call each other or text as necessary. Don't worry about using them, just be careful what you say or text, the enemy may be looking for us at any time.'

Hassan followed the Teacher as they turned left out of the building and walked to the end of Edgware Road and turned left into Oxford Street. The rain had stopped so Hassan wore his shemagh as a scarf leaving his face exposed. Someone walking with his face covered in the Arabic style, while walking with someone in a business suit, might bring the kind of undue attention they did not need. Hassan could see the Teacher knew his way around. Using no map or looking for street signs, he appeared to know where he was going. He could also see the way he looked discreetly for signs of the enemy he had talked about. He looked for people behind him by studying the reflections in shop windows. He would take his time, looking left and right when crossing the road, not just for traffic but for anyone who seemed to be going the same way. Halfway down Oxford Street the Arab flagged down a black cab. When both men were seated in the back, he asked the driver to take them to Kensington High Street. They had not exchanged any conversation since leaving the apartment and remained silent until the taxi dropped them off.

'We are going to the Iranian Embassy. They're expecting us. You will remain silent; I'll do the talking. Do you have any questions?'

'No,' Hassan replied. They continued to walk and once more both men used the training they'd been given, and in the case of the Arab had grown up with, to look for the surveillance of the enemy. There are many cameras throughout the city of London; from the usual business cameras to traffic cameras and then the security cameras that most large cities and towns relied on to back-up their security and surveillance capabilities. Most of these cameras look down at angles that give a wide panorama of the whole area. Both men knew they should walk with their heads down looking straight in front and not to look up at any time, thereby making it difficult for anyone watching to get a full-frontal face shot.

'When we get near the Embassy you should pull your shemagh to cover your face as the cameras will be covering the building.'

The Arab then took a pair of thick rimmed glasses out of his pocket. Putting them on Hassan noticed how this simple move changed the Teacher's whole appearance.

The Embassy of The Islamic Republic of Iran is a building in a row of similar terraced buildings next to the Embassy of Ethiopia and overlooks Hyde Park in South Kensington.

The building was the location of a hostage siege, when the then British Prime Minister Margaret Thatcher gave the go for Operation Nimrod. The world watched on live TV as the SAS stormed the Embassy on the 5th of May 1980, using framed window charges and overpowering firepower and training, killing all the terrorists but one and releasing the hostages. On that day, the world found out that the British would not give in to terrorists trying to hold them to ransom, and the SAS who up until then had operated in secrecy became a household name around the world. The building had been severely damaged by fire as a result and rebuilt to continue as the current Embassy.

They pressed the doorbell and were admitted to the main foyer of the building. The staircase in front of them was still the same one where the SAS had practically thrown the hostages down from one trooper to another and out the rear door into the Embassy Garden; where they were made to lie face down on the ground, with their hands tied behind their back, until everyone was identified as a hostage. In this way they were able to identify one of the rescued as a terrorist who was lucky not to be shot as there would be too many witnesses.

The receptionist at the desk just inside the main door made a quick phone call to an internal number when the Arab asked for the Deputy First Secretary and told her to say, 'Your friend Abdullah is here.' Both men then sat and waited. Five minutes later a short, well-built man, wearing a dark business suit not dissimilar to the one worn by the Arab, came down the stairs carrying a large canvas holdall.

Both men stood to greet him as he came over to them with an outstretched hand. Shaking their hands, 'As-Salam-alaikum.' he said.

'Wa-Alaikum-Salaam,' replied the Arab.

The Arab knew the Deputy First Secretary was also the main officer from its VEVAK Intelligence Agency. He would have been told to be ready for a visit from an important person who would introduce himself with the words 'your friend Abdullah is here.' That friend was here, and his other instructions were to pass on a canvas bag and offer whatever assistance was required without question.

'I'm the Deputy Secretary please come through to the office.'

Walking ahead he showed them into a room behind the reception desk and closed the door behind them.

The room had high ceilings with a desk and four chairs. The desk had a laptop and a telephone; the walls were bare except for a large poster filled with writing in at least five different languages, two of which were Arabic and English.

'Please take a seat,' said the man as he sat behind the desk.

'I have my instructions. I'm to give you this bag which contains everything you requested and to offer my services if required without question.'

The Arab took the bag and handed it to Hassan.

'Take the bag and return to the apartment, I'll meet you there later as arranged.'

When Hassan had left the Arab turned to the man behind the desk.

'You have fulfilled your instructions. I may need more assistance in the next few days. Do you have a private number where I can call you at any time?'

The man reached into his waistcoat pocket and producing a business card handed it across the desk.

'Thank you. If I do need to call you, I will say this is your brother Abdullah. As you have been told, you will provide whatever I ask without question.'

Looking into the Arab's dark eyes, the Deputy First Secretary could feel a coldness surge through his body, as small beads of sweat trickled down the side of his head. He nodded rather than spoke as he thought the words would come out in a squeak.

The Arab tapped the number on the card into his phone and placed the card back on the desk before standing to leave.

'Allah be with you,' said the Arab.

'Inshallah,' replied the Deputy First Secretary.

Throughout the short visit Hassan had kept his face covered with the shemagh and continued to do so until he had walked a good distance from the building. The bag was slightly heavy, but Hassan could easily carry it in one hand. The rain had stayed away although a slight wind brought with it the cold feeling of more to come. Hassan kept to the main streets where he knew he could find a taxi more easily. The streets around Kensington were busy and he continued to look discreetly for anyone paying attention to this man with a canvas bag and a shemagh around his neck. Trying hard not to be obvious, he decided to find a café where he could have a coffee and sit at the window to observe the street, the people and traffic without attracting attention to himself. Kensington High Street is mostly high-end retail but there were still one or two restaurants and café's. The one he entered was exactly what he was looking for, a small café with a window seat, perfect for what he needed.

The Red Team from MI5 had arrived in Kensington High Street and the surrounding area at the same time. The team's brief, for the moment, to cover the streets leading to and from the Embassy of The Islamic Republic of Iran. Report anything considered of interest and especially be on the lookout for the woman and man in the photos provided. At the time they did not know the names, but the photo of the woman showed her face as she'd passed through an airport security system. The photo of the man was split into two separate images, one sitting outside a café, the other beside a swimming pool. Although MI6 now had all three targets' photos, the third man's face was not clear enough to use for the surveillance teams and would only cause confusion.

Hassan watched the street and the passing traffic as he sipped his coffee. He realised two things: the coffee was not that bad, and even if he did spot surveillance people, he couldn't be sure he knew exactly what he was looking at. People did not wear a deer stalker hat or wraparound sunglasses unless it was sunny or walked with the collar of a raincoat pulled up around their face. He realised it would be exceedingly difficult to spot professional surveillance people. Their job, like his was not to be conspicuous, to fit in to the surroundings and look as normal as possible. He felt himself relax. He would still be careful and try to spot the danger, but it might not be there; so better to relax and be natural, the more he did that, the less likely he would raise suspicion.

At the same time, the Red Team had passed where Hassan sat drinking his coffee and, took up positions around the Iranian Embassy. It was one of the female agents who spotted what looked like the man in the photograph sitting outside the café in Tehran leave the Embassy.

'Control from Red Three I have male resembling Target One leaving the Iranian Embassy.'

'Stay on him Red Three describe and give directions, over,' came the reply.

'Heading towards Kensington High Street wearing dark three-piece suit and wearing glasses. The glasses may be a disguise so not one hundred per cent sure it's him.'

'All Red Team, converge on Red Three it's all we have for the moment so let's get on it,' said Red One, the surveillance team leader.

The Arab spotted the woman at almost the same time. She had been walking away from him but had stopped to investigate a shop window where he could tell she was following him in its reflection.

The Arab increased his pace as he neared High Street Kensington Underground Station. Red Three saw him walk into the station. Informing the rest of the team, who had yet to catch-up from their original positions around the Embassy, they approached the

Underground station from two directions. Apart from the people on foot, the first to get there and back-up Red Three was a car, with two operators and Red Five on a motorbike. Screeching to a halt they quickly followed into the station.

'Lost contact,' Red Three's voice sounded over the radio.

Allah had been with the Arab. He just made it onto the Circle Line train pulling away from the platform. The Circle Line could take him all the way to Edgware Road but that was the third stop from High Street Kensington and could take fifteen minutes giving plenty of time for the enemy forces to be there if he stayed on the train. He got off at the next stop, Notting Hill Gate; keeping his head down to avoid the cameras he knew would be looking for him. Exiting the station, he turned right and walked away from the station entrance. Over the next three hundred yards he crossed the road three times then took his time walking through the Notting Hill Market, all the while looking for the danger of enemy surveillance. After walking through the market, he climbed into the back of a black cab sitting at the end of the line of other black cabs and instructed the driver to take him to Oxford Street. He had the Glock pistol the Deputy First Secretary at the embassy had given him in his pocket. He would have used it if cornered, feeling reassured by the weight, it gave him more confidence. They may have been looking for him or just following anyone coming out of the Embassy, either way he felt he had lost them for now. He had no reason to go back to the Embassy, and London was a big place, with over eight million people; a great place to get lost in. After the taxi dropped him in the middle of Oxford

Street, he walked the rest of the way to The Beaumont Hotel, again checking for surveillance crossing the road several times and going into two large shops, one of which had doors at the rear going out into another street. When he got to his hotel room, even though it had been cold outside with rain in the air, he felt the sweat sticking to his shirt. He stripped off his clothes, placed the gun under one of the pillows and had a shower. Feeling refreshed, he returned to the bedroom and, as an afterthought he sent a text to both his students.

Be careful our friends are looking for us

Hassan read the text. He was just finishing his coffee and all the time he had been sitting at the window he had seen nothing to raise his suspicions. He knew he had to keep control of his imagination otherwise he would see danger everywhere he looked. '*Keep calm, keep relaxed, be natural'* he kept saying to himself. Leaving the café, he continued to walk in the opposite direction to the Embassy and when he saw a black cab with its vacant light on, he flagged it down and asked the driver to drop him of at Sussex Gardens, just off Edgware Road. Thirty minutes later he was back at the apartment. He placed the canvas bag on the kitchen table and poured himself a glass of water; and then sitting on the couch he turned on the TV, switching channels to *Sky News*.

Yasmin found her day less stressful. Acting like a tourist was easy, realistically that's what she was. She had never been in London before but had seen travel programmes on TV and had always wanted to go there. She had used the A–Z and had decided to walk the whole way to Trafalgar Square. The rain had stayed away; she felt the air cooler than what she was used to, but fresh despite the smell of traffic fumes. Everything looked so much bigger than she'd imagined: the shops, the historic buildings, the statues, the crowds.

Even though the day was cold, the tourists around the fountain and Admiral Lord Nelson's column were still plentiful. Yasmin took photos using her phone, the kind any tourist would take. She used the skills she possessed to observe the crowds, trying to guess who they were and where they came from, at the same time looking for the odd one out who could be surveillance. All she could see were Londoners and tourists, workers and families, no obvious surveillance; then again, good surveillance operators wouldn't be obvious. She took her time enjoying the excitement of the whole adventure. After a pot of tea in a café close to the square, she made her way back on foot to the apartment again.

Chapter 22

Reece found the traffic lighter when he drove across the city, once more he parked in the Park Plaza allocated car park. When he entered room 303, he found Mary smiling back at him from the bed. Her long black hair almost covering the pillow. She was wearing a dark skirt and a white blouse of silk that showed the outline of her breasts and Reece realised how much he had missed this woman, even though it had only been for twenty-four hours.

'You're a sight for sore eyes,' he said. 'What every man needs when he comes in from a hard day's work.'

'Well, if you feel you need to lie down be my guest.' She laughed.

The love they made brought back to Reece the memory of the first time, and the last time, always different, always better, always with love at the heart of it.

The room was beginning to get dark because of the rain clouds gathering around the city. Reece looked at his watch. He still had an hour before he needed to be at the briefing. He could walk to MI6 Headquarters in that time but even with the car he couldn't trust the traffic, or that he wouldn't get a soaking.

As they lay in the darkness of the room the clouds outside the window dark and foreboding, Mary curled up close to him, feeling the warmth of his body his skin against hers. She let her fingers stroke down from his neck to the scar on the right side of his shoulder.

'Any pain lately?'

Reece did not like to worry her, so he lied.

'No not much, just the odd stab.'

He didn't want to say that the pieces of shrapnel that remained in his body hurt like hell much more than usual. The pain killers that used to give him relief did not seem to hit the spot anymore. He knew he would need to see the surgeon again to confirm that the metal inside him had moved.

Lying close to her, he remembered that first time when he saw her in Newry, then followed her from a suspected IRA meeting house to a meeting with the head of the Provisional IRA Intelligence in the Europa Hotel in Belfast. She had become a person of interest. He made it his purpose to get to know her, the unhappy marriage she was in, and when he had pitched his plan to recruit her as a source within the republican movement, he discovered that gunmen and killers like Sean Costello disgusted her. During the months of danger and covert meetings he had fallen in love with her but couldn't tell her until after the Peace Process and The Good Friday Agreement. That was when she'd once more searched him out, with the news that there was going to be the attempt to assassinate the British Prime Minister on the streets of Manchester.

'Have you any other injuries you don't want to talk about?'

'I fell out of a tree once when I was a boy, knocked myself out and broke my wrist.'

'What were you doing up a tree?'

'What does any boy do up a tree. Climb it then pretend you're a mountain climber or hiding from the searchers.'

'Which were you?'

'Hiding.'

'Not very well, you fell out of the tree.'

'Actually, I was jumping down the last bit, but underestimated the distance to the ground.'

'That will do it.'

'Every time.' Reece smiled.

'I'm sorry but I have to go again,' he said.

'Will you be back tonight?'

'I hope so, but I'm not sure.'

'Eating on my own again?'

As he pulled on his trousers, Reece lifted one of the hotel brochures from the coffee table.

'It says here the hotel has an award-winning Brasserie. I for one want to test the veracity of that statement. If I'm not back by eight, start without me.'

'That's no fun at all, try to make sure you join me.' She smiled.

'I'll do my best.'

'Is it dangerous Joseph?' she asked, using the undercover code name he had used when she'd been his agent.

He did not want to pass her off with a glib answer, but at the same time he didn't want to worry her unnecessarily.

'I'll be truthful as I am allowed because I know you will see through me if I don't. There is a serious threat of a terrorist attack here in London. We are pulling in every resource we have, not just me and my team, but everything. I'm going to a full briefing at five and I'll know more. Other than that, I want you to try to enjoy yourself tonight and I'll make every effort to join you for dinner.'

She had stood to pull her clothes back on. She shook her head to let her hair fall once more down her shoulders. He felt it would be so easy to stay here with her. To phone his boss and say he was resigning, take her to the airport, catch the next plane back to Malta, and live the rest of their lives making love and walking hand in hand along the beach.

But that was for the Mills and Boon romantic fiction books. This was real life. His job was, and always had been, to save lives and make that dream a reality for others, not just him and Mary.

'Joseph. I've been thinking I need to go see my mother. If you don't need me here, I should go.'

This caught Reece off guard. He had been too tied up in his own world and he forgot about Mary's. She knew that was his life, his work needed his total concentration. Everything else had to wait until the job was done.

'No, I can honestly say on this occasion you can relax. I think we have enough to cover everything. You know I would love you to be here, but to tell you the truth if you were not, I'd be happier, because of the risk to anyone not involved. You know that sometimes I can't tell you anything but are you sure you want to go to Belfast after what happened in Manchester?'

Mary had been deeply involved in helping to track down the rogue IRA man Costello and had been there when Reece had shot and killed him. To what extent her name had been blown to the Republican movement in Northern Ireland was not yet known.

'My mother now lives in my old house on the Lisburn Road; a relatively safe area for me. She is getting old, and I've not seen her in a while. You don't need me here. I'll be careful and phone you every night. I'll only stay for two days, three at most.'

'If you're sure you will be safe. I can let a friend in the PSNI know you will be there and to keep an eye on you.'

Mary knew Reece still had friends in the Police Service for Northern Ireland who he had worked with in the now disbanded RUC, people he could trust.

'I'll be all right on my own. You're not the only one who still has friends in Belfast.'

'I know but I would feel better if you had someone there who would get to you quicker than I could if you need help. His name is Tom Wilson, I'll give you his private number before you go, which is when?'

'I was thinking the sooner the better. Tomorrow morning if that's OK for you.'

'If you need to go, then go. I think this job will be over in the next few days so maybe I can join you in Belfast. It would be nice to see the city as a visitor instead of a job. I'm glad you're waiting until tomorrow to go. If I can't join you for dinner at least we might be able to lie in bed together tonight followed by breakfast, it seems an awful long time since we did that.'

Reece pulled on his Barbour jacket and put the Smith and Wesson 59 in the holster. Mary knew it was the signal that he had to go and quickly jumped off the bed and putting her arms around his neck kissed him long and hard. Reece felt the warmth of her body and could smell the perfume she always wore. Kissing her back he put his arms under hers and pulled her in to him as closely as he could.

Standing back Reece kissed her on the forehead and turned for the door.

'I'll try to get back for dinner, if not, definitely for later, either way I'll call you.'

'I'm counting on it.'

On the drive back to MI6 Reece thought deeply about the future and especially the one he wanted to have with Mary. He knew he needed to get away from work and spend some time alone with the woman he loved and to really discuss their future together.

The MI6 conference room at Vauxhall Cross was set up as a theatre, with two rows of chairs facing a lectern and a large screen on the wall. One of the control room operators was sitting at a computer linking images to the screen as they were needed. Sitting on the front row of chairs were Jim Broad, Caroline Aspinall, Helen Francis, and Sir Martin Bryant, representing the Prime Minister and Chair of the

JIC. Reece knew that Bryant would be reporting through the Prime Minister to the Home Secretary nominally the overall political boss of MI5 and the British government's Foreign Secretary nominally the political boss of MI6. Matthew Simons stood at the lectern and Reece sat in the second row between Anna, and Geoff Middleton. Reece could see others he knew including Joe Cousins and Steve Harrison before Matthew Simons interrupted any more hellos and introductions.

'Good afternoon everyone I'm Matthew Simons the MI6 Officer in Charge of our Middle East desk. I intend to brief everyone with what we have so far. Some of you may have more information to add, if you could wait until I finish to ask any questions or contribute to the briefing that would be helpful. Before I start, I would like to introduce Dr Ian McLeod. Dr McLeod is one of our senior biological and nuclear scientists at Porton Down, our scientific research department.'

A slightly balding man, wearing a three-piece suit with the chain of a pocket watch showing, who had been sitting on the front row beside Bryant stood and walked to the lectern. Facing the room, he put on half-moon spectacles and reading from his notes, looked over them when he addressed the room. The accent was Scottish, his back was slightly bent. He reminded Reece of his old headmaster at his secondary school.

'Good afternoon. Prior to coming here, I've been to Downing Street to brief the Prime Minister and Sir Martin Bryant on an update we received from the Israeli Government and Mossad. The original intelligence received indicated the terrorists had brought in plutonium for a dirty bomb. Such a device is not viable, as it would be almost impossible to assemble and transport without severe radiation damage and death to the perpetrators. Therefore, the material needs to be transportable with enough shielding to protect the carrier, but not so much that it would be too heavy to transport. The update we've had now indicates that these people have transported plutonium-238 which has been produced illegally in Iran. More easily transportable, and what is more can be used to make a dirty bomb. What is a dirty bomb you may ask? Put simply, on detonation, the explosives combine with the plutonium-238. The radioactive material is vaporised (or aerosolise) and is propelled into the air. This is completely different to a nuclear detonation. Plutonium-238 is not particularly dangerous as a radiation source on its own, but, when used with explosives it becomes what we call alpha particles in the air, which if ingested or breathed in as dust is very dangerous and carcinogenic. It has been estimated that 454 grams or one pound of plutonium inhaled as plutonium oxide dust, could give cancer to two million people. However, ingested plutonium is less dangerous as only a tiny fraction is absorbed in the gastrointestinal tract, 800 mg would be unlikely to cause a major health risk as far as radiation is concerned. So basically, what we believe these people have, is not nuclear, but more of a device based on terrorising the masses and damaging us economically. Nevertheless, hundreds could still die and the damage to not only this country, but to any country that values freedom and democracy would be devastating. Sorry about the political speech there, but I think you understand what is at stake. If you have any questions?'

The SAS Captain raised his hand.

'So, what you're saying is we believe these people have a small amount of this plutonium-238 and if it's used with an explosive device, apart from the initial blast, the main danger is what people breath in. Do we need to wear any special equipment if we are close to such a blast?'

Looking over his glasses at Geoff Middleton, McLeod spoke to everyone in the room.

'If you're not injured in the blast, get yourself and everyone to a safe distance which would be outside half mile perimeter from the blast. We have people on standby here in London with the right sort of clothing and equipment to go in and spray down the area. Unfortunately, such a spray down will take some time before we can give an all clear and depending on the size and where the blast takes place that could take months.'

With no more questions Doctor McLeod sat down, and Simons stood at the lectern once more.

Holding the red dot pointer in his hand he pointed to the screen and pressed a button at the side of the device. The screen was filled with a collage of photos showing the clear faces of the Arab, a woman, and an unknown man.

'You should already have these photos and a small page of intelligence showing their connection to each other and where the photos were taken.'

Everyone opened the folders that were sitting on the chairs before they sat down.

'I don't have to tell you that this operation, now known as Operation Search, is for the time being top secret. Between our own intelligence and Mossad, we are sure that these three people, possibly more, are now in this country, most likely London to carry out a terrorist attack involving a dirty bomb. We already have people out on the ground looking for them and I'll ask that MI5 and the Met update us on anything they have to add.'

Simons continued with his briefing for another twenty minutes, bringing everyone up to date with what he had so far, from the initial intelligence after the Barcelona suicide bomb, to the operation in Malta and finally to London.

Having finished for now Simons stood to one side and Caroline Aspinall stood at the lectern.

Speaking in her intellectual clipped accent she took the screen pointer from Simons.

'Thank you, Matthew. This operation may be moving fast but we are catching up. MI5 now has some more information which may be of help. We have a CI inside the Finsbury Mosque. His duties are to allow access to people coming through the main front door. Yesterday afternoon a young man wearing the Arab shemagh arrived at the Mosque. The interesting thing was that when this man arrived and left, he had the headdress fully pulled up to protect his face from identification. Like most people who attend the Mosque, they know that we try to take photos of everyone who goes in and out of the building. The confidential informant described the young man as being of Middle Eastern appearance but speaking with a London accent. He asked for Mohammed AAyan telling the CI he was expected. AAyan is the Imam at the Finsbury Mosque, and we have a thick file on him at Thames House. The CI reported that both men held a meeting for about fifteen minutes in a room which is used for special meetings and swept for bugs regularly, so we do not have the conversation. I can confirm that photos were taken of the man entering and leaving. We have them in colour as you can see but not of much use.'

Again, she pressed the button, and the screen was filled by the man leaving the Mosque. Reece thought that with the way the photo was taken with the Mosque behind, and the man's face covered by the shemagh he could be looking at a photo taken in any of the Middle East capitals. Aspinall continued.

'We have done follow-up checks on the woman who landed in London and took a taxi from the airport. Using the airport and traffic CCTV and APNR coverage, we were able to track down the driver and the cab and follow his journey. He picked up the woman and dropped her off at the bottom of Edgware Road. The anti-terrorist people spoke to the driver. He confirmed the journey. He does not know the woman and could only say she spoke English with an accent, only speaking to give him the location where she wanted dropped off, no specific address. He said she was young no older than thirty using a silver walking stick and dressed as a European.

Unfortunately, the cameras didn't cover the drop-off or where she went afterwards. That's as far as we have her.'

'Why did the cameras lose her?' asked Martin Bryant.

Aspinall looked to where the question had come from.

'The drop-off and her movement from the car were in what we call a dark zone for our cameras. I do not know if she was aware of this but either way, we lost her. The good thing is we have a small area where we need to pay particular attention to.'

This seemed to satisfy Bryant. No more follow-up coming.

'If I could continue. We have some news on the other two men which I have only just received. One of our surveillance teams covering the Iranian Embassy were just taking up their positions when they spotted a man, fitting the description of the one we call the Arab, leaving the building. The team tried to follow him, but he was surveillance aware and made several attempts to lose the watchers. He knew where he was going, using the nearby Underground at High Street Kensington where he jumped on a Circle Line train before we could get to him. We put the word out for all the stations on the line to be covered before our teams could get in place, but we think he got off at the very first station on his route at Notting Hill Gate. We are looking at the station CCTV to confirm this, but we are fairly sure that is what he did.'

'You lost another of our targets?' again the voice of Bryant broke through the room this time a little higher pitched.

This time Aspinall looked straight back at Bryant. Her expression was that of a schoolteacher having to deal with a naughty schoolboy.

220

'Surveillance is never going to be perfect in a city the size of London. With millions of people getting in the way, and an Underground system which can move a suspect to numerous locations throughout the city. It is even tougher if the person you're following is surveillance aware as our friends will be. On this occasion our teams were just beginning to get into their positions after having received the basic information. The fact that they spotted this target, and at least have confirmed his awareness, and that we can confirm him in London, is a start, considering the circumstances I've mentioned. One of the stops on the Circle Line is Edgware Road, another pointer to that area so we should put extra resources into there. This meeting is to pull everything together that we have so far. The picture is starting to clear, we have two of our targets possibly working in the Edgware Road area of the city. The next time they're spotted we will have the resources on the ground and the camera coverage in support.'

With that Aspinall retook her seat and handed the pointer back to Simons who stood once more at the lectern.

'As you will know we will be running the operation from our control room here. All communications will be linked to our people running the boards. You should all know that this operation will be followed closely by number ten, but the final say on how it will progress will be with the MI6 Director, Jim Broad, who you all know. Mister Broad would you like to say anything?'

Jim Broad stood and turning to face the room and those seated behind him. He looked at Reece before speaking.

'Really it does not matter who runs this operation, because we all have the responsibility to work together if we are to succeed in our mission. Find these people, find them quickly because we do not have much time. In fact, we do not know how much time we really have. The operation will be running twenty-four hours a day so organise your plans to that schedule and be ready to move at a moment's notice. We will also be working closely with our friends in Mossad. Anna here, being their contact and another of their team Palo, who will be with our tech people in the control room. It is hoped that Mossad using their own people will be able to add to the information we already have. Now I believe the head of the Met anti-terrorist unit wants to say something.'

Helen Francis stood beside Broad and faced the room she looked into the eyes of Sir Martin Bryant. She wanted to make sure he understood the people in this room were united in their work, and that the message for number ten would recognise that unity.

'After the MI5 watchers followed the man from the Iranian Embassy, we had another look at our photo coverage of the Embassy around the same time.'

Taking the pointer, she pressed the button. Two photos were displayed on the giant screen. One showed two men walking into the Embassy and in the other, one of the men walking back out again.

'I want you to notice. When the men go in, we know one from his dress business suit, the surveillance, and photos to be the man we refer to as the Arab. The other whose face isn't clear; we don't know yet. After a while, the second photo shows this other man leaving the building on his own this time carrying what appears to be a canvas bag. Remember these photos were taken before our surveillance teams were on the ground.'

Pressing the zoom button on the pointer she brought the area of the man's face and head into sharper focus.

'I want you to take special notice of the black and white chequered shemagh around the man's neck. He walks with his head down to avoid a full facial photo which is partly successful as this is the best image, we have of him.'

Pressing the buttons once more she brought up the photo of the man leaving Finsbury Mosque the day before, showing his face covered in a black and white chequered shemagh.

'I believe this is the same man in both photos and is our third member of the terrorist team. He favours the Arab headdress, and that might be his downfall if we spot him again, something for our teams to watch out for. This photo is being circulated to our teams as we speak, and copies are being sent to your phones right now.'

Almost on cue the mobile phone in Reece's pocket buzzed.

Francis sat back down and Broad spoke once more.

'This man was carrying a bag, and I'm sure it wasn't containing sweets from the sweet shop. You all have everything we have, and I believe enough you will need to get these people. I'll be available here until the end of this operation. To keep things simple, we've given the three people we know simple code names. The Arab, the man in the suit Target One, the younger man with the shemagh Target Two, and the woman Target Three. I'll keep everyone informed including 'C' and I'm sure Sir Martin Bryant will do the same with the Prime Minister. Unless there are any more questions let us get out there, people, and get a result.'

No one spoke and with everyone got up to leave, Broad beckoned Reece and Anna to stay.

'I've spoken with 'C' and Kurt Shimon and they both are thinking as one on this. Mossad and SG9 will work together on this to the very end. David you will work with Anna. Palo will stay here with me and Matthew Simons. No matter what comes in from the ground, we will try to give you a heads up to enable you to get there first and if possible, eliminate this threat. We don't want these people escaping or using the justice system to become heroes to their cause. Do you have a problem with this?'

'No,' said Anna.'

Having experience of killings on city streets Reece waited a few seconds before replying.

'We know these people are here to kill. They will not care how many, and from what we know already, the Arab has killed before either by himself or by using others to do his dirty work for him. They will not worry who gets in the way if we try to stop them, so from that point of view I have no problem. But the biggest problem for us is the hundreds of people who are on the streets, not including security forces who will be around at the same time. The ideal scenario would be for us to corner them in a building where either ourselves or the Special Forces get into a one-to-one situation and take them out. That carries danger as we saw in Manchester when one of the targets set off a suicide bomb during a house assault killing one of our SAS troopers. I think in the situation we are in, any action by SG9 in the open carries more risk. In such a situation, we can back-up the Security Services and take them out in whatever way we can, but that might also include capturing them alive.'

'I understand what you're saying, David. The terrorists need to be found first. Then we can decide what we are going to do. That is why I'll be here for every second, helping with that decision, are you happy with that?' said Broad.

'Yes.'

'Then let's get out there and good luck. Your team will have the call signs Alpha One and Two to help the control team know when you're around the other surveillance teams, so that, if necessary, we tell them to hold or pull back to allow you free rein. The SAS will be mobile in two transit vans with the call signs Tango One and Two to give you back-up. Your cars have bulletproof glass. In the boot you will find police marked baseball hats and protection vests with a couple of fully loaded H&K MP5 rifles. So, hopefully everything you need. Let me know if you require anything else. If we get any more information, I'll let you know immediately. Everything else you will hear over the air.'

'I've already had a run in the BMW, it's just what we need in London. Have you seen how many German built cars there are out there?'

'That's why our surveillance teams like them David, there's so many. They blend in and the bad guys can't tell which one is being driven by the good guys.'

Broad then sat down beside Sir Martin Bryant who had remained behind listening to the conversation. Reece, like Broad, did not trust politicians, and as much as Bryant would want everyone to believe he was one of the boys, they both knew his first loyalty was to the politicians he worked for. From his years of experience in Northern Ireland, Reece knew how the politicians had helped stoke the fires of war by protecting themselves, rather than allowing the security forces to take on the enemy. Instead of demanding a complete surrender, the politicians had let them off the hook, brought in the Peace Process and The Good Friday Agreement; allowing mass killers to walk out of prison after serving just two years and giving those not captured get of jail free cards. The politicians will always go the way of the next vote.

For now, it was time to get back to work and doing the thing he was best at, tracking down bad people and dealing with them.

'Do you fancy a coffee?' Reece asked Anna.

'Yes.'

'Let's head for the cafeteria, I'm sure we will find two people you need to know.'

Reece was right, sitting at one of the tables right where he expected them to be, were Harrison and Cousins. The building had three such places, one for the civil servants who carried out all the admin chores, one for the MI6 agents where they sat now, and a private dining room on the same floor as the office of the Director of MI6, where he ate and could entertain visiting politicians and fellow heads of the world's intelligence services.

'Anna, let me introduce you to Steve Harrison and Joe Cousins, hereafter to be known as Alpha Two. Gentlemen our friend from Mossad, Anna.'

The two men stood and shook hands with Anna.

'Welcome Anna, I hope you don't have to spend too much time with David, he can get you into trouble,' said Cousins.

'That's why I'm here, he already has.' said Anna laughing.

Reece left and returned with two black coffees with milk on the side. Anna was already deep in conversation with both Cousins and Harrison.

'Your friends are typical undercover David. They tell you a lot yet at the same time say nothing.'

'I taught them everything they know, but not everything I know. Can you imagine what the conversation would be like, if we really did know what each of us were up to in our past lives, we would all have to sit here with our mouths zipped shut. Someone once said, the thing about keeping secrets; it's a lot easier if you don't know them in the first place.'

All four raised their cups to toast the sentiment.

'OK people, we need to get out on the ground both on foot and mobile. The information points to them being somewhere in the Edgware Road area. It's a long road, so that's where we start. I know the basic outline of the road so we will start out on foot, parking up nearby. It's dark now and most of the shops will be closed, so it will just be the take-aways and restaurants open at this time of the day. The rush hour traffic that lasts for three hours in London will still be clogging up the streets, so if we walk the area for now, we will find it easier than having to negotiate the traffic. Do you have everything you need?' he asked the men.

'Yes, we picked up our weapons and ear radios and the car has all the extras required,' replied Cousins.

'Good we need to keep in close contact, and at the same time be aware of the other agencies operating out there.'

Reece had been right about the traffic. Despite there being a congestion charge for people driving in the city nothing had changed. The people somehow found the money for the charge and the traffic was still congested.

As they drove through the city, they tested the comms linking in with each other and letting the control room know they were out on the ground and available for updates.

It was almost 7 p.m. when they parked up on Connaught Street just off Edgware Road itself. The street was still busy and the two parking spaces where timed for payment parking was until 6 p.m., so they were now free to park until 7 a.m. the next day.

'Steve, you stay here with the cars while we go for a walk,' said Reece.

Reece knew it wouldn't go down too well if one of the cars was stolen with a high-powered rifle inside and full of equipment. Reece also knew that Harrison had a previous life as one of the MI5 watchers. He had spent quite a few hours walking the streets of London, following suspects and he would know this area better than the rest of them.

'No problem, I can listen to my favourite hour on Classic FM,' replied Harrison.

'As long as you keep one ear for us,' said Reece.

'Always.'

Reece informed control that Alpha One was moving on foot in the Edgware Road area. He knew the communications were encrypted to avoid listening radio enthusiasts or the opposition hearing the conversation, but he still had the instinct to say as little as possible.

The rain had stopped, the pavements wet and the air cold. *Why hadn't he stayed in Malta*, thought Reece?

Chapter 23

As the SG9 team parked up and started their reconnaissance walk around the area, the Arab, now dressed in a green parka and jeans, opened the door to the apartment on the Edgware Road and walked up the stairs to meet with his students as arranged. He had called in a supermarket to pick up a bag of groceries which he placed on a bench in the kitchen.

'Good evening my children,' he spoke.

They both stood to greet him.

'You both look worried, come let us sit down at the table and talk. Hassan, bring the bag.'

Yasmin poured them yet another mug of coffee and sat down with the two men.

'Let's see what we have.'

The Arab unzipped the bag and took out the contents, one item at a time. First there were two handguns; German made 9 mm Glock pistols. He checked that each had a full magazine. He then slashed the slide of each gun putting a 9mm round in the breach. The Embassy Deputy First Secretary had already supplied the Arab with the gun that now rested in the pocket of his parka jacket. All three guns ready to fire. Beside them he placed three fully loaded spare magazines.

'You will keep these with you at all times even when you sleep. You do not surrender if cornered. If you must die for the cause of Jihad then take many of the infidels with you.'

He reached into the bag again and produced three passports and three credit cards and handed one of each to his students.

'When our mission is complete, we will use these new identities to help our escape. The credit cards are in the same name as the passports, and you can use them to buy hotel rooms and flights. After our mission, take transport as soon as you can out of the city and go to Bristol, where you will find it safe to stay in a hotel for a few days. After this short stay you will get a flight from Bristol to any European airport. From there it will be easier to get back to Iran. Don't travel or stay together you will be safer on your own.'

Once again he reached into the bag and produced three plastic Tupperware boxes. The students could see they were just like the ones they had used at the training camp in Iran. The lids were closed, and they could see the plastic explosives inside with a detonator pushed into the explosives and two wires coming from the detonator through a hole in the lid. The wires were then linked to a mobile phone which was taped to the outside lid.

'You have both seen these at the camp?'

Both students nodded.

'Good, then Kalil taught you well. That is one of the reasons I've chosen you for this mission. You have learnt well my children. Now we are going to put all that training to real use in attacking the enemies of Allah. Do you have any questions?'

'We have trained in putting this type of bomb together,' said Hassan, 'the question is, how we detonate them.'

'A good question Hassan, it is my intention that we should not be near when they detonate. Today I spotted what I think was the enemy looking for us. I lost them easily when they started to follow. They know we are here, and they're out there in the city, so we need to be extra careful. The final part of our mission will take place in two days' time. Before I answer your question, Hassan. Yasmin how was your day as a tourist?'

Yasmin took out her mobile phone and opened the photos she had taken in Trafalgar Square and handed the phone to the Teacher.

'As you can see, the square was busy despite the time of the year and the cold weather. I saw nothing of the enemy that was not unusual, just some uniformed police on foot, no more than two at a time walking through the square. Any attack would be over before they knew what hit them.'

'That is good my child, and you're sure you were not followed?'

'As sure as I can be.'

'Good, good. On Friday it will be your mission to go to the square and leave one of these boxes.'

Lifting one of the boxes he pointed to the mobile phone.

'Now, my children, to answer your question, Hassan. You will notice each box has a different coloured dot on top. The one with the green dot will be left here. It has a one-hour delay. On each box there are two buttons. The blue one switches the phone on and the red one starts the timer, then you will have time to get away. When all our boxes have been armed you will get a train or to Bristol. The enemy won't expect you to go in that direction, they will think that you are still in the city, but the timer will give you enough time to get away.'

'And the second bomb?' asked Hassan.

'The mission is two pronged. The box with the blue dot is for Yasmin to place in Trafalgar Square. It has a two-hour delay giving Yasmin time to escape. It will attack the confidence of the population and their tourist industry killing many infidels. The third one with the red dot is the most important, which Hassan and I will deliver. It has a three-hour countdown giving us plenty of time to leave the target area. It will destroy the economic heart of the infidel for many years to come perhaps even for good. Have you ever heard of Canary Wharf?'

'Yes, it's mentioned in the A–Z book,' replied Hassan.

'What it might not mention is that it's the financial heart of Europe. All the big banks and financial companies are based there. This is our main target. Using one of these boxes with what we have in our walking stick will cripple these important institutions for years to come. It will be one of the greatest blows we can make against the Great Satan and the Jihad will praise our names.'

Both students looked at the Arab and smiled.

'Why must we wait for two days,' asked Yasmin. 'Surely we put ourselves at more risk of being discovered by waiting. We could go tomorrow.'

'Have patience my child. When we visited the Deputy First Secretary at the embassy today, he told me that on Friday there'll be the unveiling of a plaque at the opening of a new office building in Canary Wharf by the Princess Royal, the daughter of the British Queen. We will time our attack to coincide with the unveiling at 3 pm. As for the risk, the risk is no more than it would be if we went tomorrow. If you remain in this area and don't expose yourselves unnecessarily, we will be safe enough to fulfil our mission.

'There is no reason to leave, I'll return on Friday morning, be ready. You have your phones. Contact me if you have any problems. On Friday morning we will make a short video describing our mission to be put on the Internet after our mission is complete.'

He reached into the bag once more and produced three full face covering balaclavas.

'As this is not a martyr mission and we will be involved in many more in the name of Allah and the Jihad, we will have our faces covered for the video. Now I must return to my hotel. Do not forget your prayers tonight my children. Pray that Allah will bless you and our mission.'

The Arab stood and drank down the last of his coffee, before leaving the two students to their thoughts and prayers.

The Arab pulled the apartment door behind him and having a quick look around, turned to walk towards the bottom of Edgware Road and Marble Arch.

It was Reece who spotted him first, the man had just pulled up the hood of his parka as he walked along the street. Reece noticed the way the man kept looking from side to side and behind while trying to appear natural. It was the years of doing this for real that made Reece realise it was anything but natural. He spoke into his radio mic.

'Alpha One to control I have eyes on a possible for Target One.'

Immediately the reply came back from the desk operator at control.

'Roger Alpha One, confirm your location.'

'Edgware Road walking towards Marble Arch wearing a green parka with the hood pulled up and blue jeans.'

'Roger Alpha One. You are the only call signs in that area. I'm alerting the Red Team who are on their way to support you. Should be with you in ten.'

Reece continued with Anna thirty yards behind him, with Cousins walking on the other side but trying to stay close to be parallel with the target.

'Are you sure it's him?' asked Anna.

'Not a hundred per cent but there's something about him.'

'Did you see where he came from?'

'No, I noticed him as we came out of the side street. He seemed to be walking with his head down and looking discreetly around him.'

The target crossed the road again taking his time to look right and left, pretending to look at the traffic while at the same time watching for followers. It had started to rain again, and the dark evening light didn't help surveillance. After crossing the road, the Arab turned into the next street down.

'Target One into Upper Berkley Street.' It was the voice of Cousins, who was now closer than he would like to be because of the man crossing the road almost in front of him.

'Be careful,' said Reece.

'Roger that,' replied Cousins.

Cousins held back to give the target time to get a little further ahead. When he turned into the street, he could see the man turn into the first street on the right.

'Target now into first street on the right,' said Cousins.

'Confirmed, Seymour Place. He appears to be walking the square may be looking for you, over.' It was the voice from the Ops room following the movement on the board in front of them.

Surveillance teams knew the term, which referred to checking for surveillance by identifying the same people or vehicles taking the same route especially if it's an obscure route.

'I'm going to try to make up some ground to see where he's gone,' said Cousins.

Reece and Anna crossed the road, keeping to the opposite side as Cousins and increased their pace to make up the ground. The loud crack of three gunshots in quick succession split the night air. They had lost sight of Cousins as he had turned into the street on the right ahead of them. Both broke into a run at the same time pulling their weapons from their holsters. As they rounded the corner into the street Anna sprinted across to take up the further footpath while Reece swept the street looking down the barrel of his gun. The rain and darkness made it difficult to focus. He could see the body of a man, lying on the path forty yards in front of him. He could see no one else, the street was empty, even the traffic seemed to have deserted it.

The closer Reece got to the figure, the more he swept the area with the gun as his pointer. Anna crossed over and knelt by the man while Reece continued to give cover. Cousins was on his back, staring up at the sky, his eyes blinking and his breathing heavy, as the rain washed down his pale face.

'He's alive,' said Anna.

'Alpha one to control, I need an ambulance and back-up to my location now.' Reece spoke into his body mic.

Kneeling beside Anna there was no sign of blood. Cousins was fully conscious but in a lot of pain groaning and trying to move.

'Stay still Joe, more help is on the way. What happened, where are you hurting?' asked Reece.

'The bastard was waiting for me when I turned the corner,' Cousins said through gritted teeth and short sharp intakes of air. 'He was pointing his gun straight at me and when I went for mine, he fired. One just missed my head but the other two hit me in the chest.'

Cousins gave out another loud groan as he tried to pull open his coat. Reece pushed his hand away and after putting his 59 in its holster pulled open Cousin's coat and saw two neat holes in the sweater. He pulled once more, this time exposing the bullet-proof vest where he could see the two heads of the flattened bullet rounds embedded in the material.

'Joe, you're one lucky son of a bitch.'

'Or one smart one,' said Anna.

'At this moment I'm not sure,' said Cousins still taking short sharp breaths.

'Take it from me Joe. A couple of broken ribs are better than a pine box,' said Reece.

'What about our man?' asked Cousins.

'Don't worry. He got away but he won't be far, we'll get him soon. For now, it's a warm hospital bed for you.'

Reece gave control a sit-rep on everything that happened while Harrison brought one of the cars to the street.

'Control. Can you have our CCTV people check all the cameras in my area to see if they can pick up our friend?' Reece also passed on the description of who he now believed to be Target One.

A few minutes later some of the Red Team and armed officers from the police SO19 unit arrived and sealed off the street. They were closely followed by the ambulance, which quickly lifted Joe Cousins, who gave a thumbs up as the doors closed.

'Alpha One from control,' it was the voice of Matthew Simons.

'Go ahead control,' replied Reece.

'CCTV has your man crossing over Oxford Street and halfway down North Audley Street. He entered a bar; we think it's called The George. SO19 and more back-ups are heading there now.'

'Roger that we're on our way,' replied Reece.

With Harrison driving, all three agents pulled into North Audley Street just as the police were sealing it off at the opposite end. Reece and Anna pulled on their police baseball hats and were getting out of the car before Harrison had completely come to a stop.

'There may be a lot of people in there so we try to do this as quietly as we can. Steve, go and tell our uniform friends that Anna and I will go in on our own and try not to look out of place. Tell them to hold back and don't shoot us by mistake.'

Harrison ran to where the police cordon was now set-up and speaking to them, pointed back at Reece and Anna who had now taken off their caps and putting them into their pockets walked through the doors of The George.

The bar was the style of a Victorian era pub with dark wood, with snugs to the left as they entered. The lights shaped as globes were connected to chains falling from the ceiling. On the right, the bar itself filled the full length of the room, with a mirror covering the wall behind. Being early, the bar was not yet full. A few of the snugs and tables were taken up mainly by couples, with at least ten people standing at the counter either drinking or awaiting service by the two women behind the bar. The light was bright enough for them to see everyone's face. It was one of those drinking establishment's where people were more interested in their own company and conversation than anyone coming through the door. Trying to look like customers was not a problem and they walked from the door all the way through to the rear with no sign of Target One. The only place left to search was the toilets. Anna checked the ladies while Reece waited. It only took twenty seconds before Anna returned to shake her head indicating no show she then waited while Reece searched the gents again after twenty seconds he returned.

'No show there either,' said Reece. There were two more doors one with the word 'Staff Only' and the other the rear emergency escape door which was closed with the bar still in place and locked. Reece stood at the end of the bar where the hatch letting the staff in and out of the bar service area was open. After a few seconds one of the women behind the bar noticed him and came over.

'Can I help you?' asked the girl who looked about twenty.

Reece discreetly showed her his Security Services ID which he always used on such occasions. He always found when people took a good look at the document their eyes would open wide with surprise and then with a touch of panic, they would always answer his questions quickly.

'It's nothing to worry about. We are looking for a man wearing a green parka who may have come in about fifteen minutes ago have you seen him?'

'It's been terribly busy. I think he was in, but he didn't get a drink.'

'Has anyone gone out the emergency exit?' asked Anna.

'No, the alarm would have gone off if it were opened.'

Reece took another look around the bar then came back to where the barmaid was standing.

'Where does the staff door go to, is there stairs?'

'No stairs they were concreted over years ago. The only thing back there is a small kitchen, the drinks store and a back door where the deliveries come in.'

Reece turned and pushed through the door followed by Anna and the voice of the barmaid shouting,

'Hey, you can't go in there.'

The room was small and filled with stock for the bar. A small cooker and a freezer made the path between narrow, leading to a closed door at the back. Both agents drew their guns once more and Reece pulled open the door covered by Anna. Outside there was a small closed in yard with another door which Reece opened to reveal a large car park. Reece swept the yard again using the gun as a pointer in front of him, but it was quiet apart from the gentle dripping of the rain from an overflowing drainpipe.

'He's gone. There's no cameras in here and about six exits out of the car park.'

They retraced their steps through the bar and Reece briefed the police on the cordon.

'You can go mobile again. Our bird has flown, thank you for the back-up. Steve, can you drop us back at the other car and we can take a drive around Edgware Road and Oxford Street? I think our friend was walking on foot for a reason, he could still be working out of somewhere local maybe even his two pals as well.'

On the way back to the car Reece updated the Ops room and requested that Jim Broad be informed.

'He knows Alpha One.' again, it was the voice of Matthews.

'Thank you. Can I request all teams to pay particular attention to the two-mile radius of where we first saw Target One? Can you also have our CCTV people check all the cameras coming out of the car park to the rear of The George within the last thirty minutes? If they get anything it would be helpful.'

'Roger that. The director asks that you return here to give a complete update before you stand down tonight.'

'Roger will do,' replied Reece.

It was then that Reece looked at the Casio G Shock watch. It was almost eight thirty. He dialled Mary on his phone. When she answered he could hear the noise of the restaurant in the background.

'Don't tell me something came up,' said Mary.

'I'm sorry I'm afraid it did. Can you forgive me?'

'Of course. I'm getting used to it, but I don't want it to be the norm between us. I hate it when you're not with me, and all I can think about is the danger you might be in.'

Reece didn't want her to worry. She was expressing the words that he was thinking about earlier in the day. The dangers were part of his life, but now he was sharing it with someone he loved it wasn't fair on her, or them both.

'No danger, just something that had to be checked out. How's the food?' Reece asked trying to change the subject.

'I don't know, yet I've just ordered, but from the smells I'm getting it's going to be good.'

'I'll get there as soon as I can. I'll pick up a bottle of Bush for the room and at least we can have a nightcap.'

'Hurry I miss you.'

'Miss you too, see you soon.'

'You should tell her you love her,' said Anna smiling.

'I do tell her, but when we are alone.'

'Knowing this type of work that won't be too often.'

'When we get back to the car remind me to find an off-licence and buy a bottle of Bushmills.'

The Arab had wasted no time in leaving the bar by the rear door. He had crossed the car park, keeping his parka hood up to avoid recognition from any cameras. He had spotted the man following him when he had crossed over Edgware Road. His suspicions were confirmed when the man turned into one street then heard his increased footsteps as he turned in behind him in the second street. He had pulled his gun and pointed it towards the street corner. It had been his plan to challenge the man, not knowing if he was just a criminal looking to mug him, or a serious threat. When the man saw his gun and went for his he fired. He saw him go down but did not wait around to confirm he was dead. He took many more diversions and checks after leaving the back door of the bar. He was confident he was alone, and he knew the shooting of the man would distract his enemies long enough to allow him to get back to the security of his hotel. He waited until he was in his room before he phoned Hassan.

'The enemy are close. I had to deal with one on the way back to my location. I'm sure they still don't know our locations, so I'll stay here and see you as arranged on Friday, understand?'

Hassan, who had listened the whole time, replied 'Yes' then heard the empty buzz of the call ended from the phone.

Reece and Anna spent the next hour driving around Edgware Road and the side roads and streets while Harrison did the same in the

Oxford Street area. Calling it a night Reece dropped Anna off at the Israeli Embassy where she was now staying and headed back to the MI6 operations room to brief Jim Broad.

'Any word from the hospital?' asked Reece.

'Joe will be all right. Two broken ribs and severe bruising. He is a smart man. That vest saved his life.'

'I know. I think we all need to take a leaf out of his book. I put mine on when we got back to the car and before I went into that bar.'

Broad walked to the back of the room where there were a few chairs and invited Reece to join him. Reece could tell by his expression he wasn't happy.

'David, the record so far is not good. We keep getting close then we lose them again. We could have lost one of our own this time.'

'I feel your pain. It is not nice getting this close and nothing to show for it. What will we do now? There's a lot of agencies involved and I'm sure Sir Martin Bryant isn't too pleased. Probably sitting sipping whisky with the PM as we speak.'

'To say the least. The only good thing that came out of tonight's debacle was that our man wasn't seriously hurt. We can put it about that it was a mugging and keep the press and media away from it. Our people will go to ground, and if their operation is still on, which giving everything we know about the Arab, it will be, then we can expect their next move to be on the day they intend to move. We are keeping our people on the streets day and night and pulling in all the information we can from all our sources including CCTV and GCHQ. The next time they move we need to be ready. We cannot rely on them to make a mistake. When they do move, we come down on them hard no second chances anymore.'

'You're talking to the converted here. I'm heading back to the hotel to get a good night's rest.'

Broad stood and stretched.

'Good idea David. I'm staying here. If anything happens, I'll let you know. Give Mary my best.'

'I will. I hope she's not too angry. I was supposed to meet her for dinner at eight, it's now ten fifteen.'

Reece went to the armoury, took the H&K from the boot of the BMW and returned it. He sent Mary a text to say he was on his way. She replied that she would meet him in the hotel's Primo bar.

Chapter 24

Mary was sitting at a table by the window looking out at the Thames. With its reflections of light, it made it look like the city was twice the size. When he looked at her, her smile made him feel that his day had just got an awful lot better. He kissed her on her cheek and sat down.

'What's in the bag?' she asked.

Reece placed the plastic shopping bag gently on the table.

'It's a bottle of that liquid gold I said I would pick up.'

'Your favourite Bushmills. The bar does serve alcohol, you know.'

'This is for the room.'

Reece beckoned one of the waiters and when he found they had Bushmills ordered a double and a Gin and Tonic for Mary.

'You look like you had a rough day, Joseph.'

Reece liked her calling him Joseph. It always reminded him how they met.

'You could say that, and it will be even busier in the next few days.'

The drinks came and Reece clinked his glass with Mary's before taking a mouthful of what he considered to be the best whisky in the world.

'I've already booked a flight for the morning to Belfast. I can cancel it if you need me here.'

'No, don't worry. Stick to your plans. This will only take a few more days and then I can join you there.'

Mary reached across the table and took his hand in hers.

'If you're sure, but please be careful Joseph.'

'I could say the same to you. You need to catch-up with your mother I know, but I'm not one hundred per cent sure about you going to Belfast. Don't be taking any risks.'

'I won't if you won't.' She smiled, as she clinked the side of his glass with hers once more.

Reece thought a change of subject was required.

'So, what was the food like?'

'Just as good as it say's on the tin.'

'What did you have?'

'I was a good girl. I had the salmon fillet with baby potatoes and a cold glass of Chablis. Every time I drink that wine it reminds me of our lunch in that beautiful restaurant in Grosvenor Street.'

Reece remembered the day just before he went to Manchester on the mission that would bring him closer to Mary moving from agent handler to lover.

'I remember. I'm a little hungry. Let us order a bottle of that nice wine and some sandwiches and get them sent to the room.'

'Now that's the kind of plan I like.' She smiled.

The wine was just as good as Reece remembered, the sandwiches excellent and making love to Mary, everything. Now he lay awake beside her, he watched her breasts rising and falling under the thin white sheet, her breathing soft in the night air as she slept the sleep of a child.

He had tried to sleep but the work of the day kept spinning in his mind. She was going to Belfast in the morning, a day that was already here. He was not happy about it. Too many bad memories of the dangers, the violence, the friends he had lost. Mary turned in her sleep and stretched her arms across his shoulders. He closed his eyes once more and at last sleep came.

The darkness of the winter morning was brightened by the streetlights through the window when he woke. A glance at his watch told him it was 06.30. Mary was up already up; he could hear the shower and her voice singing to herself. She didn't have a bad voice, and he had sung along with her in the times they'd a few too many drinks relaxing at the villa in Malta.

'You're awake.' She had come out of the bathroom a large white towel wrapped around her body.

'You're up early. I thought you would take the chance to sleep in.'

'Plenty of time for sleeping Joseph. My flight leaves at 11.30 and I want a decent breakfast before I set off. Anyway, you have a busy day ahead of you and a good breakfast will do you no harm.'

'You're right but before breakfast we have a little time.' He pulled back the bed sheet.

She smiled, then dropping the towel climbed in beside him.

Reece waved goodbye to Mary as her taxi pulled away from the hotel and headed to the airport just after 8 a.m. He had booked the room for another two nights, more for the convenience than anything else.

Twenty minutes later he was sitting with Jim Broad in the MI6 Operations Room. Broad looked like he had not slept well, and his clothes needed a good dry cleaner.

'We need to get something today David or the PM and Bryant will close down this whole city and cause a full-blown panic.'

Reece had been thinking along the same lines.

'You need to keep telling them that. You know how some of these politicians think. They will be shitting themselves. But if we catch these bastards, they'll be in front of the cameras claiming all the glory.'

Broad nodded in agreement.

'Have we received anything overnight?' asked Reece.

'We may have something. Have a look at the monitor.'

Reece crossed the room and watched the screen in front of one of the operators as Broad told him to bring up the CCTV from last night.

The black and white picture showed a man with a parka, red pointer arrows indicated the names of the location as he walked at a fast pace. The man had walked out of lower Duke Street before crossing Oxford Street and entering the upper part of Duke Street.

'Unfortunately, there aren't enough cameras in Duke Street to see where he went but he disappeared in that area.'

'He seemed to know where he was going so we could make a good assumption that he might be staying somewhere close to Duke Street. It's not far from The George and Edgware Road so we must concentrate most of our resources around there. Any spare resources should cover a roaming brief of the important high value targets in the rest of the city.'

Just then Anna and Harrison arrived, and Reece asked the operator to run the screen once more for their benefit.

'We still don't know where any of them are staying then?' asked Anna.

'No but I think we've them tied down to a smaller area and that's where we concentrate most of our resources,' said Reece.

'Alright David. I'll update everyone you get out there and see what they can do. We need a bit of luck,' said Broad.

'You know what we always say; 'They always make a mistake and when they do, we kill them.' I think last night was their first real mistake. Anna and Steve, we will stay together in one car. Steve, you drive. Then if Anna and I need to, we can follow on foot with you in the car as back-up. Happy with that?'

'Sounds like a plan,' replied Harrison.

Before they could move, Matthew Simons came into the room.

'Before you leave, GCHQ have just sent this.'

He went over to the console and typed a few words on the keyboard. The screen showed the ragged lines of an audio feed. They listened to the phone conversation between two men. The first voice was that of the Arab telling his friend of his close call with Joe Cousins and then the call finishing with a one word reply from the other man, 'Yes.'

'So, by the sound of things their plan is being set for Friday morning. We need to get the area where we believe they're hiding, screwed down as tight as we can.' said Reece.

'What makes GCHQ think these are our targets and do they have any idea where they are?' asked Broad.

'Believe it or not they've been keeping everything open for chatter and apparently Mossad were able to pass on a small voice clip from when our friend the Arab met with the Iranian General in the café in Tehran. That voice clip was very distorted, so it didn't tell them anything of significance, but GCHQ were able to keep it on their system and get a voice match when the call was picked up on their searches last night. They worked on it all night that's why it's taken until now for them to confirm it is the Arab. They were able to tie the calls down to a radius of two miles which would take in the same area where we believe they are,' said Simons.

'As I said. They would make mistakes, and this is one more. From the conversation, and the time of the call, the two men are holed up in different locations close to each other. Today we get everyone to walk it, drive it, and get to know every nook and cranny so that when they do move, we don't lose them this time,' said Reece.

'Leave that with us David. We will get everyone into that area. You'll be tripping over each other, but we will keep you updated,' said Broad.

251

Reece was feeling a little better about the future as Harrison drove them across the city. Reece sat in front, with Anna in the back seat, first stop where they left off the night before.

Chapter 25

As the SG9 team drove across the city, the Arab was eating breakfast in his hotel room, the Prime Minister was holding a meeting in his private office in Number 10. There were four others around the table. The Chiefs of MI6 and MI5, Sir Martin Bryant and Kurt Shimon had all been summoned by the Prime Minister's office for a specific reason. He wanted to look them all in the eye and watch their responses to his questions rather than over the phone.

'I've been updated about last night's fiasco and the near death of one of our people, while these people make fools of us and get away again. What the hell is going on Sir Ian, your people have overall control?'

All eyes were on Sir Ian Fraser, and he noticed that Bryant had a slight smile at the corners of his mouth, he was enjoying this; if Fraser did not know better, this first question from the PM had been set-up by Bryant.

'The first thing we should remember is that these people we are dealing with are not amateurs. They are all highly trained. The Arab himself has experience of real time operations. Some of those operations have been against the best intelligence agencies in the world and I'm sure Kurt here would agree.' Shimon nodded and Fraser continued.

'We were lucky not to lose one of our operators last night, but the Arab was lucky too. We know they're prepared to kill but so are we if we have too. Taking in the whole of Europe and this country, starting from scratch, with hardly any information to begin with, we have them narrowed down to a two-mile radius in the city. We have now concentrated most of our resources in that area, if they raise their heads, we have a good chance of spotting them.'

'What has MI5 to say about this and has anybody got anything new to indicate what the target is?' asked Bryant.

Caroline Aspinall finished sipping her coffee before answering, ignoring Bryant she spoke directly to Brookfield.

'As you know Prime Minister, we are using all our people and working closely with all the other agencies to ensure a positive outcome. The information you're getting is as up to date as the information I'm getting.'

Answered like a true politician, thought Fraser. Something he knew he wasn't good at. Caroline Aspinall had been taught how to deal with questions at a girls' private school and then at university in Oxford. Fraser had come up through the army ranks; the school of hard knocks, where the answers could sometimes be harsh but necessary to save lives. He still respected Aspinall. She was a strong personality in her own right, and would stand up for her people, just as he would.

'I believe everyone is doing their best. But I do not think it's enough. I've spoken to the Home Secretary, and she agrees that we should raise the threat level to Critical,' said Brookfield.

This time it was Fraser who spoke.

'Prime Minister, the current level is at Substantial, which, as you know means an attack is likely. The difference is that Critical is an attack that is highly likely soon. To everyone here and to the media that is a significant jump and would hopefully raise people's awareness. My own feeling is that the general population out there will not see much difference in the wording as they believe an attack is always likely. My only worry is that the press will start sticking their nose in and get in the way. It could even see our enemy changing their mind and bring forward their plan which now mentions tomorrow, Friday. It may also make them think we know more than we do, and they could drop everything disappear and come back on another day when we lack information.'

'I know what you're saying, Sir Ian, but I'm the elected leader of those people out there, and it's not only my job to protect them as it is yours, but it's also my responsibility to keep them honestly appraised of the danger they may face. We may only have twenty-four hours before this thing goes down and making the announcement now will not give the press enough time to interfere too much. The Home Secretary can handle the press for that period, and if anyone comes to any of you with questions, direct them to her.'

Fraser knew it was better not to argue as the decision had been made between the PM and Bryant before he had come into the room. It was the usual political decision. The one where they protect their arses and make sure that if things hit the fan, they can point the finger elsewhere. *Then again*, he thought, *if he were in the same shoes as the Prime Minister, he would probably make the same decision.* After all the experts had brought him nothing and the terrorists were still out there.

'I'm sorry Kurt, do you think it's the right thing to do?' Bryant asked.

The Mossad officer knew better than to get sucked into another country's political war.

'You must do what you think is right for your country. In my own country we would be kicking down doors and that would include the Finsbury Mosque. I would like to know what the Imam knows. But then you must do what you think is right for you.'

'I think you understand Mister Shimon. The British people cherish not only their own civil rights but the civil rights of others. Between ourselves I only wish I had the same power your Prime Minister has when it comes to dealing with these people.'

'Maybe that is why they think they can get away with what they intend to do, because they know you're vulnerable, and they believe because of that you're weak. In Israel we strike hard and that is the only way we can survive. We are surrounded by enemies who want to destroy us. I believe in the old saying, we call it the eleventh commandment, hit them before they hit you. I think from what I've seen, you have the resources to hit them, you just need the courage to do so.'

Fraser was impressed by the words of the Mossad officer which he totally agreed with. The difference was that the Director of MI5 and the Mossad were unaware of the true remit of SG9 that had been agreed at the highest level. To track down the terrorist threats to the UK and eliminate them wherever they were found.

'Don't worry Kurt we have the courage. If Margaret Thatcher could send the SAS into the Iranian Embassy, then an invasion fleet halfway around the world to the Falklands to kick out the Argentinians, then this country has the courage,' said Bryant.

'No offence intended we are with you in this, all the way,' replied Shimon.

The Director of MI5 had listened to this conversation and had to speak.

'You do realise Sir Martin that when we had the bomb attacks in July 2005, the Security Service came in for a lot of criticism and that's why we more than doubled the lawyers we had. The number of ambulance-chasing legal firms out there also increased because they could see big money through their distorted use of the human rights legislation. On one occasion we acted on poor intelligence that there was a biological weapon in a Muslim family house at Forest Gate. We raided it and found nothing. The intelligence was wrong, and the subsequent claims cost the British taxpayer £210,000 to refurbish the house and a further £60,000 to compensate the family. That one costly mistake almost cost the job of one of my predecessors, never mind the money. But since then, we tend to worry too much about getting it wrong, instead of doing our job despite the mistakes.'

She had made her point. Fear can freeze politicians into making mistakes. They think according to the amount of votes it could cost them, never mind the money or damage to the country. The Prime Minister stood before replying.

'Thank you for that Caroline. Can we get back to Operation Search? From my calculations we have about 24 hours, and we still need to find these people and the target. Keep me updated all the way. I'll give the Home Secretary the heads up to issue the increase to the threat level. All our forces will be put on full alert. Get me results and get them fast.' With that Brookfield and Bryant left the three intelligence officers to themselves.

'What now?' asked Aspinall.

'We find these people fast. The Prime Minister has given us more power without knowing it.'

'What do you mean 'C'? The press will be banging on our door as soon as that notice goes out.'

'Pass them on to the Home Secretary's office. In the meantime, we concentrate on the Finsbury Mosque and the two-mile area where we think our friends are holed up and knock down doors as Kurt suggests.'

'That will ruffle a few feathers,' said Shimon.

Fraser smiled.

'As I said, the PM has by his actions given us the go ahead to use all resources to find these people. If that means kicking down a few doors and ruffling a few feathers, then so be it. Better that, than hundreds dead because we did nothing. We start by putting pressure on their people. If things go wrong, we all might be dead anyway or at the very least looking for a new job. If it's war these people want, then it's war they will get.'

Reece and Anna had spent the last hour walking the busy streets between Oxford Street and Edgware Road. The winter day was cold, and both had made sure to wear warm clothes which also helped cover the fact they were wearing bulletproof vests. When Reece wore his Barbour jacket, he liked to keep his gun in the right-hand pocket rather than the holster giving easier access to it if needed. Anna was wearing a short parka coat and from the way she kept her hand in her right pocket Reece suspected she would be holding the grip of her .22 pistol.

Some of the streets being close together were not wide and they'd found on more than one occasion they'd crossed over the same road more than once. They had kept up a running conversation with Harrison in the car and Reece felt he was getting to know each street and alleyway the only way he knew best, by walking them.

'Do you fancy finding a café for something warm and wet?' asked Reece.

'Yes please, I need something to warm me up.'

'Let's walk back to Edgware Road and find one.' Reece radioed Harrison to let him know the plan. He would let him know where, and to meet them there.

They found a Starbucks, the kind of café he liked where they could get a seat by the window and observe the street outside. The café was quiet with only two other people sitting near the counter at the other end of the room. Harrison came in five minutes later and sat down with them after getting a coffee for himself.

'Do you know this area?' Reece asked Harrison.

'Yes, very well. I was part of a team a few years ago when we followed a suspected IRA sympathiser for days. He was over from Ireland working as a labourer on a building site. In those days there were hundreds of them over here working the sites throughout the city, some of them using it as cover for their other activities. Most, like him, were living in digs in Kilburn. The largest Irish area in those days. He never spotted us and went back to Ireland. But we identified his contacts and we arrested two of them later, they were planning to bomb Euston Station, not far from here. We had spotted him meeting them at a bar across from the station.'

Reece was looking out the window at the rain and the people, some of them with umbrellas for protection.

'I've stayed in Sussex Gardens a few times. I've always liked this area, its cosmopolitan shops, and restaurants. It always seemed to me to have a community atmosphere. I don't like driving in the city, it's too busy for me, and I think knowing the short cuts lets me get to where I want to be much quicker and at the same time, I can admire much of what the city has to offer. If I need to travel further out like the MI6 building or the airports, I use a taxi or the Tube.'

'I'm like you, David. When I'm in a major city like Tel Aviv, I like to walk. You can see much more, and I feel more aware of what's going on around me.' said Anna.

'Talking about being more aware of what's going on around you. I see someone we should invite to join us.' Said Reece as he looked out the window.

'Tango One from Alpha One.' Reece spoke quietly and discreetly into the body mic on his collar.

On the other side of the street from where they looked out of the café window, they could see Captain Geoff Middleton SAS stop and reply into his own body mic.

'Tango One, go ahead.'

'Roger Tango One would you like to join us in the café across the road from you?' replied Reece smiling.

Middleton looked across the road and seeing Reece at the window did not reply but acknowledged by giving a thumbs up before crossing and entering the café.

Pulling a chair over to join them at the table, Middleton sat down beside Anna with his back to the window.

'Good timing, David I was just thinking about getting something to drink, but I suppose seeing we're working it will have to be coffee.' Middleton said with a smile.

'I'll get us some refills. What's your poison Geoff?' asked Harrison.

'A double espresso please.'

'David. I saw this man at our briefing, but I wasn't introduced,' said Anna.

'I'm sorry Anna. May I introduce Geoff Middleton, a Captain in the SAS. His team are working with us on this job. Geoff, this is Anna one of our Mossad friends.'

Both shook hands across the table and Reece couldn't help but notice both smiled a little bit longer than the requisite time expected for such an introduction.

'Nice to meet you, Anna. I bet you're finding the weather here a little bit colder than where you come from.'

'If you mean Tel Aviv. Yes, but I work all over. Have you ever been to Israel?'

'Yes, on a few occasions on joint training exercises with the IDF and Sayeret Maktal. Or the Unit as you might call them.'

'Our Special Forces. I know them by both names, you must be good then.' She smiled once more.

'Oh, I'm very good.' He laughed.

Harrison came back with the coffees and placed them in front of the right people.

'Well David how is Joe? I heard he was lucky last night. Are you sure it was our man?' asked Middleton.

'A few broken ribs, but he'll be all right. We were not sure if it was the Arab when we first spotted him, but he started to take precautions right from the off. It was obvious he had done this before and knew what to look for. Joe was ahead of us when he followed him into another street. We heard the three shots. Joe said one missed his head but the other two hit him square in the chest. Lucky for him he had decided to wear his vest, or we would be talking about a dead agent today.'

'Thanks be to God he did. What's the plan now?'

'Have you been updated?'

'Yes, we've been told to get to know this area and remain on standby ready to go at a moment's notice.'

'Well, that's the plan. We are doing the same. We believe they're hold up within this two-mile radius and it's now a game of find them before they do anything, which we now believe will be tomorrow.'

Just then the mobile phone in Reece's pocket buzzed. It was a text from Mary.

'In Belfast. Call me when you can. XX'

'If you will excuse me, I need to make a call. Steve, give me the car keys where did you park?'

Harrison handed over the keys.

'Parked up in the next street down on the left.'

'Wait here. I won't be long.'

Reece found the car and pressed in Mary's name. He heard the phone ring twice before Mary answered.

'I didn't expect you to call me that quickly.' She spoke.

'You know me, you shout, and I come running. How's things?'

'Mum has had a fall and she's in the city hospital.'

'Is she OK?' He thought he could hear a sadness in her voice.

'She broke her hip. They are going to operate later today.'

263

'I'm sorry to hear that, everything will be all right. She's in the right place for now.'

'I know, I needed to let you know and to hear your voice. You know they don't allow people to use phones in hospitals. I didn't want you to worry if you couldn't get me if my phone was switched off.'

'Don't switch it off, keep it on silent. That way you will be able to read my messages or that I called.'

'How are you David, how are things going?'

It was one of the things he loved about her. She would always want him to be safe.

'Don't worry about me. You have enough on your plate. Everything is going well here. I should be finished here tomorrow and with you on Saturday.'

He could hear her voice change to one of relief.

'That makes me feel better. I'm heading for the hospital now. Please take care.'

'Don't worry. I'll see you on Saturday. Love you.'

'Love you too.' she answered before ending the call.

Reece sat back in the seat and thought about his day so far. He thought how Anna and Middleton had seemed to hit it off and compared it in his mind to the many meetings over coffee with Mary and the danger when she was his agent, code name Mike in Northern Ireland. He did not like her being there without him. There may be a so-called peace process, and the terrorists were supposed to have handed in their weapons. But the one thing that had kept him alive on many occasions, was never to trust anyone, and he certainly didn't trust the gunmen and bombers who tried to convince the world their terror was over. Reece could never believe them. They may have stopped killing for now but given the chance; because of the damage he had done to them through agents like Mike; he knew he would still be a prime target with old scores to settle. Much of this damage to the terrorist organisations was with the help of the SAS. He thought back to his close links with men such as Geoff Middleton. In his RUC Special Branch days, Reece had the job of travelling to the home base of the 22nd SAS Regiment in Hereford which had at first been named Stirling Lines after the regiments founder Colonel David Stirling. The name had then been changed to Bradbury Lines but Reece always preferred Stirling Lines. Being an Ulster man himself he had also thought they could have named the Headquarters after one of the regiment's most famous officers Colonel Robert Blair Mayne another Ulster man. He would travel to the base for a few days every six months. His job was to update the incoming Squadron taking over from the current one in Northern Ireland. He would be picked up and dropped back at Birmingham airport. Over the next few days, he would stay in accommodation provided for him in the Officers Mess. He remembered the long corridor, with bedrooms on each side. The walls were filled with the plaques showing the badges of the different regiments and agencies throughout the world, who had visited the base and worked with the famous regiment. One of the plaques showed the harp and crown badge of the Royal Ulster Constabulary and had been presented to the regiment by himself. At the end of the corridor was the Officer's Mess, itself with a bar where, if no one was available to serve, officers and visitors could serve themselves and sign a chit which would be presented to them for their bar bill at the end of their stay. Reece had had a few beers in the mess with some of the SAS team and signed his chit, only to find at the end of his visit, he was presented with a receipt showing the regiment's crest of the winged dagger and the bill marked as paid with thanks. Above the bar there was two AK47 rifles presented to the mess by Major Mike Keeley. These were a souvenir from one of the most famous battles in the regiment's history. Keeley himself had fought against the communist backed guerrillas in the battle at Mirbat during the Dhofar Rebellion in Oman in July 1972.

Keeley had died from hypothermia during an exercise on the Brecon Beacons in Wales. Reece had a photo of himself standing at the bar with the rifles above him.

He would brief the incoming team in a type of theatre classroom on the current threat and intelligence in Northern Ireland using visual displays as well as answering questions. He would work with many of the men in the future months, and he would always remember the drinking session with them that evening after the briefing. The SAS men also took the time to show Reece around the main training areas of the base including the famous killing house, where the men would practise their close quarter combat firearm skills and hostage rescue. Reece had done most of his specialist firearms training and anti-ambush escape and evasion drills at a secret location in Northern Ireland. Over several days, he would fire every weapon under the sun; most of them captured from the terrorist organisations he was working against. Everything from Armalite and AK47 rifles to Thompson Sub machine guns. They would enter and clear buildings, engaging cardboard full size human silhouette targets. The last two days of the course included anti-ambush training that simulated the agent's car being attacked. He was taught how to fire and reload while still inside the car. Then the instructors brought in the bomb disposal officer (ATO) who would detonate a small charge in front of the vehicle to simulate disabling it. He had to get out of the car and moving up a narrow pathway that they nicknamed the Ho Chi Minh trail, engage more cardboard targets to the right and left taking cover to reload. It was as realistic as they could make it and after the course Reece felt a little like John Wayne in that he was confident he could draw his pistol and hit the target in the centre of the body every time. When he had joined SG9, his MI6 bosses sent him once more to Hereford to receive more specialist training. The SAS training was tough. They taught him the unarmed tactic of Krav Maga, a self-defence fighting style use by Special Forces the world over. They taught him that rather than back off in a fight it was better to engage quickly with your opponent to give you the element of surprise, especially if you don't have a weapon to hand. Reece ended up a qualified marksman with the handgun and could handle himself in a close combat fight, either with a weapon or his bare hands.

One of the main lessons he learnt was 'You are not John Wayne,' if you must take out your gun, you shoot to kill, two in the chest one in the head. If necessary, you keep shooting at the target until it's eliminated and no longer a threat. Lessons he would never forget.

Reece headed back to the café where he found Harrison standing outside.

'Are they all right in there?' he asked.

'Getting on famously. Two's company three's a crowd if you know what I mean. I was the gooseberry.' smiled Harrison.

'That good eh, lets break them up. We have work to do.' Reece handed Harrison the car keys. 'You head back to the car we will do another hour then head back to base to see how the other teams are doing.'

When Reece entered the café Anna and Middleton were laughing and leaning close across the table their hands almost touching.

'Right, you two, let's keep this professional; we have work to do. Geoff, I'm staying in the Plaza Westminster Hotel. I'm sure Anna would like to join us there for dinner tonight, say eight? Are you up for that, provided nothing happens in between of course?'

Sitting up straight in the chair with his eyes still on Anna.

'Sounds like a great plan. I look forward to it. See you both later then.' Middleton stood and turned left out the door to move in the direction Reece had first seen him.

'I've told Steve to shadow us in the car for an hour and then we can head back to HQ unless you have other plans?'

'No, none for now, or for dinner at eight.' She smiled.

Chapter 26

In a small hotel in Kensington the Deputy First Secretary of the Iranian Embassy was enjoying his second bottle of champagne in his bedroom. The woman he had just had sex with was showering in the bathroom. When it came to breaking Islamic law, he knew he would be hanged if his bosses in Tehran knew he was drinking alcohol and having afternoon sex with a woman who was not his wife. He had met her not long after becoming the new London Embassy Deputy six months ago. He had been out for a morning jogging session in Hyde Park when he spotted her. She had been jogging in front of him and he had noticed the firm shape of her body and her bouncing blonde ponytail hairstyle before he saw her take a bad tumble falling a few yards in front of him. As there was no one else around, he stopped to help her to her feet enquiring if she was all right. She had said her ankle was sore, and he could see a small amount of blood coming through a tear in her tight Lycra training tights.

She rested her hands on his shoulders as she got to her feet and he helped her through the park to the main road, where he flagged down a taxi to take her to the hospital. She smiled and thanked him for his help. Her accent was English, and she was softly spoken and educated. All he could think about the few days after was how stupid he had been not get her name or contact details or even introduce himself. It was to be three weeks later, when jogging the same route at the same time of day, that he saw her once more in front of him. Quickly catching up he had called out hello. She stopped, and turning, she seemed to recognise him so smiled and said hello back. He asked how she was, and she reassured him she'd made a full recovery. The ankle was twisted and the cut on her knee was only a scrape. She had felt foolish and when she thought about it afterwards, she was embarrassed that she'd not asked him for his name or told him hers. With everything now mended she had started back in her jogging routine only that day. He thought this must be fate. Fate had brought them together twice and he intended to make the most of it. He asked for her contact details and if he could take her out to lunch or a coffee. She had hesitated for just a few seconds then smiling agreed to lunch later that week. The lunch went well. He did not tell the Embassy security or the ambassador that he had met this beautiful woman. He had not told his wife either, she'd gotten fat from eating too much at the Embassy events. Sex with her was a chore and they hardly spoke anymore with more shouting arguments than talking. He had decided to keep this woman to himself, and he found the secret liaisons made the love making even more exciting. It had started with the lunch date where he had found himself laughing with the woman. He enjoyed having a glass or two of wine in the afternoon and over the weeks they'd met up when jogging, going for a coffee afterwards. The lunch dates had led to dinner dates and eventually, after about four weeks, to a hotel room and bed. There was no comparison between the young woman and his wife, her body was slim and fit. She was a single businesswoman, with the intelligent mind that went with it. She made love to him the way he wanted her to, he would tell her what he liked, and she obliged, seeming to know how to bring him to a special height of passion. He liked to think he pleased her, and he always felt relaxed in the time afterwards, when they lay in each other's arms and spoke openly about the world and their lives.

The woman in the bathroom was indeed beautiful. She looked in the mirror applying a little lipstick, just enough to keep a man interested, but not enough that he could get it on his clothes and give the game away. To her it was a game, ever since she'd been a girl of seventeen and realised that men liked how she looked and were willing to pay to be with her. She was twenty-six now and she'd made a small living from letting men enjoy the experience of spending a short time with her. That was until two months ago when she was having her end of the week glass of her favourite white wine in the Grosvenor Hotel in Mayfair. A man had sat at her table and asked if he could join her and buy another bottle of wine to share with her. She had been approached by men offering to buy her a drink many times but for some reason this time it was different. The man, tall and of athletic build clean shaven with dark brown eyes and hair, he was not the kind who needed to pick up women. *If anything,* she'd thought, *women would flock to him.* His open white shirt and dark grey suit

271

were made of expensive material and design and his accent was foreign, although she couldn't place it.

He introduced himself as Ari and she readily invited him to stay while he ordered the wine. She was intrigued, and for the rest of that afternoon enjoyed the conversation finding he could make her laugh easily with his beautiful smile enhancing his appearance. It was when he had poured the last glass from the bottle that the conversation changed, he said he had a business proposition to put to her. He said his company were interested in the oil industry in Iran and hoped to complete contracts worth billions of pounds. Through business contacts he had been given her name and where to find her when she visited the hotel for her favourite glass of wine. He had given her a plain white business card with the words Eastern Oil and a mobile telephone number.

The proposal was simple and would bring her the kind of wealth that would make her immediate future financially secure. She was intrigued and invited him to tell her more, without asking anymore questions until he had finished speaking. The man ordered another bottle of wine and talked for the next hour. What it came down to he had said, was that his company needed inside information, and she was in an ideal position to get it for them. What they wanted her to do, was contact one of the Iranian Embassy staff in London, get to know him and let them know whatever he told her. He then told her if she could do this, they would be grateful and to show their thanks they would give her an apartment overlooking Hyde Park and pay her handsomely enough that she wouldn't need to have any other clients and she could concentrate on just the one.

When she told him she was interested but wondered how she could contact such an Iranian without raising his suspicions, he had the answer to that question as well. He would provide her with all the details and how to make such an approach without raising suspicion. It did not take her long to decide before the second bottle of wine was empty, she agreed that she was interested but would need to hear more and see the apartment he promised before she signed on the dotted line. She had asked him would it be dangerous, was she going to be a spy? The question she thought was a sensible one and one she needed the answer to or there would be no deal. Once again, he calmed her fears. She would be doing what she'd been doing for many years, seducing men to like her and give her what she wanted. In this case the money would be coming from his company at a larger rate than her usual fee. She would only have one client, the Iranian, who wouldn't know she was working for his company. She would always have his phone contact details on speed dial if she should need him and they would meet after every date she had with the Iranian. Over the following weeks she'd moved into the Hyde Park apartment and met with Ari. He had provided her with the answer to the questions that she'd asked at that first meeting. She would go jogging in Hyde Park at a specific time on a specific day. He showed her photographs of the man they wanted her to get to know. They agreed she would instigate the meeting by falling. Before she would go on her run, she would tear her training trousers at the knee, and he would provide her with a small vial of blood to pour over the knee area. She was to pretend to be injured and allow the man to get her a taxi but not give him any information, just to thank him and leave in the taxi, which she should take back to her apartment where Ari would brief her further. It had all seemed a bit melodramatic, but she was intrigued, and if she admitted it, a bit excited at being involved in a new experience, where her talents were being used for reasons other than just for sex.

On the day she'd fallen in front of the Iranian everything went just as Ari had said and he was waiting for her when she'd returned to the apartment. She had done wonderfully well he said. Now that the first part of the plan had been completed, he gave her a bank card. He explained they'd opened a bank account for her in a new name which she was to use from now on so that the Iranian would never find out who she really was in case she wanted to call off the deal for any reason and go back to her previous way of working. From that day she was to be known as Martha Fleming. Ari had made her day complete when he told her there would be £5,000 per month in the account but not to go mad as lavish spending would bring unwanted attention to her. She was to say she'd received an endowment from her dead parents, and she'd worked in the travel industry thereby showing her interest in anything foreign. She was currently out of a job and was enjoying some time off. She knew this was a good cover as she loved to travel and had visited most countries in the Mediterranean, including Egypt and had travelled to New York. She had to wait for three weeks before Ari would tell her to go jogging again. The plan had worked just as he had told her it would and as she had dried herself down in the bathroom, she knew the man in the bedroom had believed everything she'd said and accepted the invented story of her past life as fact. He was like most middle-aged married men she knew. A little flattery and a glimpse of her cleavage and she could have most of them eating out of the palm of her hand. Over the weeks he had started talking a little more each time they met. He talked about his work, a little about his family and how living in London compared with his home in Iran. She had been an enthusiastic listener. It was his work that Ari was interested in, and he had told her to let the Iranian bring the conversation up and not to question him just to let him lead the way. It did not take many meetings before she found the Iranian beginning to talk freely about his work and his life. He was not happy with his work and was angry that he was only the Deputy Secretary at the Embassy. He believed he would be better at the senior job than his boss. Today she'd tried to get him to talk about the Iranian oil business with the intention of impressing Ari, but to her surprise the Iranian said he did not know much about it instead asking her why she wanted to know about oil. She was thrown for a few a seconds before replying that she was thinking of investing some money in the oil industry on the stock exchange. It was then that the Iranian told her he had a secret. When she innocently asked him what it was, he would only reply that he had recently met with an important man who had advised him that the financial district of London was about to experience some difficulty and it wouldn't be sensible to invest in a stock exchange that might not be there tomorrow. She pretended not to hear and replied I need a shower, but I'll be back soon so keep the bed warm. This seemed to please him. She knew that Ari would need to hear about the stock market and how the oil industry might be affected.

It was after ten when she left the hotel and pressed the number on speed dial for Ari. After a few rings he answered.

'Hello'

'Ari, I've just left our friend. I know it's late, but I think we should meet tonight.'

'I can be at the apartment in an hour.'

'Great see you there.'

Chapter 27

Alpha One had signed off for the night and Reece, after checking that there were no updates, returned to his hotel room where he cleaned up, changed his clothes, and headed down to the hotel bar. He sat on one of the stools at the bar and ordered a Bloody Mary. When he tasted it, he realised it wasn't as good as the last one he had drunk in Malta. Just then he saw his Malta drinking companion walk into the bar and walking closely behind was Geoff Middleton. *Did they come together or just happen to arrive at the same time?* Reece thought.

'I see you're having our drink,' said Anna.

She was wearing a tight-fitting white trouser suit and Reece thought she must have her gun in her purse as she couldn't hide anything in the suit.

'Hi David, what are you having?' asked Middleton.

'I'm OK. You two go ahead. I've booked us a table for eight.'

'Let's share a bottle of wine,' said Anna.

Middleton looked at the wine list then spoke to the barman.

'A bottle of Lindeman's Bin 65 Chardonnay please and two glasses.'

'Good choice,' said Anna smiling back at Middleton.

'Unfortunately, this will be about all we will be able to drink tonight and possibly until this bloody thing is over,' said Reece.

The dining room was busy, but their table was near the window overlooking the city and in one of the few quieter places in the room. It was obvious to Reece that his two dining companions had been speaking earlier. There were no personal questions. Are you married? Is there anyone else in your life? Where do you live? The kind of questions two people who are getting to know each other ask. Instead, they'd moved to the next phase. What do you like to do when you're not working? What are your likes and dislikes? Where do you like to go to get away from it all? Reece now knew what Harrison meant earlier in the day when he said he had felt like a gooseberry. When the time came to order dessert, Reece asked for the cheese and biscuits with a small glass of Taylors vintage port. Middleton said the same but Anna who asked for Cointreau with ice.

'Any news or updates?' asked Middleton.

'Nothing new on our side,' said Reece. 'The plan stays the same. There will be people out all night in the two-mile area we think, or should I say, hope they're in. We are back on the ground from 7am.'

'Nothing new from my side. All our people across the globe and here in London are working to find answers.'

'What if we don't find them? What happens if they get through?' asked Middleton.

'I don't want to think about that. You remember when we were in Ireland, Geoff? We worked night and day to stop attacks. The public didn't appreciate that we stopped nine out of every ten terrorist attacks. People only remember the ones that got through, the ones that took lives and devastated communities. We don't have the comfort of worry. We need to do our best and I'm sure if we do, we can stop these bastards.'

'Amen to that,' said Middleton.

'We have been stopping these bastards as you put it David for a lot longer than any of you. When they do get through the blowback is way above our paygrade,' said Anna.

'It's not only a time for good soldiers but good leaders as well,' Middleton replied.

'I don't like politicians at the best of times, but I have to say Brookfield is one of the strongest Prime Ministers we've had in a long while. I saw how he worked in Manchester up close. Even though he knew there was a terrorist hit squad out to assassinate him, he still went about his normal business and let us get on with our job, giving us the OK to take them out when we found them.' said Reece.

'It's always been my experience that politicians look for a way out to blame someone when things go wrong,' commented Middleton.

Reece raised his glass.

'Well, when I finish this port and cheese I'm off to bed. Early start in the morning provided nothing happens tonight.'

'Don't forget to call Mary before you go to bed.' Anna said.

'of course, she would never forgive me if I didn't say good night.'

Reece left the two diners alone and headed to his room. As promised, he called Mary to say goodnight. She told Reece her mother had come through the operation and was resting well.

'How was your day, Joseph?'

'Busy. I just had dinner with Anna and Geoff Middleton. Do you remember him from Manchester?'

'Yes, I think so, the SAS Captain?'

'Yes, that's the guy. I think him and Anna are getting on very well if you know what I mean?'

'If I know you, you're not happy about that, you're too much of a professional.'

'I know they are too, or I would have to remind them we have important work to do.'

'That sounds more like the Joseph I know. I'm tired my darling, so I think I'll hit the pillow. You do the same, by the sound of things you have a busy day tomorrow.'

'You're right, and that's exactly where I'm heading. All being well tomorrow, I should still be OK for Saturday in Belfast.'

'I'm looking forward to it and you can meet my mother. Good night. I love you.'

'Good night, Mary, sweet dreams I love you too. I'll try to call or text you tomorrow if I'm not too busy and you're not in the hospital quiet zone.'

He poured himself a small glass of Bushmills taking a few sips while looking out the window across the city. He thought about Mary and then his enemy across the river somewhere on the other side of the city. He was glad Mary was safe and far enough away to make his job that bit easier not having to worry about her.

Reece felt warm and decided to lie on top of the bed. Following old and trusted habits he placed his gun within reach on the bedside cabinet. He closed his eyes for what only seemed minutes when his phone, which he had plugged into a charger, started to buzz loud enough to wake him. Looking at his watch he could see it was only 2 am and he had been sleeping for two hours. Lifting the phone, he could see the name Broad on the screen. And he pressed the button to answer.

'What's up, Boss? I hope it's good news. I was having a beautiful dream.'

'Sorry to interrupt your dream but we aren't getting any sleep here. We have just been given some new information I think you need to know.'

Reece didn't know whether it was the warmth in the room or being awakened in the dark, but he could feel small beads of sweat rolling down his back and his forehead.

'Is it good information or bad?'

'Why don't you come here and see for yourself I'm in the Ops room.'

Reece took another look at his watch.

'I can be there in twenty minutes.'

'Try and make it fifteen.'

What the hell's going on, thought Reece, as he began dressing. No one likes to be rudely awakened and Reece knew from experience such awakenings were not only rude but not welcome usually bringing bad news. No matter how fast he moved it was seventeen minutes later when he walked into the operation room at MI6. He was surprised to see Kurt Shimon sitting at a table beside Jim Broad.

'What brings us here at this time of night?' asked Reece, sitting down opposite them.

The two men looked at each other then back at Reece before Broad spoke.

'I won't say I'm sorry to get you out of bed David, but if I have to be up at this time of the day then so do my people.'

'You know me Boss, you say jump and I say how high.' Reece smiled.

'Thanks for jumping. Kurt has some new information which you need to hear, I'll let him explain.'

Kurt Shimon pulled out a small notebook from his inside jacket pocket and started to read from it looking up at Reece as he spoke.

'As you might expect, like your Security Services, we have operatives all over the world especially in the major capital cities. This is not just for the benefit of Israel but also for our friends and allies in the war on terrorism.'

That's the politics out of the way, thought Reece, as he listened without commenting.

'One of our operatives has been working with a casual contact to obtain information from one of Iran's diplomats who works in their Embassy here in London. Late last night our contact was able to pass on something that the Iranian said. The contact thought the comment odd enough to pass on, and we think the same. The Iranian commented that your financial services might suffer a problem tomorrow. Our contact had been asking about investing in the stock market. On its own it could mean several things, even something as small as insider trading or a market slump concerning oil prices. But when we think that we are expecting the terrorists to attempt some sort of attack tomorrow it started me thinking and I contacted Sir Ian and Jim.'

Again, Reece kept quiet looking across at Broad as he felt there was more to come.

'Kurt contacted me just after midnight at just about the same time I received a call from the director at GCHQ. As you know they've been monitoring everything, and they found a text message that was sent from the Arab's mobile earlier. With the help of our friends in the NSA, we were able to clarify the message around the same time as Kurt contacted me, so I asked him here and then called you to join us.'

Broad pushed a piece of paper across the table on it he could see two lines of type.

'Light of the Sun, Tomorrow Friday, Allah Akbar.'

'Interesting. You are sure this was the Arab?' asked Reece.

'GCHQ are happy it was the same phone we identified earlier.'

Reece read the words once more.

'Were they able to say where he is?'

'Unfortunately, no, because the phone was switched off immediately afterwards, but they did confirm from what they were able to get that he's somewhere in the two-mile radius we are covering. At least it confirms our theory, and we will continue with our main efforts there.'

'Was your GCHQ or the NSA able to identify who he sent the message to?' asked Kurt before Reece did.

'Now that's where it gets interesting. The person at the other end of the text was none other than our Quads General Malek Hasheem Khomeini. Even though his phone is encrypted we can decipher the message.'

'Ah, more confirmation we are on the right track and looking for the right people. I'll contact Tel Aviv tonight and tell them to listen out for anything coming out of Iran. We have found in the past when these terrorist operations take place, we can expect a build-up of chatter to all their Arab friends to expect news from their Jihad friends.'

'Thank you, Kurt, between our people and the Americans, I'm sure we can point the finger in the right direction when this is over,' replied Broad.

'How are things out there right now?' asked Reece.

'As you can see it's quiet. We have updated everyone relevant with the information that our terrorist friends are still in that area and we believe the attack will be tomorrow. The police are going to hit the Mosque in the morning before Friday prayers. They want to be in and out before people start to gather so they'll go in at six. At the same time, they will hit the Imam's house and other suspect's houses.'

'I don't think they'll find much,' said Reece.

'Neither do I, but the powers that be want to send a message. If not to the Jihadis in our midst, then to the ones involved in this operation, in the hope it will scare them off, at least until we get more concrete information,' replied Broad.

'I know these people. They have come this far. They won't wait or run, they're here, and they'll complete the job or die trying,' said Shimon.

The phone on the main Ops desk began to ring and one of the two desk officers answered it before looking across at the three men and replying, 'Yes sir he's here. Mister Broad it's 'C' for you,' holding out the phone.

Broad crossed the room and took the phone and listened. As Reece and Shimon watched Broad's expression gave nothing away.

'Understood, Sir.' said Broad before putting the phone down and crossing the room to sit down at the table, joining the two men once more. They waited for him to speak. He was working out what to say and from his expression they knew the news wasn't good.

'As you will have gathered that call was from 'C'. When we spread the latest intelligence and all the other agencies were updated, he was contacted by both the Met Commissioner and Sir Martin Bryant who informed him that the Princess Royal is expected to open a new banking firm in the financial district of Canary Wharf today at 3 pm'

Broad waited for both men to take in what he had just told them.

'That's all we bloody need, a blue blood in the middle of everything. Can we stop her from being there?' asked Reece.

'Apparently the PM has already asked the Palace that same question. This is a new office in the city of the Bank of South Africa. The South African ambassador and a lot of high-ranking businesspeople will be there, and it's been arranged for some months. The Palace have refused to alter their plans, so yes, we have the added problem of the daughter of our Queen right in the middle of where our terrorist friends might be going.'

'Finding these people before they get there is more important than ever. I presume the Princess will have her own security?' asked Shimon.

'Correct, all the usual diplomatic protection. And Canary Wharf comes under the jurisdiction of the City of London police. It's my understanding they will all be briefed by the Met Commissioner and MI5 that there is an increased threat and that several security agencies will also be operating in the area. It's not unusual and something they've seen in the past, and they're happy they can work around it,' replied Broad.

'Have they been told it might be a dirty bomb?' asked Reece.

'No, that part they won't be told. With too many people knowing the full story, the worry is that someone will leak it to the press and all sorts of panic would ensue. The Home Secretary has increased the threat level so that's all they need to know for now.'

Reece looked across at the two men before speaking again.

'Realistically nothing has changed for us. The object of our task is still the same; find these people before they get to their target and stop them. With the added outside security for the Princess we need to ensure their people wear their identification such as the baseball caps and arm bands, we don't want people getting in each other's way. Our surveillance teams need to be aware of the Canary Wharf and especially the area that will be covered by the Princess's visit.'

'Agreed David. We will keep the night people out on the ground and have the day teams here for 7 a.m. for a full update and briefing.'

Reece looked at his watch.

'It's 03.30 so I'm off back to my hotel to try to catch a few hours' sleep. Can you organise a small A4 paper for the morning showing where the Princess will be with times and call signs for her protection? You could also give us a map of the area.'

'No problem I'll get Matthew Simons on to it. See you at 7 am'

'A good idea, Mister Reece, I think I'll do the same. See you here later Jim,' said Kurt Shimon.

Reece and Shimon travelled down in the lift to the underground car park.

'Thank you for looking after Anna for me,' said Shimon.

'Don't worry about Anna. I'm sure you know she can look after herself.'

'Oh, I know that, but still, it's her first time in London and she could be distracted.' Smiled Shimon as he got into his car.

Reece waved as Shimon started the engine and drove towards the exit. *I wonder,* thought Reece, *was he talking about the tourist attractions or a certain SAS Captain?* Kurt Shimon was the type of person who does not miss much, especially when it came to his Mossad agents.

Reece never slept well when he was in the middle of an operation and tonight was no exception. Between the dark dreams and the thoughts that were running through his head, he slept lightly for no more than two hours. At six he gave up and decided a shower would at least freshen him up ready for this day and whatever it would bring.

Across the city Yasmin was doing the same. She couldn't sleep, and a picture kept flashing through the screen in her head. It was a picture of herself playing as a child on the streets of Baghdad before all the wars and death. She got up and made herself a cup of black tea and scrolled through the photos on her phone, the ones she'd taken in Trafalgar Square and found the one she was looking for. A woman of about her age was smiling down at her daughter as she held her hand in front of one of the fountains, both laughing at the pigeons running around the feet of the people passing by. The young girl in the photo had triggered the dream of her childhood days on the streets of the Iraq capital. Carefree days when all she had to worry about was to be home in time for dinner when her father came home from work. She had always wanted to have children of her own and to meet and fall in love with the man of her dreams, but a cruel police inspector in the city of her birth had changed everything. It was no good to think of what could have been. She had taken a path to where she now sat, in a room in a foreign city, ready to complete her mission and punish the people who brought the war to her doorstep, and by their action changed her life forever.

288

She knelt on the floor and prayed to Allah for the strength to complete her mission to his honour and name. When she stood and opened her eyes Hassan was sitting in the chair watching her.

'I'm sorry, did I waken you?' she asked.

'No, I was awake, I couldn't sleep either. I hope you prayed for both of us.'

'Of course.' She lied. 'What keeps you awake?'

'I don't know. Thinking about the morning I suppose. All the training all the planning now it will be real. We will kill the enemy and they may kill us.'

'I was dreaming of my childhood in Baghdad. Before the war when you could play in the street without fear. The war changed everything and everyone. I suppose that is why I'm here. Everything changed for me I grew up from being the girl playing in the street and found that the circumstances changed to make me recognise the enemies in my life.'

Hassan stood and smiling he walked to the kitchen and switched on the kettle.

'Would you like another cup of tea?'

'No thanks.'

Bringing his tea back into the room he sat back down in the chair by the window. Yasmin was stretched out on the couch.

'What time is it?' she asked.

'Four,' he said looking at his watch.

'I'm looking forward to this being over and getting back to somewhere warm. I could never live in a country this cold.'

'I've lived here. You get used to it, and it's not like this all the time, the summers are usually great, but it's a different kind of heat to the one you're used to.'

Yasmin stretched, yawned, and closed her eyes. Hassan could hear her breathing change as she drifted off to sleep. He finished his tea and returned to the bedroom to kneel and say his own prayer to Allah and to try to sleep for the short while he had before the day's work would begin.

Chapter 28

Two hours later at 6.00 am. police had knocked on the door of Mohammed AAyan at his home in Finsbury, he inspected the search warrant, then accompanied them the short distance to the Mosque to find two police transit vehicles stuffed with police officers. Using his keys and switching off the alarm system he allowed them into the building under protest. Two officers stayed with him in the small office where he had met Hassan and made sure he did not use a phone. Two of the officers who continued to search the main building were in fact MI5 operators, they knew they wouldn't find much. They were aware of the informant working inside the Mosque and that he had brought everything he could find of worth to the attention of his handlers. They also knew that the building was swept regularly for listening devices, so it was part of their remit to leave behind two listening devices one covering the main hall and the other in the office where the Imam now sat. He would be brought into the hall to be questioned by the search team leader while they completed the task. What the Imam did not know, and because he lived alone, was that at the same time this search was taking place, another MI5 team were installing the same top of the range bugging devices in his home. He might carry out a sweep looking for them when he returned home but they would be left switched off for a few days until they felt sure the sweep had been done and then they could safely be activated. The Anti-Terrorist Squad contact in the Mosque was now able to let his handlers know when a sweep looking for bugging devices was to be carried out. When that happened, the devices would again be switched off reducing the chance of them being discovered; then turned back on to record again after the sweep had been completed.

It was when the Imam was brought into the main hall under more protest, that the two MI5 men discovered the hidden panel behind the office mirror. There were a few documents which they photographed before placing them back and closing the mirrored door. It took them another thirty minutes standing on one of the chairs to remove the main light in the ceiling and install the microphone and lithium battery pack above. They did not need to drill any tell-tale holes for the microphone, as the new equipment could easily pick up the voices below through the ceiling. When they screwed the light back into the ceiling, they used the small battery powered handheld suction device to collect any dust or debris left on the chair and the floor. They left the room looking exactly as they had found it. By 8 am the operation was complete. At the same time several suspect's houses had been raided throughout the city. Again, little was found and only one person arrested for breaking the nose of one of the search team.

As the searches were finishing Reece and the other team members had just finished their briefing. Matthew Simons had brought everyone in the room up to date with the latest information. They had the suspect's most recent photos, text, and phone messages. Everything indicated that the terrorists were still hold up in a two-mile radius, but in a city the size of London even this held thousands of locations and people. A small jungle to hide in and get lost, a needle in a haystack situation. The only good information from the day before was the possibility that the target was somewhere in the financial district of Canary Wharf. Simons had told those in the room that the Princess Royal was to open a new office at Canada House. He also told them that Canary Wharf, where the financial district was located, was an area of six million square feet with thousands of workers, tourists, and everyday Londoners: yet another needle in a haystack. Everyone in the team knew that GCHQ would be monitoring the phones and a special team would be looking at every inch of CCTV coverage. Anything of interest would be sent out to the teams from Simons and the men in the operations room. Reece had noticed that Anna had sat beside Geoff Middleton throughout the briefing and afterwards he sat down pulling a chair around to face them.

'I hope you both slept well last night, we are going to have a busy day,' said Reece noticing how Anna's cheeks turned slightly red as she blushed.

'We're well rested and ready to go,' replied Middleton answering for both.

'My boss has agreed for me to work with the teams today. Where do you want me?' asked Anna.

'You can stay with me and Steve Harrison today. He has gone to check out the MP5 and other bits and pieces. Have you any idea where you will be placed today, Geoff?'

'We have enough people to split them into two teams in two transits. One will be located near Hyde Park and the other near Canada Square in Canary Wharf. SO19 will have their own people on the ground. They will be working mostly with the Princess's protection detail during her visit to Canada House. They have the training and firepower to take down anyone who gets too close. Our job will be as a quick reaction force to back them up and deal with any fast-moving hostage situation. I'll be call sign Tango One at Canary Wharf and the other team at Hyde Park will be Tango Two. Both teams know what their jobs are so I hope you spot these people before we have to follow up, because if that happens, they will already be on the move with their bombs.'

'Any word on Joe?' asked Anna.

'I phoned the hospital before coming here this morning. He should be getting out today but with two broken ribs he won't be allowed out on the ground, but if I know him, he'll make a beeline straight for here to sit in on the operation.'

Jim Broad had been speaking to Simons and now came across to speak with Reece.

'David, can you come with me, 'C' wants a word before you go out on the ground.'

Both men took the lift to the director's floor where the secretary in the outer office told them to go straight in. Sir Ian Fraser was sitting behind his desk and invited the men to take a seat. Reece was surprised to see Kurt Shimon sitting in one of the three chairs.

'Gentlemen I hope you're up to date with the latest information. I've asked you here with Kurt so that you fully understand what we need to happen today when we find these people if you get the opportunity. David, you know the reason SG9 was brought into existence, not only to track and find the people who threaten this country but if you can, and the circumstances are right, eliminate that threat. It might surprise you David that I'm saying this in front of Kurt, as your team and your remit are most secret and only a select few know of your existence. Like MI6 the Mossad make it their business to know these things and I'm sure the existence of SG9 is known to them, just as we know about the Kidon teams in Mossad who are given similar tasks. Kurt told me this morning that the Israeli government have three people who sit on what they call the X Committee, the Prime Minister, the Minister of Defence, and the head of Mossad. They meet on a regular basis to discuss intelligence reports, specifically those concerning people or organisations that are a threat to the people of Israel. When they have enough information, the X committee then issue the order for the threat to be eliminated, just as we do when we use our SG9 team to eliminate specific threats against this country.'

Reece had known from his own Special Branch days of the existence of such a special force and committee in Israel.

Kurt Shimon waited for 'C' to finish before adding his own thoughts to the conversation.

'Thank you, Sir Ian. As you can see from what Sir Ian is saying the terrorists involved in this operation are also of great interest to Israel. We have been trying to find Abdullah Mohammad Safrah, known better to you as the Arab, for some time. This is the closest we've ever been. As you know from your own files and intelligence, it's for that very reason that the X committee have placed him on the list for elimination. This is also the reason I'm here today, the Mossad Director of the Kidon, sitting in the office of the directors of MI6 and SG9. Both our countries and our intelligence organisations have come together, to aid each other in the important task of protecting our people, by tracking down and if possible, eliminating the enemy of both our countries. I'm glad you've met Anna and Palo and that they'll be working with you today. You can be sure of their full support. I've briefed Anna and Palo that as we are working together on your soil, they should take their instructions from you. However, if they should find themselves on their own with the terrorists, then they should engage them and eliminate them.'

It was the turn of 'C' to add his voice to the conversation once more.

'So, as you can see David, your remit is just as clear today as it was on the first day you joined SG9. You know the target, go out, find it and eliminate it.'

Reece understood that the whole conversation was to reassure him that both governments and the directors of their various intelligence agencies were together on this. They knew the task was going to be dangerous, and the kind of people Reece was dealing with. It was also their way of giving him the go-ahead to use lethal force if necessary, even if not necessary.

Reece went back to the Ops room and found that Middleton had left to join his team and Palo was with Harrison and Anna. Like Reece everyone had dressed in suitable clothing that served the dual purpose of being inconspicuous and waterproof taking care of the British weather. Anna had her hair tied in a ponytail again and as Reece had noticed before, she could dress in a bin bag and still look stunning.

'I left your vest in the car, and both vehicles have everything we need from baseball caps to the fully loaded MP5. The radios are tuned in to the Ops network and we have the most up-to-date satnav map displays with a back-up A–Z just in case,' said Harrison handing Reece a folder.

'Inside you will find the most recent photos we have of our targets which might come in useful if we find them.'

'Great, thanks Steve can you work with Palo and Anna will stay with me? I think we can leave the rifles back in the armoury. I don't think our enemy will have big weapons and between the SAS and SO19 there'll be plenty of those on the street. Our small arms will do for now. All we need now is a bit of luck and the rain not to be too heavy. There are other teams out there from MI5 and the police to the SAS and SO19. Everything goes through here so Matthew and the team will keep us up to date and stop us from running into each other. Everyone happy with that?' All three nodded. Reece turned to face the men covering the communications desk.

'Matthew?' Reece called over to Simons. 'That's Alpha One and Two out to Edgware Road. Will let you know when we are there.'

Simons answered back with a thumbs up.

'Don't worry, David. All those little dots you see on the screen are our people. When you're on the move the tracking device in your car will let us know where you are and that goes for the ear and radio mics as well,' said Simons.

'Nice to know Big Brother is alive and well,' replied Reece.

Chapter 29

The Arab had slept well, and had breakfast in his room, then leaving the hotel he walked towards Oxford Street, as ever checking for surveillance. He had dressed for the day to blend in with the employees of the financial district of London, a three-piece grey business suit, white shirt, dark tie, smart shoes, and a dark blue overcoat. To complete his disguise, he wore thick rimmed glasses and a tweed flat cap. He had watched the news in his room and there had been no mention of a shooting which was unusual and another indication that the Security Services might know about him and his plan. The rain was staying away for the moment, but the dark clouds gave an indication that it would come later in the day. He knew because of any heavy rain there would be less people walking the same streets as him. This would make it easier for him to spot surveillance. Turning down the side streets, crossing the roads checking reflections in windows; all to help him spot someone appearing in his line of vision more than once in the same streets.

The wind was strong, and people were walking with their heads down for protection from the biting cold air. A surveillance operative would more likely have to keep their heads up to follow a target.

Even the weather was in his favour, he thought, *Allah is with us today*. After crossing a few streets and making the customary checks, he felt there was no reason to worry yet, so he flagged down a black cab and asked to be taken to Sussex Gardens. Just as before, when he was walking, he watched the traffic and noted the vehicles and motorbikes taking the same turns or keeping to the same speed. Everything had looked clear when he got out of the taxi and started walking towards Edgware Road. Near to the end of Sussex Gardens, and just before he turned right to walk down the Edgware Road, he noticed a dark BMW car in a parking bay with two men inside, even though they were talking, their eyes seemed to be focused on the street and the people walking along it. Immediately he was wary and concentrated his attention, watching the men and at the same time increasing his pace slightly so that he could turn right into Edgware Road and get lost in the larger number of pedestrians. Entering the road, he walked a few paces before crossing over to the other side and stopping to look back and then up and down the street. No one seemed to be paying him any attention and he walked further down the road before crossing directly and turning the key in the apartment door. He took the stairs two at a time and entered the living room where he found Hassan and Yasmin sitting at the kitchen table.

'Good morning, my children how was your night?'

Before they could answer, he took off his overcoat, threw it on the couch then went to the main window overlooking the road. He watched through the net curtains standing back so as not to be observed from below, but from where he could observe. He watched for the next five minutes without there being anymore conversation. To the untrained eye everything seemed normal, but the same man and woman had passed twice in five minutes then disappeared. Neither of them had paid any attention to the building he was standing in, but at this time of morning he expected most people on the street to be workers, heading directly to their place of work and not normally retrace their steps, unless perhaps they had forgotten something. Was he being paranoid? The couple could be early morning shoppers who were just browsing the shop windows but hadn't looked in any windows; he wasn't sure but still he trusted his instincts. He turned to his children who were watching him closely.

'You did not leave here since we met yesterday?' he asked.

'No, Teacher, as you requested, we've been here all night,' replied Hassan.

'Good. We do not have much time. I feel our enemies are close, but they don't know exactly where we are yet. Have you both had breakfast?'

'Yes, we've eaten, and I've just made a pot of coffee,' answered Yasmin.

'Then I will have a cup of your coffee,' said the Arab as he joined them at the table.

Yasmin poured a cup for him and taking it black, he looked at his proteges and smiled.

'Don't worry my children. Today is the day when we will make the Devil nation fall to its knees and tremble. Our plan is unchanged. Yasmin you will bring your package to Trafalgar Square and leave it where it will cause the most pain to our enemies. Do not forget the timer is set so you must not press the start button before 1 pm, it is set to go off at 3 pm. Hassan and I will be working to the same time so we must leave here at eleven. Hassan, please bring me the bag from yesterday.'

Hassan crossed the room and from behind the couch pulled out the bag and brought it to the table. Reaching inside the Arab brought out the three Tupperware containers with the explosives in them and set them on the table. Then he took out two plastic shopping bags, the walking stick, two small backpacks and finally what looked like a roll of brown packing tape.

'You remember which button to press?'

Both students nodded. The Arab then placed one device into one of the plastic shopping bags then into one of the backpacks and pushed it across to Yasmin.

'This is your weapon with which you will attack our enemy Yasmin. Treat it as your child, to deliver it in the name of Allah.'

The Arab unscrewed the knob of the walking stick and tipping it up, slid out the three six-inch-long items from its tubing. The items looked like sticks of black rock, the kind you would buy at a holiday resort each, wrapped in a thick plastic type substance. *In a way they also looked like sticks of black dynamite*, thought Hassan. The Arab placed them next to the container with the red dot. Taking the three black sticks he held them against the container and secured them with packing tape. Finally, Hassan noticed he secured the end of the tape into a slot at the side of the phone timer. Satisfied, he placed the box with the taped sticks into the remaining rucksack and pushed it in front of Hassan.

'The plutonium does not need to be attached to the explosives themselves. The blast itself will be enough to disperse the poison into the air and will not only kill many of our enemies but its financial strength as well. It has been that same financial wealth that has paid for its wars against our people and killed many of our children.'

The Arab moved the third container with the green dot to the centre of the table.

'This one will remain here when we leave. It will be set for ninety minutes after we've gone just by pressing the button. That way if they find this location, we will leave them a surprise, it will distract our enemy from our true target and give us the time we need to succeed.'

The Arab removed his mobile phone from his pocket.

'Are you ready to make your statement my children?'

Both Yasmin and Hassan stood, and the Arab placed two of the kitchen chairs in front of one of the white walls. Taking a black flag with white letters in Arabic, he then pinned it to the wall behind his two students. Yasmin and Hassan sat side by side facing the Arab. Hassan fixed his shemagh around his head showing only his eyes and Yasmin did the same placing her red scarf around her head, her brown eyes the only visible sign. The Arab set his phone to video and recorded their statements. Yasmin first, then Hassan; stating they were soldiers of Allah and the Jihad. Hassan with his English accent said that their actions were necessary as the West and Britain had killed the children of Allah and they had to pay for this sin. Yasmin then continued, her strong Middle Eastern accent coming through, by stating that the West had brought terror to her people, she quoted Churchill by saying, 'You have sent the wind, now you will reap the whirlwind.' Both finished together, 'Allah Akbar, God is Great, Allah Akbar.'

The Arab played the video back and satisfied linked it to a number in his phone and pressed the send button.

'Very good my children. Now, let us have some more of your wonderful coffee and we will talk some more about our mission.'

As Hassan placed the chairs around the table, Yasmin brewed fresh coffee while the Arab watched the street through the net curtains. People were going about their business. It was still raining, and many walked with umbrellas up. Satisfied he returned to join his two students at the table.

'What do you think our enemy is doing?' asked Hassan.

'A good question. If the other night is anything to go by and my close call when I came out of the Embassy, then they're working hard to find us, and we can expect them to be alert. When we leave here, we must be alert. If they find us, we cannot surrender, we must fight. We have our bombs and our guns, and we must kill as many of the enemy as we can but always try to escape. Today, we will be two teams. Yasmin, you leave by the front door at 11 am. You will travel alone to your target and then, as we discussed, try to get to Bristol. At the same time Hassan and I will leave by the rear door. The Arab then spread a small map of the city on the table.

'Yasmin, using your own route make your way to Trafalgar Square and complete your mission. Hassan, we will follow this route and take a taxi from here, then the train from here to our target. When we leave, I'll walk ahead of you and the only times we will be physically together is when we are in the taxi and when we reach this point, we need to travel alone in case one of us is compromised. When we reach this location, then and only then we will agree on the best place for our attack. By doing it this way if we are compromised there'll be a better chance for us to escape. You both must ensure you have the bank cards, money, and passports with you for we will not be coming back here. Only take what you need for today leave everything else, you can buy whatever you need afterwards. Leave the flag pinned to the wall as part of our message if the enemy finds this place before our surprise gift finds them.'

At that same time Reece and Anna were passing the apartment in the black BMW. He was able to turn the wipers to intermittent as the rain seemed to be slowing down against the windscreen.

'How do people live in this country?' asked Anna.

'What do you mean? I'm sure it rains in Israel.' replied Reece with a smile.

'Yes, but not with the coldness as well.'

'Warm rain. At least you could have a shower outdoors then and save on the electricity bill.'

Anna laughed at this idea.

'The neighbours might not like such a sight.'

'I don't know, maybe if it was me, but not you,' replied Reece.

Edgware Road was quieter than usual, thought Reece. Maybe the weather, the rain, would make it a little easier to spot someone, but it would be the same for them.

'You know I was just thinking in this weather with more people using umbrellas it will make it more difficult to spot our friends using CCTV, as most cameras are looking downwards. Our eyes on will be even more important,' said Reece.

Anna nodded in agreement.

'All the more reason we have cars and people on foot.' Anna replied.

'Therein lies a problem,' said Reece.

'What do you mean?'

'At any one time the likes of MI5 and the Met have at least three thousand active targets in the country. Many of those are already using up a great amount of their resources. I guess that's only one of the reasons that both our bosses are pleased for us to be working together, it reduces the odds of these people getting through, even though we haven't been too successful on that score.'

'Control to Alpha One come in over.' It was the voice of Jim Broad.

'Roger control, send over,' replied Reece using his body mic.

'Can you call me on your phone? Need a quick chat.'

'This car has a hands-free phone.'

'I know but apologies to our friend with you, but I need to speak to you on your own.'

'Roger, give me a few minutes to park up.'

Reece knew it could take up to five minutes to find a parking space in the area but in the event, as it happened it only took two as he parked outside a hotel in Sussex Gardens.

'Sorry about this Anna, but when the boss says on my own.'

'It's the world we live in. It must be important.' Anna smiled.

Reece left Anna in the car and found a low wall to sit on. He was glad the rain had stopped, and the wall was dry. The traffic, although noisy, was far enough away allowing him to hear Jim Broad's voice when he got through to him.

'Thanks for getting back to me,' said Broad.

'You asked me to call, so here I am. What's up?'

'The reason I don't want your friend to know, is that it's to do with the searches we carried out on the Mosque and suspect houses this morning. MI5 bugged the Mosque and the Imam home, so you know how they can be about need-to-know and especially when it's to do with their capabilities and the results coming from them. So basically, what their saying is that our friends from Tel Aviv don't need to know.'

'Understood. So, what you're saying is that you have something to tell me that's come from one of these devices?'

'Correct, it's not much, but it definitely confirms that we are on for today. Normally five would keep the device switched off for a few days to avoid it being found in a sweep, but on this occasion, it was decided by the gods on high that as all our intelligence indicates something is imminent, they would keep it switched on. Our friend the Imam had a conversation in his office with an unknown male.

The unknown lives in one of the houses we also searched so he's not a friendly. The Imam told him to stay at home today as the Jihad will be hitting the city. This is the interesting bit, he also told this unknown that the people who will be carrying out the Jihad are staying in an apartment he supplied to them on Edgware Road. So, you're in the right area. They must be close.'

That is what we've been thinking all along. So, if the target is Canary Wharf, then they'll be moving soon if they're not already on their way.'

'I hope we find them before they get to Canary Wharf. It is more open there with too many ways to escape.'

'Exactly David. But we have another problem now. The Home Secretary has been getting some sticky questions from the press. The kind of questions that would indicate someone is talking. That is another reason I didn't want to talk in front of your car passenger. I'm not saying it's coming from them. It might just be some over enthusiastic reporter throwing out some bait to see who bites. I think it's all down to the politicians raising the threat level.'

'More likely one of our own politicians. People in our line of work usually know how to keep a secret and why we keep it.'

'I'm inclined to agree with you there David. You can tell her we have information from a source. If she is as good as I think she is, she will be able to work it out for herself. Find these bastards David. Find them soon and deal with them.'

'I'm trying too. Do we have any air cover?'

'We are trying but the rain has made for low cloud which we hope will rise just enough to get a spotter helicopter up. I've authorised a CCTV and camera communications van to park up and cover Canary Wharf, especially where the Princess Royal will be this afternoon. That will give us access to all cameras in the area, with or without the permission of those who own them.'

'Thanks for the update, will you be there for the rest of this?'

'Yes, me and Matthew.'

'In that case I'll get back to the car and do some more passes up and down Edgware Road.'

Reece looked at the sky and he could see the greyness that indicated the rain clouds wouldn't be lifting any time soon. He returned to the car to find Anna finishing a call on her own phone.

'So, David, what's up, anything new?'

He wasn't going to tell her everything, but he knew she was professional enough to understand that what he did tell her was what she needed to know.

'They have definitely confirmed that our targets are in this area, so we can concentrate on this road. It's a lot less to cover than the two-mile radius we were working on initially. No air cover because of the weather, but extra cover to assist on the ground at Canary Wharf has been dispatched. The press are starting to ask awkward questions which might make our job a little more difficult. Do you have anything new?'

Anna held up her phone.

'That was Kurt Shimon asking how things were going. I couldn't tell him anything more than we had already been briefed. I did tell him that both Palo and I were embedded with the operational team, and we were out on the ground working the area. He told me he'll be in the office of 'C' until this is over. He also said that as we expect it to be over one way or the other by tonight, he has booked us on the late flight to Tel Aviv; so, let's get the right result when we leave.'

Reece started the car engine.

'Let's get the right result then.'

Chapter 30

In the apartment the Arab was looking out the window once more. The street below appeared to be normal, shoppers, tourists and workers all going about their business. The rain had stopped, and his watch showed the time to be 11 am exactly.

'Now my children it's time to complete our mission. Yasmin put on her red scarf, tying it tightly around her face. She pulled the rucksack over her shoulders placing her arms through the straps and pulled up the zip on her long brown overcoat. Hassan pulled his shemagh around his neck under his parka, using it as a scarf which he could pull up to cover his lower face if necessary. The rucksack he placed over his right shoulder.

'One more check, my children. Are you happy with your mission as soldiers of the Jihad and in the name of the holy one?'

Both students nodded.

'Good, you have your guns fully loaded and ready to use. You have your money and passports. I bless you my children, I have sent the video which will be circulated to the world at the end of this day.'

The Arab pulled on his own coat and placed his gun in the right-hand pocket. Then he kissed both students on their cheeks before he activated the small device, they were leaving behind on the kitchen table.

Leading the way out of the room, he watched from the landing as Yasmin went down the stairs opened the front door and closing it behind her, stepped out onto Edgware Road.

The Arab and Hassan walked down the same stairs, turned at the bottom and left by the rear door that led to a small, enclosed yard.

'Keep close but not so close that someone would know we are together,' said the Arab. He opened the yard door and walked into the street that backed onto Edgware Road. He had memorised the names of the streets and locations he was to pass through to protect his identity. A London businessman would have no need to keep stopping to look at maps. He would know exactly where he was. He was happy with his new appearance; it was surprising how a simple pair of glasses and a flat tweed cap could change his appearance, adding to the confusion of anyone looking for him.

The Arab continued his walk; watching, ever watching pedestrians, cars, reflections.

He crossed Paddington Green and felt the rain starting to fall gently and he knew this was why there were not too many people on the green. In summer, the grass would be covered by people lapping up the sun and enjoying a bit of quiet peace in the middle of the city. Leaving the green, he turned and walked in the direction of the City of Westminster College that he could see in the distance, a quick look over his shoulder and he could see Hassan keeping his distance but stayed close enough to watch his every move.

Yasmin walked slowly to the end of Edgware Road, stopping occasionally to look in shop windows as any shopper or tourist would. At the bottom of the road, she took her time. Using the pedestrian crossings, she crossed over into Hyde Park to Marble Arch. She had read somewhere that parts of Oliver Cromwell's body had been buried near there. She stopped short of the Arch and taking out her phone took a photo of it and the park in front looking every part the tourist.

Reece and Anna watched Yasmin as she raised her camera. They had spotted her on their third drive pass down Edgware Road. Reece had let the rest of the team and control know that they might have eyes on one of the suspects, the woman. He did not want to do anything yet, until he was certain. Although she fitted the general description and looked like the woman he had seen for a fleeting moment in Malta and on the screenshot security photos, in the light of day and with her wearing a headscarf, he had to be sure. They had parked the car in one of the side streets off Edgware Road, then called for Harrison and Palo to stay mobile close by, in case any of the woman's friends appeared. Reece asked control to get the rest of the team to carry out a block surveillance for now. The team's mobile and on foot would now hang back and cover the routes the target would need to use when moving to another location.

'We can't jump on her yet. Until we confirm her identity, or if her friends are nearby, we hang back,' said Reece into his body mic.

'Understood, will wait for your instructions. But if she tries anything funny you know what to do. I'm moving the troop vans into the area in case you bump into the other two and need back-up,' replied Broad from the control room.

'Understood.' replied Reece.

Reece and Anna started walking on a path that was parallel with Yasmin, never taking their eyes of her, but watching in a way that would look like they were tourists themselves, taking in the bigger picture, rather than focusing on the woman who stood in front of the Arch.

'What do you think that rucksack on her back contains?' asked Anna.

'I think it contains exactly what you think it contains.'

Yasmin turned and walked back in the direction she'd come then crossed the junction into Oxford Street.

'We need to close-up on her. If she takes that bag off her back, we hit her. What's your location Alpha Two?' asked Reece.

'Just turning into Oxford Street from the Circus end heading towards you,' replied Henderson.

'Try and pull in and wait. We are heading towards you.'

'Roger, will do,' came the reply from Henderson.

'I don't like the fact she is moving into a more crowded area. It will be harder to close her down before she tries anything,' said Anna.

'If there is no sign of her friends by the time we reach Steve and Palo, then we will make a decision on whether to move in.'

Reece could see that the woman was taking her time. If she did have a target in mind, she was in no hurry to get there. The woman continued to look in shop windows and crossed Oxford Street twice, before reaching where Henderson and Palo were parked at the top end of Duke Street facing towards Oxford Street. Both men watched the woman cross over keeping to the main shopping street.

'Alpha One, that's her past us. What do you want us to do?' asked Henderson.

'She's going into the West One shopping centre. Stay in the car, we will go in after her,' replied Reece.

Reece had walked through the West One shopping centre in Oxford Street many times. He knew this would be the ideal place for the woman to carry out a suicide attack. Stepping up the pace Reece and Anna entered the centre twenty yards behind the woman. Her walking pace had slowed even further as she continued to investigate shop windows. Reece knew that there was a train link at the back of the centre. *Was she heading there,* he thought?

'Alpha One, I think the woman is the same one I saw in Malta,' said Palo.

'Roger that, I'm ninety-nine per cent sure it's her. She is still playing the part of the tourist shopper, but I'm beginning to think that whatever she's doing, today she's on her own. I don't want a Barcelona incident here, especially as I'm too bloody close to her now.'

'Take her out if there's any doubt.' It was the voice of Jim Broad in his ear. 'I have the Tango team deploying to you if you need them. We don't want a fuck up here and we don't know where the other two are.'

Reece could feel some of the pressure Broad must be under. He could imagine the calls coming down from Downing Street via 'C'.

Reece remembered being under similar pressure when his bosses in his Special Branch days always wanted more. He used to remind them, do you want it done right now, or do you want it done right?

'I know the risks control. Tell Tango to hang back.'

Yasmin had looked in several shop windows before finally appearing to make up her mind. She went into the Starbucks coffee house and joined the small queue at the counter.

'What do we do now?' asked Anna.

Reece watched from across the corridor as the woman ordered coffee and sat down at a table near the window. Reece felt she was using the window as he would, looking for followers.

'I have an idea that might save time and a lot of lives,' replied Reece.

'What do you mean?' asked Anna.

'Stick with me and follow my lead,' said Reece walking across and into the Starbucks.

Anna couldn't believe her eyes but quickly fell in behind Reece.

Reece walked straight over to where the woman was sitting. She was taking off her backpack, placing it on the seat beside her. Reece sat down on one of the two chairs opposite her at the same time pulling his gun out of his pocket and pointing it at the woman under the table. Anna sat in the chair next to him. It took two seconds for the woman to register what had just happened. Her instinct kicked in and she started to reach for the rucksack, but Reece spoke first.

'My gun is pointing directly at you under the table. Don't make any stupid mistakes or it will be your last.'

Yasmin pulled her hand back to rest it on the table. The man's blue eyes were cold, and she realised she'd seen that type of seriousness before in the eyes of the Teacher.

'Who are you. What do you want?' asked Yasmin.

Reece was glad she did not panic or appear nervous. The one thing he did not want was a shoot-out in a packed coffee shop.

'I'm pleased to meet you and to see that you're not stupid. The last time I saw you was in a hotel in Malta,' replied Reece.

Reece saw the moment's surprise in her eyes.

'My question is still the same. Who are you and what do you want?'

'To answer the first part of your question, we work for the British government. As to the second we just want to talk for now. Do you mind if we join you in a coffee?'

Yasmin felt herself nodding even though she just wanted to run. The man never took his eyes away from her and she knew he was not joking when he said he had a gun under the table. She also knew from his eyes that he would kill her despite the many people sitting around them.

'Anna, would you get us three coffees please? I think we might be here for a while.'

When Anna had gone, Reece leant closer so that he could whisper the words directly.

'Do you have a gun and what's in the rucksack?'

Yasmin felt the weight of the gun in her left-hand pocket. For a second, she thought about going for it, but the next thought said *no he'll kill you.*

'I have a gun in my left pocket, and as you seem to know more than you should, there is a bomb in the rucksack.'

'Is it armed?'

'Not yet.'

'When Anna comes back you will hand her the rucksack with your left hand only. She will then sit down beside you and take the gun out of your pocket. Any stupid move and I assure you it will be your last.'

'What is your name?' asked Reece.

'I'll tell you mine if you tell me yours.'

'Joseph,' he replied using the undercover name.

'You can call me Yasmin. Are you Jewish with a name like Joseph?'

'No, I told you we are British.'

Anna returned with the coffee.

'Anna meet Yasmin. She is going to hand you her rucksack with her left hand. There is a bomb in it, she says it's not armed, she also has a gun in her left-hand pocket. When she gives you the rucksack, take it then sit down beside her and remove the gun discreetly from her pocket. Bring both outside and ask control to have the Tango team and ATO to pick them up and check the device asap.'

Yasmin handed over the rucksack and Anna sat beside her and neatly removed the gun, placing it in the rucksack. She left talking into her body mic as she walked back to the shopping centre exit.

'Now we can just enjoy our coffee and have a little chat as friends do. We are friends now aren't we Yasmin.'

Reece had decided to use his training and experience as a recruiter and handler of agents. His instinct was telling him this woman wasn't the dangerous terrorist they'd thought her to be; despite the fact she'd ruthlessly killed a man in a hotel bedroom in Malta. He saw something in her brown eyes that verged on the edge of tears. She took a deep breath and started to speak.

'I couldn't do it. I was awake most of the night and then this morning. I found myself going along with the plan but wanting to scream no, no, no.'

Reece kept quiet allowing her to continue now that she was opening up. He just hoped there would be time for questions and answers that would help find her two friends. Between sips of coffee and deep breaths she continued.

'To tell you the truth Joseph, I was hoping someone would stop me.'

'Why?'

'When I checked out Trafalgar Square and took photos. I was determined to return there today and leave the bomb to kill as many people as possible. But then when we reviewed my photos back at the apartment, I started to have second thoughts as you would say.'

'What apartment, where is it, are there others there now?' it all came out fast when Reece realised the Arab might still be there.

'The apartment on Edgware Road is an upstairs apartment number 137A. There is no one there now they've left to carry out their mission. But, oh my god, they left a bomb which is timed to go off ninety minutes after we left.' Her eyes opened wider as the memory came to her.

'What time did you leave?'

'Eleven.'

Reece looked at his watch the digital display showed 12.05 he grabbed her arm and pulling her to her feet made for the door and the street.

Anna was standing at the opened side door of a white transit. Two heavily armed SAS troopers stood beside her.

'Cuff this woman and get her into the van now,' said Reece to one of the troopers.

'There is a bomb in the apartment ready to go off in twenty minutes. We don't have time for bomb disposal all we can do is clear the streets and buildings.'

Reece jumped into the transit followed by Anna. Talking fast but clearly into his radio he informed control of the address and told them they were on their way with Tango One and one prisoner. Reece told the transit driver to get to the Edgware Road fast.

Anna held up the device they'd taken from Yasmin.

'What should we do with this?' she asked.

'It will only work if you press the blue button to start the phone, then press the red, it will explode two hours later,' said Yasmin.

Reece took the device and handed it to one of the troopers.

'There will be a bomb disposal team on the way to where we are going, give it to them. Tell them what you just heard about arming it but also tell them to trust nothing.'

The trooper nodded, took the device, and placed it inside the rucksack.

The transit driver had switched on the two-tone sirens and flashing lights while weaving the way through the city traffic. Turning into Edgware Road, Reece could see at least four police cars and two police motorcycles all with their blue flashing lights parked across the road barring the traffic from both directions. Police officers, some armed, were shouting at the startled pedestrians and herding people out of shops and buildings away from the area surrounding 137A. Reece was impressed at the speed they were closing the road.

'Have you the keys?' Reece asked Yasmin.

'No, I left them in the apartment. We were not returning.'

'Anna, you stay here with our friend. Two of you come with me,' said Reece pulling on the police baseball cap.

Reece had intended trying to break down the door. After that with fifteen minutes to go, he didn't have a clue. As they moved towards the building, a man in civilian clothing ran towards them from the opposite direction waving his hands in the air stopping Reece and the two SAS soldiers in their tracks.

'Stop, stop where are you going?' the stranger called loudly.

'Who are you?' asked Reece stopping outside the door with 137A written on it.

'I'm Felix,' replied the man.

Reece knew that Felix was the code name given to the bomb disposal officers or ATO Ammunition Technical Officer. When Reece had worked in Northern Ireland, he knew the code name Felix was because they were named after the cat with nine lives. He knew that once Felix was on the scene of a suspected device the rules were that he was in charge and must be obeyed. As a bomb disposal officer once told Reece when he was just a young police constable in Belfast and was sealing off the street because of a suspect package in a building, 'I get paid to do this you don't.' Another he met when dealing with an abandoned car bomb told him, 'I'm a bomb disposal officer. If you see me running, try to catch-up.'

Reece had great respect for these men and women who, no matter what the equipment they had, always had to take that last walk right up to the device to declare it safe. He knew the danger of any device being booby-trapped was one of the greatest dangers any ATO faced.

'I'm David Reece, Security Services. We've been told there is a device in the upstairs apartment in this building ready to go off in less than twelve minutes.'

'Is there anyone up there now?'

'We don't think so.'

'Well then, Mister Reece, if that's the case all we can do here is clear the street and buildings of people and sit back and wait for those twelve minutes to tick down. I suggest you and your team get back to your vehicle and park a bit further down the road.'

'In that case we have another device and the lady who was carrying it in the back of that transit. Perhaps you could use your time to look at it for me?'

'I will, now let us get away from this building.'

'You're the boss.' said Reece and turning on his heels with the two SAS men ran back to the transit. He was sure he could hear Felix shouting from behind him, 'You better believe it.'

Felix took the device out of the rucksack and having asked Yasmin once more how she was to set it, carried it further down the road, where he sat down on his own and spent five minutes inspecting it from every angle. From where he stood Reece could see that the ATO had a small penknife which he used to gently pry open the lid of the device, then he appeared to remove or cut something away before placing the lid back on and standing, walked back to the transit.

'I've seen this type of device before when I worked with the army in Afghanistan. One button, as the lady said, switches on the phone and the second usually sets a timer in motion counting down to detonation. But young lady,' He spoke to Yasmin while holding up the disabled device, 'in the case of your bomb, this one was set to go off as soon as you pressed the red button, and these little items are four-inch nails, combined with the Semtex there wouldn't be much of you left.'

'Oh no!' gasped Yasmin.

'Yes, young lady. Whoever gave you this bomb expected it to explode immediately, making you a suicide bomber. If you even know what that means.'

Reece saw that Yasmin was shocked at hearing these words, her eyes were wide and full of tears, and he thought, *fear*.

'Now, Mister Reece, if you're right we have two minutes left before the device in that apartment explodes, so if I could suggest you make sure everyone has taken cover before then and that the fire service is ready to go in to preserve as much evidence as they can. I'll get back to my own people before then.'

Felix then walked slowly back to his own green transit and Reece could see him waving his arms as he shouted for people to take cover.

Reece gave Broad a quick update over the radio and had just finished and was taking his place beside Anna and the rest of the transit passengers at the back of the vehicle when the bomb exploded. The blast was just as Reece remembered from his days in Northern Ireland the bright flash, followed by the loud low boom of the explosives detonating followed by the noise of flying debris and breaking concrete and glass tumbling to the earth from the sky. Then came the smoke followed by the smell and finally the flames starting to lick the outside of the broken windows. As the bomb was small and inside the building when it detonated, the flying debris had not travelled too far and fell well within the cordon perimeter reducing the danger to those taking cover. Reece slowly lifted his head to watch the flames start to take hold. He knew the fire service would wait at least five minutes to allow time for a secondary device to go off before they would approach the building, working from the outside to deal with the flames. By the look of things, no one was hurt and the agencies working in harmony with each other had reduced the chances of anyone getting injured. Reece was already thinking ahead. The Arab and his friend were still out there. If they had access to the Internet on their phones, it wouldn't be long before they heard about the blast. Reece hoped the news would please them and keep them thinking they were on track to finish their operation. Turning to Yasmin, he grabbed her by the arm.

'Now Yasmin. You know that your friend the Arab was happy to see you go up the same way as that building.'

The tears started to roll down her cheeks.

'No time for tears, many more people will be crying if we don't stop these people. They've shown they're no friends of yours. The Arab was happy to see you die, and he would have told everybody you're a martyr, now tell me where they are?'

Yasmin had been sobbing with her head down but at these words she lifted her head her eyes that were angry now, looking directly into the eyes of Reece.

'I don't know exactly where they are. They left by the back door when I left. All I know is they're going to Canary Wharf.'

'Do they have the bomb with them?'

'Yes, and the plutonium.'

For the first time Reece noticed that Steve Harrison and Palo had arrived and were talking to Anna.

'Steve says you need to talk to Matthew at control. With the explosion going off our radio mics were down for a few minutes,' said Anna.

Reece spoke into his body mic.

'Control, this is Alpha One, you have something for me?'

The voice of Matthew Simons came back.

'Roger Alpha One. We have had a couple of updates from GCHQ. Our friends have sent a video to Tehran which will go out when they complete their mission. We were able to confirm the end user as the Iranian Quads General so everything on for today. It then appears that the mobile phone this end has been switched off so we can't track it.'

Reece felt like saying, *no shit Sherlock,* but kept his thoughts to himself for now.

'Understood. The people here have things in hand, luckily no one hurt just some damage. The only problem is that the city will go into lockdown and the Tube will stop running. We need to get to Canary Wharf fast, so I need a chopper right now.'

It was Jim Broad's voice that came back this time.

'You're right about the lockdown Alpha One. The emergency Cobra meeting is already under way in Whitehall, and they're working to the book with boots on the ground and transport being brought to a standstill. The weather has cleared slightly meaning we only have one helicopter in the sky, just taken off from the city airport. I can get it to where you want it, but there'll be plenty of people on the ground at Canary Wharf so you could stay where you are and let them deal with it.'

'This fucker has got away before. Canary Wharf is a busy place, and we have the woman, we can use her to help us spot him.'

'OK, I can get you a Gazelle, where do you want it?'

Reece had flown in the RAF Gazelle helicopter many times, but he knew it only had five seats, the pilot and a spotter up front and three passengers.

'We can get to the top end of Hyde Park near to Marble Arch.'

'Leave it with me it will be there in fifteen minutes.'

'We will be there, and can you make sure there is an ATO at Canary Wharf, I have a feeling we are going to need one. The one here is following up on the bomb that has just gone off making sure there are no other devices. No matter what this woman tells us I don't trust the Arab and I don't trust her.'

'Roger will do,' replied Broad.

Reece turned to the others who were all hearing the conversation over their own radios. Yasmin was sitting in the back of the transit her hands tied with plastic cuffs.

'Steve and Palo go with the troop and use their sirens and lights to get across London as quickly as you can to Canary Wharf. I'll take Anna and Yasmin in the chopper and will be there before you. We will use Yasmin to help us identify the Arab and his friend, hopefully you will get there in time to take them out, if not, we will have to stop them on our own. Geoff Middleton already has an SAS team there. The more people we have the better.'

Reece leant in the door of the transit.

'Yasmin, you're coming with me.'

Chapter 31

The Arab and Hassan had continued their journey with Hassan walking a few yards behind the Arab. Outside the City of Westminster College, they had taken a taxi to Baker Street station, where once again, they separated before entering the station and the CCTV camera coverage. Keeping a distance between them, they had taken a Tube train on the Jubilee Line to Canary Wharf. The journey of almost one hour, brought them into the station at 12.30 just as the bomb had gone off at the apartment. They left the station and, with Hassan still behind, crossed over the road disappearing into the crowds of workers and tourists that filled the streets and walkways of Canary Wharf.

The Arab decided to use the next half hour to check out possible locations to leave the device, look for security surveillance, both people and cameras.

He crossed over Upper Bank Street and walked past the large building that was the home of Citibank UK then turned left and walked along the South Colonnade to the iconic skyscraper that was One Canada Square. He crossed over the square passing the Canary Wharf DLR Station and on into the shopping centre at Cabot Square.

The square was named after John Cabot and his son Sebastian, Italian explorers who had settled in England in 1484. He had read on the Internet that Cabot Square is one of the largest in Canary Wharf. Passing the large fountain in the centre he knew that the inner perimeter had more fountains and was surrounded by trees, which would make it more difficult for observation via CCTV. What made it more interesting for the Arab was he knew there was a large car park under the square with glass ventilation holes to allow the car exhaust gasses to escape. He stopped by one of the fountains and sat down on the park bench. Turning he waved for Hassan to join him.

'We have made good time my child. Now it is time to complete our mission. I've not seen any of the enemy.'

Hassan looked around him. The rain had stayed away and now there seemed to be hundreds of people walking about. It would be almost impossible to spot surveillance in this crowd.

'Where have all these people come from?' he asked.

'You have to remember my child this is the very heart of the financial district of London. All these tall buildings hold thousands of offices and employees working there. It's lunchtime now and they walk about looking for their coffee lounges and restaurants. Our target is not just these buildings and banks but the very people who work in them, the same people and banks that have financed the killing of our women and children.'

'What about the Princess. When will she arrive?'

'According to our friend in the Embassy, she will be here at three, just around the same time we will send them a message from Allah they will never forget.'

Just then the roar of a low flying helicopter brought their eyes to the sky. The machine was flying low and appeared to be coming down to land somewhere nearby.

'Maybe the enemy is awake. We should find cover and set the timer. Follow me,' said the Arab.

Reece, Anna, and Yasmin had kept their heads down when they boarded the French Aerospatiale Gazelle helicopter when it had landed in Hyde Park, not far from Marble Arch. Reece could still hear many sirens above the noise made by the fast-whirling blades as they sped through the city, placing important areas into lockdown and the troop transit was now on its way to Canary Wharf. Strapping themselves in behind the two crewmen, Anna and Reece took the outside seats with Yasmin in the middle. Within seconds the machine took off and turned towards the Thames to follow the winding river towards the Isle of Dogs or as Reece knew it Canary Wharf. Looking at his watch he saw that it was almost 1 pm. Talking into the mic on the headphones they were all wearing, Reece decided to use the time to ask Yasmin more questions.

'Yasmin, can you hear me?' he asked above the noise of the aircraft. She nodded.

'What is the plan. What are they going to do now?'

Her voice when it came sounded weak and the radio static did not help.

'I only know they have a device like mine. They intend to set the timing switch at one to have the bomb go off at three, when they hope to be far away.'

'Where will they place the device?' asked Reece.

'I don't know.'

'You must know, you must have heard them talk about things and what they're going to do.' He could see her lip drop and the tears start to well up once more, but he couldn't be sympathetic. The helicopter banked to the right, and he could see that they were getting lower almost touching the rooftops of buildings.

'OK, tell me why Canary Wharf?'

'All the Teacher said was that they were going to deal a blow to the financial system in the West. He also said that a Princess would be there about the same time.'

Reece knew she was trying to be helpful. He had seen the same in many agents he had turned in the past who wanted to change their lives. Only in this case he believed it was too late for her, she'd gone too far down the rabbit hole.

'So, the device is the same as the one you had?'

Again, he could see from her expression she was thinking and wanted to tell him everything she knew.

'It's different. The Teacher placed sticks of plutonium in the bag with the device. He said it would disperse into the air with the explosion, that was the reason the timer was set to give them plenty of time to get to safety.'

'Where will they go?'

'All he said was that we were all to get transport to Bristol and book into any hotel there, where we could link up later.'

Reece could feel that the pilot was pulling slightly back on the controls, and they were slowing down getting ready to land. He looked out of the window and could see a large, grassed square between the skyscrapers and people in military and police uniforms pushing the public back to clear the landing area. Within a minute they were on the ground and opening the doors. Two men in military uniform ran up to Reece as he stepped down from his side of the aircraft, while Anna, took Yasmin out of the other side, her hands still tied with plastic cuffs. All three kept their heads down and moved out of range of the turning blades allowing the aircraft to lift vertically into the grey sky once more. As the noise died down Reece could see that one of the military men was Geoff Middleton.

'Good to see you David and you have one of our friends with you.'

'I'm sure you mean Yasmin here and not Anna.' Reece smiled.

'Correct, although I'm glad to see Anna,' he replied smiling at Anna as she approached holding Yasmin's arm.

'Where are we here? Any sightings of our friends?'

'No sighting yet, but we have this part pretty much tied down between ourselves and the police. The Princess is opening offices in One Canada Square at three and we've been told she refuses to change her plans.'

Reece brought up a google map on his phone. The location arrow showed they'd landed in Jubilee Place.

'This is a big area; we are a bit far from One Canada Square. When we were coming in, I could see there was many people about. That might be a problem when it comes to spotting our friends. Yasmin has told me they're probably already here. We do not know the exact target, but we do know if they're on schedule, they're setting a two-hour timer at 1pm on the device which is connected to the plutonium to give them time to get well away before it goes off. That is one of the reasons I brought Yasmin along, she knows them and if she spots them, then we have a chance.'

'There is a communications van in One Canada Square. I've been in it, and you wouldn't believe the radio and surveillance equipment it has. I would get over there if I were you, they might be able to help her spot our friends on the CCTV. I have our transit on the road it can get us there quickly.'

Reece looked at his watch as he jogged to the transit alongside Middleton and the trooper followed by Anna and Yasmin, the digital display showed 12.55.

'If they're here already, then we have five minutes before they set the timer running.'

Three minutes later Reece, Yasmin and Anna were in the back of the large HGV size communications van. Middleton wasn't exaggerating when he said it was well equipped.

Reece immediately recognised one of the two men sitting in front of the monitors.

'Jonesy, what are you doing here?' He had last seen Constable Jones doing the same job in the command room at the Conservative Conference in Manchester when the SG9 team had tracked down a terrorist squad and prevented the assassination of the Prime Minister. Then Jonesy as Reece had called him was doing the same job monitoring screens trying to identify suspects.

'Hello, Mister Reece. I decided the Gold Commander in Manchester was such a dickhead I just had to get away. London called and here I am.

'Great to have you on-board Jonesy. I presume you're up to date with who we are looking for?'

'Yes, sir. We have been looking and using facial recognition but so far nothing. There is a lot of people about so fingers crossed.'

'Everything crossed Jonesy and I'm not a Sir just call me David and as you're probably linked into our comms, Alpha One as well.'

Reece was looking over Jonesy's' shoulder at the screens and could see the problem. He suspected the crowds not only included shoppers, tourists, and workers but the extra people drawn to the prospect of seeing the Princess Royal.

'Tell me Jonesy does any of these screens do a playback showing say the last half hour of footage?'

'Yes, the one in the corner can do that and it can be divided into a four-square screen showing different angles and footage.'

'Can you get in front of it and run it through for us?'

'No problem,' said Jones, moving chairs and manoeuvring the mouse on the pad to show the four screens on the monitor. He typed on the keyboard and Reece could see all four screens flicker as the timers in the corner showed 12.30. Jones pressed another button and the screens started to run their pictures at normal speed.

Reece pulled two chairs and placed them behind Jones he pointed for Yasmin to sit in one while he sat in the other; Anna stood behind them. They were watching the screens over Jones' shoulder and Reece noticed each camera view on the screen was also imprinted with the name of the area it was covering, One Canada Square, Cabot Square, Churchill Place, and Columbus Courtyard. Reece looked at his watch again, 13.00. If the Arab was on schedule, he had just armed the bomb and started the countdown.

Chapter 32

The helicopter had passed over the square and by the sound of its engine the Arab knew it was preparing to land. The noise in the distance died down as both men walked through the doors into the Cabot Square shopping center. The Arab once more walked in front of Hassan. Leading the way, he could see a lift ahead and a sign which showed the types of shops on the upper floors, but he wasn't interested in the shops. Looking at the bottom of the sign he could see a downward pointing arrow and the words 'Underground Carpark'.

He pressed the lift button and waited with Hassan standing behind him. Both men entered the lift when it came, and the Arab pressed the button for the car park. They were the only two in the lift. The Arab turned to look into the eyes of his student.

'Now my son, I will not be getting out with you. The mission is now in your hands. Find a place under the air vents in the car park, set the timers and leave. I will meet you in Bristol or Tehran. Allah bless you and be with you this day.'

'Thank you, Teacher, Allah akbar.'

'Allah akbar.' replied the Arab as the lift doors opened.

As Hassan left the lift as two men got in to join the Arab on the upward journey to the first floor of the centre. Looking at his watch he noted that it was almost one o'clock. He put his hand in his pocket and wrapped it around the gun, he knew this was the time of most danger.

'You said your name is Joseph,' said Yasmin who had been listening to the conversation between Reece and Jones.

'I have many names and many faces Yasmin, a bit like your teacher. Now I want you to concentrate on these screens. Find your friends and maybe this day will end a little better for all of us.'

Yasmin leant closer to look at the screens, taking her eyes away from Reece, she had seen something similar in his eyes to the Teacher's, now she realised what it was, death.

'I'm going for a walk around the square,' said Anna.

As she was leaving the van Reece called on her to not go too far.

The phone in his pocket buzzed and Reece could see from the screen it was Broad calling.

'Yes boss,' he replied.

'Anything David? Everyone is getting a bit jittery now we've passed the one mark?'

'It's a bit jittery here too. We have hundreds of eyes looking and now our lady friend at the camera for the last thirty minutes footage. We are doing everything we can. I can assure you I would rather be somewhere else right now.'

'I know David. I'll keep out of your hair and let you get on with it. But let me know when you have something positive I can pass upstairs.'

'Will do.' Reece put the phone back in his pocket.

'David I might have something here.' It was Jones.

'What have you got?' Asked Reece, looking at the screen over the Constable's shoulder.

Using the cursor, Jones pointed at a man walking away from the shopping centre. He zoomed in and the man in an overcoat and wearing glasses looked familiar.

'Yasmin come here quickly!' called Reece.

Standing beside Reece she looked at the man being followed by the camera.

'Can you get closer?' she asked.

Using the mouse Jones zoomed in on the man's face just before he walked into the centre of the square and disappeared into the cover of the trees surrounding the park.

'I think it's him, but he is wearing glasses, it's hard to say.'

'The Teacher?' asked Reece.

'Yes,' she replied.

'Keep eyes on the exits from the park area Jonesy and inform control I'm going after him and to get people to the shopping centre and park. Yasmin, you're coming with me.' Reece grabbed her arm and opened the door.

Reece with Yasmin trying to keep up walked at a fast pace and pulled her along with him heading in the direction of Cabot Square.

It took nearly five minutes for him to reach the square. A five minutes which meant the Arab could be anywhere. In the distance he could see armed police and men in military dress starting to seal off the park exits. It was then that Reece felt Yasmin try to pull back on the grip Reece had on her arm. Turning to look at her he could see the look of shock and fear in her eyes as she looked over his shoulder in the direction they'd been walking. Reece knew instinctively there was danger and turning he saw the man in the overcoat and thick rimmed glasses ten yards in front of him. The man had stopped walking. Reece knew by his reaction that he had recognised Yasmin the same time she'd recognised him.

How is she still alive, and who is the man with her? he thought just before the realisation sunk in.

'It's him, it's the Teacher,' screamed Yasmin pointing.

The Arab was quick. He pulled the gun from his pocket and fired three times. Reece tried to pull Yasmin to the ground, but he heard her cry out and he felt the warm spray of her blood on his cheek as the bullet hit her. He pulled out his own gun as he hit the ground and rolled over once as rounds hit the concrete close to his head; he rose to his knee and taking aim, he fired double tap as he was trained. He could see one round impact the man's shoulder and spin him round. The man started to run. This time Reece took careful aim, controlled his breathing, and fired. The round hit the man squarely between the shoulder blades. He staggered for a few steps then fell, first to his knees then face down on the ground. It was only then that Reece realised there were people stood staring, some were screaming, some their phones already filming, him, then some running and Yasmin lying still. Anna came running up with her gun drawn.

'Are you OK?' she asked.

'Yes! See to Yasmin.' Reece shouted as he ran to where the man was lying face down, his blood, a small stream staining the pavement. As he got close to the man, he could see he was still breathing. Reece pointed his gun at the man's back, then he saw the man's fingers tighten on the grip around his gun. Reece fired twice more from the Smith and Wesson into the man's back, the 9 mm parabellum steel jacket rounds causing his body to rise in spasm, before he let out a loud groan, the last rattle of dying breath, letting the grip on the gun ease before it fell from his hand.

Reece remembered his special firearms training. Never take it for granted they're dead until they are dead.

Bending slightly, he placed his foot under the man's body and rolled him over. The glasses he had worn had fallen off his face, and although his eyes were closed Reece was able to reassure himself it was the Arab. More armed police started to appear, and Reece realised he still had his own gun in his hand and the police baseball cap was still in his pocket. Kneeling beside the man's body he quickly exchanged both, his own gun to his pocket and the baseball hat to his head.

'Security Service,' Reece shouted towards the arriving officers who now surrounded the small area where the shooting had taken place, their automatic rifles pointing in his direction.

'Alpha One to control. Get a couple of ambulances to my location two people down neither of them friendlies.' Reece knew ambulances were not much use for dead bodies, but he wanted the scene tied down with as many emergency services as he could get, to move the crowd of curious watchers and their cameras.

'Roger, Alpha One, on the way. Update when you can.' It was the voice of Matthew Simons who would appreciate that Reece would be too busy to give a running commentary right now.

Turning to one of the police officers who seemed to be in charge, he told him that the ambulance was on its way and to seal off the immediate area and to start moving the crowd of onlookers away and if possible, seize their phones.

'And while you're at it, cuff this man, he's dead, but I still don't trust him.' He said pointing at the Arab who he could see was bleeding out fast, the pool of blood now flowing quickly into a drain beside the path. He ran back to where Anna was kneeling beside Yasmin.

'I'm sorry David, she's dead.'

Yasmin was lying on her back. Reece could see the ragged hole in her coat exactly where her heart would be, at least it had been quick but despite this he felt her death was such a waste.

'You're bleeding, David,' said Anna pointing at his cheek.

'No, it's Yasmin's,' he replied wiping his hand across his face.

He spoke into his radio mic. 'Control, can you get Alpha Two here to take control of the scene? Targets One and Three are dead.'

'Roger. They're on their way. Should be there soon.'

'Good, we will get back to the Cabot Square shopping centre. We still need to find Target Two and the device, we are running out of time. Get the comms van to keep looking at the playback on the CCTV to see where Target Two might have gone.'

'Roger understood. Units are sealing off the centre as we speak,' replied Simons.

Turning once more to the police officer Reece pointed to the Arab.

'Keep a close eye on him. Our people will be here shortly to take control.'

'Understood,' replied the officer.

'Anna come with me now,' shouted Reece over his shoulder as he ran towards Cabot Square and hopefully the third terrorist.

Chapter 33

Jim Broad had been standing behind Simons in the operation room listening to the ongoing communications from Reece. Simons was passing on the request from Reece to the communication van. Things were moving fast he thought: the end game not far off. He picked up the phone and spoke with Sir Ian Fraser who was now in the Cobra Room in Whitehall with the PM, Sir Martin Bryant, and the head of MI5 Caroline Aspinall. They had been listening in through the communications panels in what was effectively the government equivalent of the American situation room in the White House.

'I take it you've heard everything Sir Ian?' asked Broad.

'Yes Jim, thank you. We are also linked into the area CCTV and communications. At this moment I can see Reece and Anna running towards Cabot Square.'

Broad looked at their own screens and he could see the same feed.

'Can I suggest, in the light of what has happened, and given the time scale, there is at least one more terrorist out there. He's close and most likely has the device with him, given the current time he has probably started the countdown. I'm not happy that one of the Royal family and her security detail are going to arrive slap bang into what is a fast-flowing scenario. Can we not stop her?' asked Broad.

There was a pause and Broad could hear mumbled voices in the earpiece.

'Jim. The PM is currently on the phone to the Palace bringing them up to date with what is happening. Now, the Palace wants to go ahead with the visit but only on the understanding that the issue will be dealt with before they set out to drive to One Canada Square. Realistically if we've made no progress in the next thirty minutes bringing us to two o'clock, then the Prime Minister will have to order the evacuation of Canary Wharf. It is a massive area and thousands of people. I don't believe we could get everyone out by 3 pm. Your priority now Jim is to find the third terrorist and, more importantly the device, and eliminate the threat from both.'

'Understood,' said Broad as the line went dead.

'Matthew, we need to know where this guy is and fast. Anything, anything at all get it to Reece.'

Simons knew the pressure was on, and they were all under scrutiny. Not only were thousands of people and the country's economy on the line, but the very survival of SG9.

As Reece and Anna reached the trees and the park at Cabot Square, he could hear Jonesy's voice in his earpiece.

'Alpha One, come in, over.'

Reece slowed to a stop taking a few seconds to catch his breath.

'Go ahead Jonesy,' replied Reece.

'I've been looking at the feedback from earlier and I can see both men from the time they were together until they enter the Cabot Square shopping centre. The man with the glasses walking slightly in front of the younger man. I'm currently trying to get access to the CCTV inside the centre to see where they went. I've looked at the pictures from then. As far as I can see only the man with the glasses has left the centre so by the look of things the younger man is still in there.'

'Great work Jonesy. Can you capture a headshot of the younger man and send it to me?'

'As you speak, sending now,' came the reply.

'Thanks, Jonesy I'm going to cross the park and enter the centre. As well as trying to find this man's movements, can you also try to find where he is now?'

'Ahead of you. No sign of him currently but hope to have info of where he went shortly.'

'Thank you, Jonesy. Control, we are going into the centre. Please have uniform seal off entrances to prevent anyone going in and check people coming out and let them know we are on the ground inside the centre.'

'Roger Alpha One, on it,' replied Simons.

Reece and Anna continued to walk across the park and then into the centre. The time on his watch showed 13.40.

The shopping centre was crowded with lunchtime shoppers, many of them queuing up at fast food take-aways and filling up the restaurants. Reece took off his police baseball cap. No sense in giving the third terrorist any early identification of himself and Anna. Surprise, in any operation, was important. The faces of the many people around them seemed to swamp them. Reece felt it was like trying to find that needle in the haystack.

It was Anna who spotted Hassan first. He had just come out of a lift about fifty yards in front of them and was walking towards them. He was still wearing the black and white check shemagh; the same as the one in the most recent photo sent by Jonesy.

'David, I think that's him, just coming out of the lift straight ahead,' she said coming close enough to Reece to whisper in his ear.

Reece pulled Anna in front of him her back now to Target Two. Reece looked slightly over her shoulder and could see him walking towards them. Reece was pretending to talk to Anna as two friends might talk, up close and indifferent to the world around them. He whispered in Anna's ear.

'I've just realised that we need to take him alive. He is probably the only person who knows where the device is. When he gets close, stand in front of him as if you're going to ask a question.'

Hassan had felt relieved when he had completed his task. The buttons had been pressed, the countdown had begun, now to keep moving and find his way to the nearest train station to take him to Bristol. He was thinking what the evening's news would be like, the word of his mission being flashed around the world. An attractive woman was standing in front of him asking something about Boots chemist. The next voice he heard was a man speaking into his ear from behind. At the same time, he could feel something cold and hard pressed into his neck.

'Hassan don't make any sudden moves, or I'll blow your head off.' said Reece quietly.

Hassan thought for a split second to pull the gun from his pocket. His hand had been holding it tightly since he left the lift. The woman changed his mind moving closer she pushed a gun into his stomach reading his thoughts.

'Now don't be a naughty boy Hassan,' she said as she pulled his arm backwards and with a quick movement took the gun out of his pocket and placed it into her own.

Reece was impressed at how fast Anna had moved. No one had noticed how quickly and quietly this danger had been removed from their midst as they went about their daily lives.

'Now Hassan let's move quietly outside I have a few questions for you,' said Reece moving the barrel of his gun downwards to press it into the man's side. Gripping him with his other hand Reece moved Hassan towards the exit while Anna walked on his other side.

Being so close, Reece could smell the fear in Hassan as small beads of sweat trickled down the back of his neck. Maybe this was one terrorist who wasn't too sure about wanting to die for Allah.

Outside the exit armed police were stopping shoppers from entering the building. Reece could see the SAS transit with Middleton standing beside it and he guided Hassan towards it.

'Captain, can you get this man cuffed and place him in the back of the transit? I'll update control and start to get this place cleared.'

'No problem,' said Middleton pointing his MP5 at Hassan. 'Right this way sir.' One of his men quickly pulled Hassan's hands behind his back then searched him before placing him in the back of the vehicle. The only items on him were a mobile phone, a wallet with a bank card, pound notes, and a passport.

Reece quickly briefed Broad in the control room.

'He was coming out of the lift. When he went into the centre, he had a rucksack with him but now he hasn't so it's still in there somewhere with the device in it. Can you order the centre to be evacuated while we try to find it and get Felix here asap?'

Broad's voice came back. 'Will order the evacuation right away. That's a big place to search in time. As for Felix we only have one available and he is trying to get to you through heavy traffic after clearing up on Edgware Road, so it will be cutting it fine for him to reach you. At least we have some good news. The Princess Royal has decided to postpone her opening and stay at home for today. Do what you can but be careful David.'

'Oh great. I was always told to stay away from bombs. I'll have a word with our friend here and see what he can tell us.'

Anna was already in the transit and Reece sat beside her to face Hassan. The terrorist stared back at both his dark brown eyes filled with hatred and thought Reece, a little fear. Reece decided to take it slowly even though the clock was running down.

'Hassan. As you already know we do not have much time so do not fuck around with me. Your two friends are dead.'

Reece could see the change in the man's expression and the look of surprise in his eyes, but no reply.

'To tell you the truth, I'm surprised to see you alive. I bet you didn't know that your friend the Teacher had given Yasmin a suicide bomb to go off when she pressed the button on the phone timer.'

Again, the surprise in the man's eyes.

'We know you and the Teacher went into the shopping centre together and you had the rucksack with you. He left on his own, leaving you to finish placing the bomb and setting the timer. Now we can sit here until it goes off meaning we all die, or you can tell me where it is and stop this madness.'

Hassan continued to stare back but saying nothing. Reece decided to change tack.

'Alright Hassan, if you're not willing to talk we can clear this whole area, and no one will get hurt but as you know the plutonium will damage not just this country's, economy but the world's economies for many years to come. If you think it through that will bring great hardship to the many countries in the Middle East including yours. Families will suffer, many of them will starve, and all because you thought it a clever thing to do. I don't think you realise how much you've been used by your friends in the Jihad.'

'That's why it's called a Holy War, because in war people die and if the people who die are true to Allah, then they'll enter paradise to be with him,' said Hassan.

'That's funny. Because when we stopped you in the shopping centre you could have been in paradise already, but you decided not to. Do you think you're not good enough?' asked Anna.

Hassan looked at the woman but said nothing. Reece knew from experience they were getting nowhere fast.

'OK Hassan. We will go and search for the bomb without your help. I know it's supposed to go off in one hour. If we do not find it in thirty minutes, I'll pull everyone out of here, chain you to a pillar and let you count down the minutes to your meeting with your teacher in paradise.'

Again, no reply.

Reece and Anna left Hassan in the care of Middleton and his men and returned to the entrance to the shopping centre.

'We need get as many people in there as possible to find this thing,' said Reece.

'David this is Jonesy. Come in over.'

'What have you got Jonesy?' Reece replied.

'I have the two men on CCTV taking the lift down to the car park level. The man with the glasses stayed in the lift, came back up and left the centre. The one with the shemagh and rucksack got out. I then have shemagh man with no rucksack getting out of the lift twenty minutes later, just before you jumped him.'

'He didn't get out anywhere else other than the car park. You are sure, Jonesy?' asked Reece.

'Yes, I'm sure, down to the car park and return to the same floor.'

'Thanks, Jonesy that's helpful,' replied Reece.

Reece called to the police officer who seemed to oversee the evacuation.

'Chief Inspector can some of your officers search this floor and the upper levels, they should look for an abandoned rucksack. If they find it, they are not to touch it. Bomb Disposal are on their way, and they'll deal with it. Can you let me have two of your men to help us search the car park level?'

'No problem, understood.' Replied the Chief Inspector as he returned to his people, Reece was pleased to see he was the kind of officer who got things done without question.

'I guess the car park will be down to us, are you up for it?' asked Reece.

'That's why I'm still here,' replied Anna.

They took the lift to the underground car park accompanied by two uniformed police officers.

There were more cars than Reece expected, but they all seemed to be here on one level. Reece asked the officers to cover the area to his left and Anna to search to his right. He would take the central isles.

'Don't forget our man was down here for no more than twenty minutes he's fit enough to use the stairs, so that's why I've asked for the upper floors to be searched, not only for the rucksack, but for anyone still stupid enough to have ignored the evacuation call.' They had been searching for ten minutes. Reece knew that Hassan wouldn't have left the rucksack under a car or anywhere else it could easily be spotted. It was then he saw the large cabinet containing the emergency fire hose attached to the wall at the end of the aisle. He moved closer taking his time to check the outer door of the cabinet. He could see the wood where the door lock had been damaged. Someone had prised it open with something sharp. It could have been damaged by vandals, but Reece didn't believe in coincidence. He carefully pulled the door open and there squeezed below the curled firehose was the rucksack.

'All right, everybody stop. I think I've found what we are looking for,' shouted Reece.

Turning to the police officers he told them to return to the main entrance and tell the Chief Inspector to move his cordon further from the building. The officers quickly left using the stairs. *'Smart',* thought Reece if this thing goes off the lift could be a death trap.

Anna had joined Reece and looking over his shoulder she blew the air slowly from her lungs through pursed lips.

'I don't know about you, but I don't like being too close to these things,' said Anna.

'I know what you mean. I thought my days of being this close were long over.'

'What are we going to do now?' asked Anna.

'We can't use our phones or radios they might trigger the thing. But it will only pick up transmissions over a short distance so we should be OK upstairs. The last time I spoke to control they said Felix was stuck in traffic. If we are to believe Yasmin, we should still have around one hour before this thing detonates but we can't trust these bastards especially the Arab. He was willing to make Yasmin a suicide bomber without her permission. He left Hassan to plant it and again he made sure he would be out of the way when Hassan pressed the button. I have no choice; I must check it out, at least that way I can give Felix the best information possible allowing him to deal with this thing quickly. You get out of here, no sense in both of us taking the risk.'

'No chance, David. I've been with this all the way from Malta to the back streets of London to here. A young woman died in my arms today, I'm not going to see you die as well. You might need someone here, right now I'm the only one.'

Reece knew by her voice this was an argument he wouldn't win.

'It's your funeral.'

'I hope not.' She smiled.

Reece slowly and gently pulled the rucksack out from under the fire hose. Turning he placed it on the ground and knelt on one knee beside it. He could feel rather than see Anna's eyes looking over his shoulder. Again, taking his time he pulled back the zip on the top of the rucksack. He switched on the torch on his mobile phone and pointed it into the rucksack. He hoped no one wanted to call him right now, either way he wouldn't answer it.

He could see a square plastic Tupperware box with a mobile type of phone on top. The clock on the phone screen was counting down in large letters 57 minutes 32, 31, 30 seconds and on. The box was covered with what looked like packing tape that was holding three dark tubes, Reece assumed was the plutonium.

'Well, here goes nothing,' said Reece as he steadied his balance and took hold of both ends of the box and lifted it clear of the bag, carefully setting it down on the floor beside him before standing and stepping back beside Anna, he looked around him.

'These bastards are clever,' said Reece pointing to the air vents in the ceiling.

'That humming noise you hear is the air vents to take the car fumes away from the car park and up into the air outside. If this bomb goes off the plutonium would get into the water system through the hose while the air vents would spread it twice as fast and twice as far, God knows how far. I need to separate that plutonium from the box and get it out of here. The bomb can then be dealt with by Felix if he gets here on time, if not, bomb damage can be repaired but not if it goes off with the plutonium. We have about fifty-five minutes, and I need something sharp to cut the tape around the box to release the plutonium.'

'I said you would need me,' said Anna pulling a small flick knife from her shoulder bag.

'You wouldn't happen to have the bomb disposal manual in there as well,' said Reece taking the knife.

He knelt beside the container taking a firm grip of the tape with his left hand, with his right he slipped the knife under the tape and pulled upwards. The knife was sharp and cut easily through the tape. Reece handed the knife back to Anna and gently began to roll the tape back from the foot-long tubes at the side of the box. When the tape was free of the box, he lifted the tubes and placed them inside the rucksack. As he placed the last one in the weight and pressure of the tubes on the box was removed. At that moment Reece could see the numbers on the phone start to run down at a much faster speed as the minutes became seconds 30, 29, 28, 27. Reece picked up the rucksack and shouted to Anna.

'It's booby-trapped run, run!'

He did not have to tell her twice with Anna in front they ran to the door that led to the stairs.

Both made it through the door and Reece had slammed it behind him when he felt a powerful rush of air, heard the noise of the blast and he felt as if a giant hand was pushing him through the space. He landed at the bottom of the stairs, concrete and metal fragments shredding through the air around him. He lay on his back looking at the hole in the ceiling above him which held several large concrete slabs in a precarious position over his head. He started to stand, the rucksack still in his hand, but he felt a sharp pain at the back of his left thigh. He felt around and could feel what seemed to be a long thin piece of metal embedded in his leg. When he looked at his hand it was wet with blood. The air surrounding him was full of dust particles making it difficult to see.

'Anna! Anna!' he shouted but couldn't hear his own voice.

Moving around the space he almost tripped over her body lying face down at the bottom of the stairs. As the dust began to clear he could see she was covered in debris, and the hair at the back of her head had a small bloodstain, she wasn't moving. He turned her over and knelt beside her. Her face was untouched, but her eyes were open, staring at the ceiling, the light gone from them in death. Reece sat down beside her and lifted her head into his arms brushing the dust covered hair from her face and closed her eyes with his hand. Reece could see the trail of blood from his leg wound to where he now sat. It was then he realised there was quite a lot of it, and he felt cold, and it was getting dark but something yellow like a cloud was moving above him; then it went black.

Chapter 34

When Reece woke up in the London Hospital there were three people round his bed, Jim Broad, Matthew Simons, and Mary.

'Where am I, where's Anna, what happened?' he croaked. His mouth felt dry.

Mary rushed to his side and held his hand.

'You're all right my darling. You're safe in hospital, you're going to be all right.'

'I'm sorry, Anna didn't make it old boy,' said Broad.

The memory of her face came back to him, and he knew it was true.

'Mary, I know you want to be with David right now, but we need to talk to him alone for a few minutes then you can have him all to yourself,' said Broad.

Mary looked at Reece who nodded.

'Five minutes. He needs rest. I'll get a coffee but when I return your gone, understand?'

'Understood, Mary, thank you,' replied Broad.

She kissed Reece on the cheek and left the men alone to their secrets.

'I'm glad you're alive David,' said Broad.

'So am I. How long have I been here?'

357

'Two days. The doctors said that four inches of steel in your leg nicked the artery. If you had pulled it out you would have finished the job and bled to death,' said Broad.

'I could see yellow moving all around me before I blacked out what was that the plutonium?'

'No, it was the people in the Hazmat suits, they'd arrived just before the blast. Getting the plutonium away from the bomb was vital. You'll be glad to know the stuff it was wrapped in protected it from getting out into the atmosphere and the whole area including you was clean,' said Matthews.

'What about Anna? What happened to her?'

'One of those bad luck stories. A lump of masonry hit her on the back of her head. She died instantly I'm told. The ATO was badly stuck in traffic and according to him even if he had got there in time, he would probably have done exactly what you did. From his examination of what was left, the tape that surrounded the box had tiny metal strips running through it that were linked to the countdown of the timer. Any interference with the tape would set the timer in a faster count. He told me to tell you it's a good job you can run fast.'

There were still times when there seemed to be smoke in front of his eyes, but Reece knew it was the beginning of tears which he always held back.

'The Israeli Government have already flown Anna back to Israel where she will be buried on Mount Herzl in the graveyard for the heroes of the state,' said Broad.

'What happens now?'

'Your friend Hassan is being interrogated at one of our safe houses. When we are finished with him, he'll be handed over to Mossad who will take him to Israel. After that he'll no longer be our problem. The Prime Minister and the Queen want to give you a medal, but 'C' has told them you don't exist. Your instruction to the police to seize those mobile phones from onlookers was a good decision. The footage showed the Arab starting to move on the ground with his gun in his hand. The Met and the Attorney General have both agreed your decision to fire was the right one. The press has been told that he was shot by a member of the Security Services involved in a surveillance operation against a terrorist cell. David, I want to thank you myself. You had a tough job to do, you need to take time out to rest and recuperate. Get back to Malta with Mary and enjoy some of that sun.'

Broad's timing was perfect as he finished speaking Mary walked back into the room.

'Times up! He needs his rest,' she said.

'My words exactly, Mary. We will leave you two alone, David, you're in good hands,' said Broad. The two men left them alone.

Mary sat on the bed looking down into his eyes.

'You look tired my love. They say you should be ready to leave in a few days. Try not to worry. Mr Broad contacted me in Belfast and got me a flight back. He has told me to call him when you're ready to go and he'll take care of the flights to Malta. Mother's a lot better and getting all the help she needs.'

Reece pulled Mary close to him.

'I can't wait to get back to Malta. But first, we need to go to a graveyard in Israel to leave some flowers and pay our respects.'

The End.

https://www.davidcostaauthor.com

Email: david.costa.writer@outlook.com

About the Author

The author has twenty-six years of experience working in anti-terrorist operations throughout the world and has used that knowledge writing this book.

Because of this background David Costa is of course a pseudonym.

Printed in Great Britain
by Amazon

68446799R00220